One True Place

One True Place

Margaret P. Cunningham

Black Lyon Publishing, LLC

Our books may be ordered through your local bookstore or by visiting
the publisher:

www.BlackLyonPublishing.com

Black Lyon Publishing, LLC
PO Box 567
Baker City, OR 97814

This is a work of fiction. All of the characters, names, events,
organizations and conversations in this novel are either the products
of the author's vivid imagination or are used in a fictitious way for the
purposes of this story.

ISBN-10:   1-934912-27-1
ISBN-13:   978-1-934912-27-0
Library of Congress Control Number: 2010923195

Published and printed in
the United States of America.

Black Lyon Contemporary Romance

For my mother,
Gertrude Nicholson Relfe Pearson.

1.

A Tidy Demise

Burkett Cowley had just finished up with his last patient of the morning—Kayla Mitchell, who'd lost yet another retainer—when his shoulder began bothering him. The new receptionist at Vista Palmas Orthodontics, a marvel of efficiency named Kimmie, turned off the state-of-the-art sound system that kept the kids coming through the door and got the office ready for the afternoon. She was on her way out with just enough time to make her lunchtime kick-boxing class, when she heard him fall.

The first thing she noticed upon entering his office was how he'd neatly missed the recently installed chrome and glass shelves holding his golf memorabilia.

Having spent the last four years working in one kind of doctor's office or another, Kimmie hurried over and put her fingers to Dr. Cowley's neck, but she knew he was gone. Probably before he hit the faux zebra carpet.

True Cowley got the call just as she was wrestling the final stems of heliconia and bird of paradise into a centerpiece on the Ponce DeLeon Room's oval Empire banquet table. The flowers were an unsettling contrast to the solid English furniture, but True had to admit that they reflected nicely in the house's latest acquisition, an early 1800s Federal gilded mirror. A gardener's truck rattled by the side loggia, creating shadows and causing the mirror to throw arcs of afternoon sunlight onto la casa's bleached walls, which gave a pleasant, other-worldly ambience to the room. Such was the substance of her thoughts before plucking the chiming cell phone from the pocket of her linen pants.

The slacks were a last-minute departure from the usual washed-out jeans she wore when volunteering at Casa Vispera. She had no idea why she'd opted for taupe linen over blue denim on this average south Florida Friday in early fall. Perhaps it was the anticipation of the weekend. Maybe it was in response to the hot flash that had attacked out of the blue that morning, mocking her new hormone replacement patch. For all she knew, she'd been visited by some subliminal premonition that by day's end she would be making arrangements for her husband's memorial service.

The thought made her shudder, but she would be grateful not to be wearing some shabby, undignified get-up when she sat before Mr. Crane, the pompous funeral director in his overly air-conditioned office. Being attired as a competent adult would help her feel less like the frightened little girl cowering inside of her.

After Kimmie, the now-unemployed receptionist dialed 911, she'd had the foresight to call Joe Davis, Burkett's lawyer and closest friend. Joe, per Kimmie's instructions, went directly to Casa Vispera. At True's insistence, Joe drove her to Serenity Shores Mortuary and Crematorium.

"Better to get it over with," she explained.

As Joe maneuvered through the afternoon traffic, True slumped against the window, her cheek resting on the soft inside of her arm for comfort. Joe ignored the peculiarity of her posture and instead talked to her gently about what a good wife she'd been to Burkett, "though he'd had his shortcomings, that was for sure." None of True's senses seemed to be working properly, yet when she made herself sit up straight and look at him, she was aware of something in Joe's eyes, something in the tone of his voice beyond grief and sympathy.

Mr. Crane was walking her through the details with Joe running interference, urging her toward the less expensive "interment accessories" when she noticed a discreet sign on the director's desk. It was a reminder to the bereaved that Serenity Shores Mortuary and Crematorium accepted an assortment of credit cards. This, in turn reminded her that she had very little money in her checking account. True fished the Visa out of her purse and handed it with a surprisingly steady hand to Mr. Crane. It was the American way, right? Besides, Burkett had always encouraged the accumulation of frequent flyer miles.

Mr. Crane paused for a few seconds then cleared his throat. The next order of business was the plot, he said.

"Plot?" asked True. "There was no plot. He just had a heart attack. Or maybe a stroke. But there was no plot."

The immediate association in her overloaded brain was the convoluted story in Rio Rendezvous, which she had been reading the night before. Then she realized what he meant.

"Oh, the burial plot. That would be in St. James churchyard," she said. "It's in Belle Hill."

"Oh, of course," said Mr. Crane. "That's Belle Hill, Alabama?"

"Yes."

True's thoughts floated back to the place of her and Burkett's births. Her memories of Belle Hill were dreamlike and vague, reminding her of the watery renderings of her favorite impressionists.

The town itself was a grand mélange of ante-bellum, French and Spanish influences scattered beneath a canopy of live oak dripping with Spanish moss and situated on a bay that emptied into the Gulf of Mexico. The inhabitants, due to their geographical (literally, the end of the earth) and philosophical (a fluctuating hierarchy of God, family, country and football) positioning were a fairly quirky crowd.

"Burkett's family was from there," Joe was saying. "And True was born there, too, weren't you, True?" he added, more to rein in her wandering mind than anything.

"That's perfectly fine," interrupted Mr. Crane, shuffling papers and scooting his chair back silently over thick, colorless carpet.

True figured there was probably another fresh widow pacing the hall, so she didn't take offense. Besides, she couldn't wait to vacate the icy premises.

But Joe requested a minute with Mr. Crane.

True thought this a bit strange but chalked her confusion up to grief, perched herself on the edge of a mauve velveteen wing chair and tried to rub some feeling back into her freezing arms.

The last and by no means least fortuitous circumstance on this beautiful, tragic Friday was the absence of True's daughter, Katie, who was out of town and could not be reached in time to be of any assistance with the immediate arrangements. Guilt, who always rode shotgun in True's relationship with her daughter, quickly replaced the initial feelings of relief, however, and she decided to turn the flower and hymn choices over to Katie. That would ease things a bit. Besides, at this point she was past caring if Katie hired the entire Tabernacle Choir and ordered a truck load of orchids, which was only a slight exaggeration in regard to her over-achieving offspring.

As True and Joe left Serenity Shores Mortuary and Crematorium, the tidiness of it all dawned on her, and despite the shock and grief she was feeling, she was grateful. For a while, anyway.

True couldn't remember at exactly what point during the whole process of burying her husband that Joe broke the news to her. Dr. Burkett Cowley, top orthodontist in the greater Vista Palmas area, had mortgaged himself up to his molars in order to expand his state-of-the-art orthodontic center. But this wasn't the worst of it. Though the practice and the new, overblown building that housed it could be sold, the proceeds would just manage to cover Burkett's gambling debts.

True was aware that her husband's affection for betting and his lousy golf game were a bad combination. She just hadn't realized how out of hand it had all gotten. *I mean who would risk that much on a putt, for God's sake?*

"You would be surprised," was Joe's answer.

The upshot was that her lifestyle was about to undergo a radical change.

Even though she had maxed out the Visa at Serenity Shores, True had been feeling a trifle guilty about her choice of Burkett's interment accessories. She knew, for example, that Burkett would have chosen what Mr. Crane referred to as the Rolls Royce of caskets. When she realized the financial bind her husband had left her in, however, she called Mr. Crane and substituted her original middle-of-the-line choice with the "green funeral" which consisted of a pine box with an all-over banana leaf design painted on it. And the icing on that morbid little piece of cake was that Katie, who was inordinately prideful about her high degree of environmental sensitivity, couldn't say a word about it.

At least True didn't have to worry about shopping for a cemetery plot. Thankfully, when Burkett's father was running through *his* family's fortune, he'd overlooked the Cowleys' holdings in St. James's churchyard, the place where everybody who was anybody in Belle Hill, Alabama ended up. It was said that St. James's was harder to get into than the Belle Hill Country Club. And that was almost impossible. True was merely grateful for one less expensive decision to make. She hadn't thought she'd ever return to Belle Hill, but in the name of Burkett's memory—and fiscal responsibility—it made perfect sense.

The Thursday following Burkett's unexpected departure dawned cloudless and almost crisp (actual crisp doesn't occur until sometime late in October along the gulf coast). Camellia sasanquas softened the austere lines of St. James Chapel where a well-attended visitation and service took place. True was appreciative of the turn-out, but sadly, she didn't know most of them.

When Burkett left Belle Hill for college in Miami, his family had followed, opting for the perennial summer of south Florida. The Cowleys kept up with the "folks back home" for awhile, but after a year or so everyone gave it up, and they all lost touch with one another. Being an adaptable kind of guy, Burkett never looked back, and Florida instantly became home to him.

But really, that's sugar-coating things a bit. The truth is, the glitz of Vista Palmas fit Burkett Cowley like a tailor-made golf glove whereas Belle Hill was more like a wool sweater that had somehow gotten into the washing machine. It was just never right.

True hardly remembered the first four years of her life as a resident of Belle Hill. This was just as well according to her aunt and namesake, Beatrice Gertrude, known to all with great affection as B True.

The cemetery was close enough and the weather mild enough that everyone walked to the gravesite. A train beckoned from a distant track, the sound barely audible. But to True it was strangely compelling. Compelling and comforting.

Through the oaks and magnolias and towering camellia bushes, True could see the front porch of Oak View House, the house she'd lived in with her mother before the accident. She felt drawn to the house, though she'd barely given it a thought over the years. She actually turned in its direction, the feeling becoming so intense that it replaced all thoughts of Burkett's memorial service. But Katie's arm caught her mother's, steering her back toward the cemetery.

True soon found herself sitting with her family in a line of chairs facing her husband's environmentally friendly casket. The group consisted of her daughter, Katie, Katie's husband, Parker and their two sad little children, Tommy and Mary Kate.

The rector, George Baker (aka Speedball Baker in his Belle Hill Prep days) was starting in on the Lord's Prayer when it occurred to True that this was the last time she and Burkett would be together on this earth. It also occurred to her that she was sitting on what was to be her future resting place—the plot next to Burkett's recently excavated one.

"Hallowed be thy name," intoned George. He had a lovely, resonant voice. True figured it had probably been a toss-up between minister and radio announcer when George was making career choices.

"Thy kingdom come."

How did she get here? Wasn't it just the other day that she and Burkett were making out in the basement of the Phi House? No, that would be over thirty years ago.

Father Baker threw her a glance as if he knew her mind had wandered off to the Phi House basement.

"Thy will be done."

•

Because of his height, Jackson Bean habitually stood to the back of the crowd. This afforded him a kind of bird's eye view of things not available to those of shorter stature. The main proceedings of whatever function he attended were rarely obstructed. Nor were the reactions and interactions of the spectators in front of him. He had come to value this as an asset to his profession as sportswriter for the Belle Hill Courier, and as the years rolled by, these observances had given Jackson quite a bit of insight into human nature in general. Now he watched his fellow Belle Hillians as they watched the widow of his old teammate, Burkett Cowley.

In high school Jackson Bean had played baseball with Burkett. Though the deceased was several years younger, in the way of small towns, Jackson felt duty-bound to pay his respects. He'd known nothing about True Cowley except that she'd been born in Belle Hill to a wild, red-headed beauty — Jackson's preferred type, now that he thought about it. He realized that an inappropriate smile had formed on his face. No one noticed — another bonus to his back-of-the-crowd position. However, he cleared his throat and shook off memories of wild red-heads.

No one seemed to know the identity of True's father, though there had been endless speculation. When True's mother had fallen off a party boat and drowned, her four-year old daughter was sent to live with an old aunt somewhere. That the child had grown up to marry one of Belle Hill's native sons put the mint in the julep as Jackson's Aunt Maisy was fond of saying. In other words, the story kept the town's grapevine juiced up for decades. Jackson shook his head. In all of his years and all of his travels, he had never seen village gossips that could hold a candle to those of his home town.

Knowing her back story, Jackson was surprised by his first glimpse of the widow Cowley. She was pretty, but not the ravishing beauty her mother was reputed to have been. The black dress showed off a well-kept, shapely figure, however. Her hair was dark and cut just beneath her jaw, thick and shiny in the sunlight, trying to curl in Belle Hill's soft air.

There was an air of vulnerability about her. This was unexpected and at odds with her age, the DNA inherited from her mother and the unconventional nature of her childhood. True Cowley actually looked a bit ditsy, Jackson decided, and he shrugged off the soft-hearted feeling that was beginning to overtake him.

Jackson found an old uncle of Burkett's, murmured condolences and shook the man's hand firmly while placing his left hand gently on a bony shoulder. He started toward True, watching as she tried to make sense of who was who and thanked each one for coming. She knew as well as he that most of them were there to satisfy their curiosity. That and their taste for the fried chicken, tomato aspic and cucumber sandwiches Jane Ellen Jackson Jones (third cousin on Jackson's daddy's side) had waiting for them back on the lawn behind the church.

Then Jackson remembered that his column was nearing its deadline. Besides, he was starting to sweat in his coat and tie. It was enough that he'd spoken to Burkett's uncle, he told himself. The thought of Jane E's fried chicken almost made him change his mind, but he turned back toward the shortcut that led through the woods and right up to his back door.

2.

Restorative Cocktails

Predictably, True's daughter, Katie; Joe Davis, Burkett's lawyer and faithful-to-the-end (and beyond) friend; and Mr. Crane of Serenity Shores Mortuary and Crematorium had seen to Dr. Burkett Cowley's final trip home as well as to most of the funeral arrangements on the Belle Hill end. Maisy Downey, True's only contact in Belle Hill, had taken care of the rest.

The old lady had made the fifteen minute drive from her house in downtown Belle Hill out to St. James' cemetery and checked on the grave site. She'd engaged her niece, also the best caterer in town, to serve the gawkers (her word) at the après-interment get together. She even insisted that the out-of-towners stay with her.

Finding themselves in the unusual situation of throwing a funeral in a town where they knew almost no one, the out-of-towners had fallen on the invitation to stay in the rambling house of Maisy Downey. True described Maisy to the others as elderly but spry. And the tiniest bit eccentric. They rightfully understood this to be respectful verbiage for crazy old character, but bunking at Maisy's was better than a stay in the Whispering Pines Motel out on the highway. Due to the arrival of the Mobile Home Extravaganza Show and the Gulf Coast Azaleas Growers Convention four days prior to Burkett's funeral, everything but the Pines was booked.

Maisy had earned her reputation for eccentricity in many ways over the years, but her inclination toward impromptu séances and fortune-telling gigs really put her over the top. The Belle Hill gentry feigned detached amusement when Maisy's gold and yellow tent went up at various soirees, however. They choked back snickers when the tiny, old lady showed up in full gypsy regalia complete with a luxurious black wig that didn't quite cover her own shoulder-length platinum blonde hair.

The truth was they overlooked Maisy's "bizarre behavior" primarily because she was wealthy as all get-out and secondarily because she was pretty much dead-on in her predictions. And so the good citizens of Belle Hill congratulated one another on humoring an old lady's whims—it was their Christian duty, when you thought about it—as they stood in line outside that tent and then hung on Madame Maisy's every word in the flickering green glow of her malfunctioning crystal ball.

Maisy also happened to be the life-long friend (and not-so-distant cousin) of True's dead aunt, B True. B True had reared her great niece and namesake, little Beatrice Gertrude—known simply as True—since True's mother's untimely death by drowning in the Mississippi Sound.

B True had refused to step foot in Belle Hill (lest she and little True be reminded of her niece's fatal fall from grace—and Johnson Boudreaux's party boat—that fateful summer night). So Maisy frequently made the two-hour drive to the home of True and B True. Since B True also refused to acknowledge unpleasantness of any description and therefore Belle Hill's existence, Maisy was True's only link with her birthplace and her mother.

True and her small entourage arrived on Maisy's doorstep the day before the funeral. Following a light supper of gumbo, French bread and several bottles of very good wine, True fell exhausted and a little drunk into the rosewood tester bed in the front guest room.

Someone in the neighborhood had blooming ginger lilies. Maisy's loquat tree was in flower. Their scents—a recipe for nostalgia—slipped in through the open windows and swirled around True. She breathed it all in, feeling protected. A train called to her from somewhere far off. This was the last thing she remembered before passing out on Maisy's monogrammed linen sheets, her cheek resting on the soft inside of her arm.

She awoke in time for a quick breakfast of sausage and grits and hair-of-the-dog in the form of a screwdriver before making the ride out to St. James's.

After a full day of making acquaintance with people she was meant to have grown up with had fate not intervened, True ended up back at Maisy's. She and her diminutive hostess sat on the back porch enjoying one another's company and Maisy's self-described "mean margaritas." The old lady kicked her heels off, propped her little feet on the coffee table and wiggled her granny toes at True.

"You must be worn to a nub, sweetie," she said and True realized that it was Maisy who was likely exhausted.

The old character was in her eighties, after all, and had hosted the bereaved horde with an ever-flowing kitchen and bar (not to mention unfailing good humor) for two days.

"If I sleep as well tonight as I did last night I'll be fine tomorrow," said True. "I can't thank you enough for putting us all up, Maisy."

Maisy waved her gnarly fingers dismissively. "I've loved having you all here—except for the circumstances, of course. If you thank me again, you'll embarrass me, so I don't want to hear another word. Besides, it would've been pretty heartless of me to stick B True's great niece and her family out at the Whispering Pines Motel during her husband's funeral."

"And the other hotels were all booked? I didn't realize that Belle Hill had that many visitors."

"Not one vacancy." Maisy bobbed her head for emphasis. "The azalea growers' convention and the mobile home show have been in town all week. Yep. Things are happening in Belle Hill, Alabama, baby."

She took a noisy sip of her drink and moved her toes around a little, watching them wiggle. "You're good company, True. Always were one of my favorites—and not just because of B True, either, though you remind me of her a little. You got her sweet nature." She looked at True with a funny expression on her old face. "You're welcome to stay here as long as you want, you know."

"Oh, Maisy, that's very kind, really, but ..."

Maisy put her empty glass on the table. "I tell you what.

Since the rest of the group has headed for the hills, how about I give you a tour of your birthplace tomorrow? There's no need to rush back down to Florida, is there?"

"No, just a big, empty house that will go on the market soon. Then I don't know what I'll do. I haven't had time to think about it."

True noticed Maisy smiling at her, and there was a peculiar shine in her eyes. Was it the mean green concoction she'd just imbibed or was the old lady up to something?

3.
The Road Less Traveled

Jackson Bean pressed the send-now key and officially ended his modest work week. His column, *Bean on Sports*, covering the latest football prodigy to come out of Belle Hill as well as a heartfelt interview with the kid's coach, was the kind of stuff his editor hyperventilated over. It would need no revisions.

Jackson's knees creaked in the quiet as he unfolded himself from his desk chair and turned the Dell off. He unplugged the laptop and looked around the room, checking the open windows and door for unexpected guests, then crossed over to a large watercolor of a Blue Marlin leaping from bluer water. He slid the painting to one side on an unseen track, turned a combination lock this way and that and swung open a door almost the size of the marlin picture. He placed the laptop inside next to neat stacks of books and carefully reversed the process, finally clicking the marlin into its original position.

"Juju," he yelled. "Come're, girl! Ready to go fishing?"

In response, an oversized adolescent lab crashed through the azaleas by the back door. There was a path, but a lab always takes the road less traveled. And it is the nature of an immature Labrador (maturity happens at approximately three years to never) to leap before looking or at least to do both simultaneously, so in her excitement at hearing the word fishing, Juju misjudged the distance between the door and Jackson, applied the brakes a hair too late and slid into the desk. Her head made a sickening thud as it made contact with the solid oak. Unfazed, she shook it off, scrambled to her feet and gazed adoringly at her master, her pale eyes and pink tongue resplendent against the Hershey Bar brown of her coat.

To Juju's credit, when Jackson opened the driver's side door of his new green truck, she waited—not sitting as she had been taught—but still, she did not claw her way over her master or pee all over herself or, in a paroxysm of excitement, take off in the opposite direction.

As you may have guessed, these were some of JuJu's previous responses to being offered a ride in the truck. But she had come a long way in learning the curious ways and expectations of humans, and so she waited.

"Okay, girl! Let's go!"

Juju leaped into the truck and sat at attention in the passenger seat.

Jackson owned a cabin, high above the threat of flood waters in the alluvial flood plain known as the Alabama delta, a wild and spiritual place full of gators and pelicans, herons and the occasional black bear. He and his father had built the cabin, floating the materials upriver in a wooden skiff.

He would soon meet up with three other men—fishing gurus who knew the ways of speckled trout, redfish and bass better than the fish knew themselves. Though they had been fishing and hunting together for years, Jackson knew nothing of their lives outside the delta. There was an unspoken agreement that theirs was strictly a business relationship—the business of hunting and fishing was how Jackson explained it to anyone curious enough to ask.

The men would spend the night at Jackson's cabin. One of them, Booger Favreaux, cooked almost as well as he fished and could whip up anything from grits and grillades to fried softshell crabs. Jackson could taste it already.

He thought of the soon-to-be-well-received column popping up on his editor's computer. Then there was the aforementioned breakfast-to-be and the near certainty of hauling in a mess of fish. He looked over at his dog, and his good feelings intensified. She finally seemed to be getting the hang of who was the master and who was the pet. JuJu looked back at Jackson and barked. It was a short, fierce statement that caused him to wonder if she was having the same thought. Only, in her mind, who was the master and who was the pet? But she yawned and lowered her head submissively, and Jackson's sense of well-being righted itself.

To top things off, the pleasant weather was holding. This convergence of fortuitous events put Jackson Bean in such a superior frame of mind that he decided to take a spin through the campus of St. James college to enjoy the local flora (blossoming co-eds playing Frisbee in front of the library) before getting on the highway. He rolled down the windows of the truck and gripped Juju's collar with his right hand, lest she see a squirrel — or God forbid, a cat, and go flying out of the window.

The detour turned out to be such a good idea that he rode along the narrow, winding streets a second time, feeling a bit homesick at the idea of leaving all of this for a night with three guys suffering from gas and sleep apnea. His house was just a little too quiet lately, though. Being with the guys — yeah — it would be great.

Still, he should probably get to work on renting Pap's place. Not that he needed the income. Or the company of a neighbor so close. God, that could be more trouble than it was worth. He shook his head at the memory of a previous renter, the buxom Ms. Whitley. She had adopted the habit of dropping in on him (with her tight sweaters and tales of marital discord) every night after Mr. Whitley passed out in his recliner. Years of experience had honed Jackson's skills in the gentle dissuasion of unwanted female attention, but no, he certainly didn't need another Ms. Whitley.

It was just that it wasn't good for a house to sit empty. Everybody knew that. He also didn't need his over-interested friends and neighbors wondering why a man living on a Belle Hill Courier sportswriter's salary would let an income-producing house remain unrented. He would get on it as soon as he got back from …

This train of thought was interrupted by a familiar car coming his way. As the convertible sped beneath a flickering lacework of sun and shadow, the driver's platinum page boy was barely visible behind the steering wheel. It was Aunt Maisy.

She had someone with her — Burkett Cowley's widow. She was laughing at something Maisy was saying as they passed.

The sun caught her dark hair, the flash of white teeth, the strong line of her jaw, and Jackson remembered the feeling he'd had at the cemetery. There was something about that True Cowley… something that Jackson couldn't exactly put his finger on. But it was something he liked.

4.

Return to the Future

After a spin through Belle Hill's charming downtown, a zip along Bay Front Road where cottages laze behind pickets and hydrangeas, and a dash through the tiny geranium-and-fern adorned shopping area adjacent to St. James College, Maisy finally relaxed her size-five lead foot and turned to True.

"I know you'll want to see Oak View, and I'll be glad to take you to see your mother's and grandparents' graves too if you'd like. They're not far from Burkett's, you know."

But True couldn't visit those graves. Not yet.

"It's all so unreal, just being back in Belle Hill … I know you must think it's strange of me …"

"I understand perfectly. One thing at a time, sweetie," said Maisy.

She patted True's knee and turned the Miata onto the campus of St. James College. The entrance she chose was the oldest and prettiest—a wide street lined with sprawling azaleas and a canopy of oaks. Framed plantation-style, at the end of this avenue was a white raised cottage, its front porch scattered with wicker furniture. Floor-to-ceiling jib windows were shuttered with louvers the rich green of surrounding magnolia leaves. The driveway made a deep half circle around a splashing fountain in front.

True remembered walking through the tall windows as a little girl, careful not to trip over the sills, hurrying lest the top half of the double-hung window drop down on her. She had dipped her toes in that fountain, heard approaching visitors as their tires crunched over the oyster shells in the drive. That she recalled it so perfectly amazed her.

"Would you like to go in?" asked Maisy, gliding to a stop near the fountain. A sly smile crinkled her eyes. "I have a key."

True watched the splashing water for a second, recollecting the sound and thinking about her mother. Thinking about Burkett. She had come full circle to this spot. Or had she? She had a beginning and possibly an ending, but the stories themselves lay somewhere in Oak View's shadows.

"Sure, Maisy. I can't believe I haven't been back until now."

They mounted the steps and crossed the porch but before Maisy could insert the key in the lock, Oak View's imposing front door swung inward.

"Whoa!" said a man slapping a hand to his chest. In his other hand was a tool box.

"Woo, you ladies gave me a start." He blew out a breath and stepped out onto the porch. "I'm just here checkin' the wirin' and all. Reports of lights in there again last night. You ask me, it's them college kids, doin' Lord knows what. Didn't smell any funny weed or burnin' wires though. Can't be too careful in a old house like this one, you know. Guess it's haunted after all." He rolled his eyes dramatically then contorted his features into a ghastly wink to let them know what he thought of "hants." "Some of them church ladies from over to the Baptist church—I do work over there, too. Call myself a certified, all-denominational electrician, heh, heh. Anyway, them ladies said it's some ghostie guardin' somethin'—they figured it was voodoo-based." He raised his free hand, wiggling the fingers. "Woooo," he said, and he looked so comical that True had to laugh. Woooooo," he said again, wiggling his fingers right up in True's face. When she stepped back he said, "Okay, I got to get goin'. You ladies have a nice day, okay?" And he was off around the side of the house. Seconds later his pick-up rattled away down the street.

"Well, that was weird," said True.

"Yep," said Maisy, stepping through the door and dismissing the subject.

True was confused. For a fortune-teller with her own personal key to the house, Maisy was surprisingly uninterested in the man's story of supernatural goings-on. Before she could broach the subject, however, True's attention was diverted by the magic of stepping back into her forgotten childhood. The first sensation was the smell. Musty, flowery, with a hint of pine and scent of the bay. Next she remembered the light and the spaces the light settled into.

The house's interior had received more of a gentle facelift than a restoration. Though changes had been made, in its bones Oak View was the same. The walls had been painted in soft neutrals and the pine floors refinished, but mantels, hardware and most light fixtures were as True remembered. Claw-footed tubs and original pedestal sinks remained in the bathrooms.

The women's steps echoed in the wide "dog-trot" hallway. As far as True could tell, no walls had been moved, no closets added. Big wardrobes overflowing with her mother's dresses and shoes flashed in True's memory. And there had been hat boxes, full of outrageous hats.

Each of the house's six main rooms opened onto the center hall. One now held a large Queen Anne dining room table and chairs. The others were sparsely furnished since the space was now needed for receptions and parties. At the end of the hall, encompassing the entire rear half of the house was a magnificent curved ballroom. It was a sudden, perfect recollection.

"Surely you remember this room," said Maisy as they entered it. "You used to ride your tricycle in here on rainy days." She chuckled. "Your mother let you do the most outrageous things. She was more fun than a bucket of margaritas. I'll say that for her."

Further exploration revealed that the curved, windowed expanse beneath the grand ballroom which had served True's grandmother as a potting shed and green house, now housed wooden folding chairs, a Prie Dieu, assorted candelabra, vases, urns and cleaning equipment.

And there was the doorway that creaked and opened to her vague and unsettling memory of the twisted stairway leading to that storage room.

"Your mother's parents—your grandparents—were quiet, sweet people," Maisy continued. "They had Nick … that's what everyone called your mother. But I guess you know that much.

Anyway, they had Nick late in life. I don't think they ever knew quite what to do with her—she was so different from either of them. Your mother was one those up and down people, happy one day, sad the next. Like I said, lots of fun. But easy to get the blues.

"Anyway, your grandmother spent most of her time volunteering at St. James library or pouring over seed catalogs and books on camellia cultivation. She was a great gardener, you know."

"B True told me that Nick loved camellias, too—that she always had bowls of them in the house."

"That's right. Nick and your grandmother both had a thing for camellias. They did have that in common." Maisy shook her head. "But that's about the only thing, I'm afraid."

"What about my grandfather?" asked True hopefully.

"Well, your grandfather always had his nose buried in collections—stamps and things. A philatelist, I think the word is. Or is it a numismatist? I always get them mixed up." She shook her head. "Where was I? Oh, yeah. Nick wasn't a thing like either of them, but she sure put the blue in their sky. Sadly, your grandmother died a few years before you were born, and if memory serves me, your grandfather passed away just six months before Nick. In a car accident."

True said B True had told her about it, but had gotten so upset in the telling that True never had the heart to ask her the details.

"Just as well," said Maisy. "It was just one of those terrible things. He had a heart attack and ran off the road. On his way to visit B True—that's why she took it so hard. We were all sad, of course, but then when your mother died, too, we were heart-broken. And just worried to death about you.

"When B True decided to take you home with her, it seemed like the best solution—to have you reared away from all the sadness." Maisy gave True's arm a final pat and said, "I'll be quiet now, let you get the feel of the place." She walked over to one of the ballroom's tall windows and stood looking out to the back lawn and the golf course beyond.

True closed her eyes and heard the rain from all those years ago tapping on the tin gutters. She felt the warm metal of a tricycle seat pressing into the backs of her thighs. She had ridden that tricycle back and forth, back and forth across the bare floors, then fast over the wooden threshold, frightened by the unbalanced sensation, then on down the center hall. On every rainy summer day, it seemed.

"I remember it, Maisy. I couldn't have been more than three or four, but I remember it. And I remember this …"

Other than riding her tricycle across the fabulous floors, it was mostly a hodgepodge of rather inconsequential things that she pointed out to Maisy as familiar—a sink's chipped pedestal, the bare bulb hanging from a braided wire in the pantry, stained porcelain doorknobs. How a chandelier seemed suspended not from some unseen rafter but from a medallion of feathery acanthus leaves and curlicues on the ceiling of the parlor. True had wondered how the delicate arrangement of painted leaves and circles could hold the weight of the heavy chandelier. She'd asked someone (her mother?) about it.

"Since the time of the ancient Greeks, folks have been using acanthus leaves to hide things," was the response True had gotten.

At the time she hadn't realized that the medallion was hiding an ugly hole in the ceiling and instead imagined a secret tucked in the leaves above her.

Maisy led the way into a room that comprised half of a symmetrical pair of wings set back from the main body of the house.

"Oh my gosh, Maisy. This was my mother's room." True stared at the back wall. "Her bed, the one I still have, was right there. She used to let me sleep with her sometimes." True walked across the room to a window, her footsteps echoing in the emptiness. "We would have the windows open and the big fan on and the curtains—white, gauzy curtains would float around. Like ghosts."

Maisy sat on a tufted Victorian settee, the only piece of furniture in the large room. She patted the brocade fabric. "Let's sit for a minute. Tell me what else you remember."

True closed her eyes for a few seconds.

"The trains," she said softly.

"The trains," Maisy repeated, nodding her head, thinking.

"B True told me you had a thing about trains. I sure miss B True. She was my best friend, you know. So tell me about you and the trains."

True closed her eyes again, sitting there on the ugly settee that occupied the very spot where she and her mother had slept the summer nights away in a lovely heirloom bed.

"The only real memory I have ever had of my mother and me is us lying here in this room in her mahogany four-poster. Outside that very window …" True nodded toward it for emphasis. "It was raining."

She paused, thinking, and Maisy could tell that scraps of True's childhood—minor, but important things—were coming back to her.

"The end of Mama's cigarette danced like a fairy in the dark. I always loved that. And there was a train. We heard its horn in the distance. And I remember her voice—kind of a cross between mine and B True's. I remember her saying 'That train sure sounds lonesome, doesn't it?' I didn't know how to answer, but then later I wished I'd said, 'The trains do sound lonesome, but you don't have to be because you have me.'"

The words came out in a rush, and True knew she sounded childlike, but going back to that night was having an odd effect on her—she felt four years-old again.

"I think that's the last time I was with her. There's no way to really know."

Maisy patted True's knee.

"I remember how she let me get right up close to her in the dark and put my leg up on hers and put my cheek against her arm where it was soft. I knew I was crowding against her, and it was hot, but she let me do it anyway." True sighed. "I think that was the last time.

"The next thing I know, I'm living with B True. My mother and the first four years of my existence are nothing but a dream of a dream I can hardly recall." True sighed again and shook her head.

"I couldn't ask B True to fill me in because she'd get upset, Mama being her dead baby sister's daughter and all. And she was so good to me—taking me in to raise at her age and everything."

"B True was bad to get the fall-aparts," agreed Maisy. "But she had the biggest heart I ever came across."

"Once I did ask B True about my daddy—it had just occurred to me that everyone has to have one at least in the beginning—and she started crying and said, 'Believe me, some rocks are best left undisturbed.'

"Then she dabbed at her eyes with her hanky, and frowned at me. 'Put your arm down, True,' she said. 'I don't know what's wrong with you.' But I couldn't. The inside of my arm, up at the top felt so soft against my face, it could've been satin or a baby's cheek."

"Or a mother's arm in the dark," said Maisy.

"The trains would come by B True's at night, and I could hear their wheels as they moved on to who knows where. They made a low sound—like a whisper at first—and sometimes I would think, it's not the train at all, but the heater or the attic fan. It wasn't. It was the train, leaving town."

True and Maisy sat there for awhile wrapped in the morning's stillness and thinking about True and trains and the things a child manages to find comfort in.

Finally True said, "Maisy, I want to know about my mother, know her story. I can't think about it just yet, but soon, I'm going to start looking into it."

Maisy smiled up at True. "There's plenty of time, sugar, plenty of time. You don't have to decide just yet."

True wondered if the old lady was trying to dissuade her from digging into the past and waited for her to elaborate, but Maisy seemed lost in her own thoughts.

Finally she said, "Do you know what entrainment is, True?"

"Something to do with trains?" True teased.

Maisy laughed. "Well, yes, but that's not the definition I'm thinking of. Your story is probably what got me thinking about it, though. Entrainment is a delightful phenomenon in nature. An example would be two rhythmic beings gradually altering until they are in the same rhythm—like crickets."

"Like pendulums in clocks—they do that."

"Exactly."

True was confused at first. "Well, it is interesting, but … "

"Like I said, it's a gradual thing. Just something to think

about," said Maisy.

So True decided to think about it and in a minute or two understood what Maisy was getting at. The pace of it here, it encouraged deep breaths, relaxing stretches and long walks. It allowed True rare moments of rhythmic, coherent thought. It was her rhythm. True leaned over and kissed the old lady's papery cheek.

"Thanks, Maisy."

"For what?"

"For bringing me home."

5.

A Turnip Amid the Palms

"Katie, I'm tired of arguing. I've made up my mind. I'm moving back to Belle Hill."

"Back? Mother, do you even remember living there? This is your home. You've been here for what—thirty years?"

"Something like that." *Actually, twenty-seven and a half, but like they say, who's counting?* But after just a few days, Belle Hill felt more like home somehow. *Is it possible to be from a place as much by nature as by birth? A genetic predisposition to call a place home?*

"What about Mary Kate and Tommy? Your own flesh-and-blood grandchildren? How can you leave them?"

The truth was that Katie had her children's social lives ramped up to warp speed. Lessons and parties and trips and team sports kept them so occupied that as they had gotten older (and True's baby sitting services were no longer needed) weeks could go by between openings in their schedules. Their father, Parker, was a good man and a loving if often absent parent. And God knows, he was a good provider, but he lived as manic a lifestyle as his wife and children. True felt as if she needed an appointment to see any of them. They made her tired.

And though True had, as Katie pointed out, lived in fabulous Vista Palmas for approximately thirty years, unlike Burkett, she'd never really gotten her roots comfortable in the sand. She felt like one of Belle Hill's azaleas, pretty but paled by the raucous confetti of bougainvillea; a bubble-headed hydrangea languishing in orchid elegance; a humble turnip, invisible amid the flashy fronds of the palms; a … well, you get the idea.

True had survived more than thrived, feeling dwarfed and unimportant in the rampant tropical flora and the sizzling climate—not to mention the glitz and the glam of new wealth the place attracted like bees to its balconied condo-hives. She had tried to fit in, but most of the time hanging out at the posher-than-posh golf club, she'd just wanted to escape when the latest "it girls" blew into the Vista Palmas and attempted to take over everyone's lives.

The whole picture had emerged with blinding clarity the day she'd sat in that musty room at Oak View talking to Maisy. For the first time in years—since leaving B True's, now that she really thought about it—she'd felt a part of a place. She had come home that day.

And then there was her mother, Gertrude Nicholson Hunter. Nick was what everyone called her. Not True or Trudy or even Nicky, but Nick. The name itself fed True's need to give substance to the shadows that taunted her.

In middle school when her friends were doling out nicknames, they'd called her by her initials, B.G., for awhile, but it didn't suit her, and she was soon just True again. What kind of woman could carry off a man's name so well that it sounded cool? It was one more wonderment that fed True's desire to know things—things she had a right to know about her mother. But the catalyst was the house itself, seducing her with its memory-evoking rooms and nooks, its creaks and smells. Like Nick herself, it had been wonderful and comforting and exciting—and frightening with its dark places and high places and harbored secrets. The house itself planted the seeds of curiosity that sprouted into a tangle of craving to know Nick and her story.

In contrast to Oak View, the Cowley home in Vista Palmas, Florida was a stucco showplace, an estate really, with its manicured lushness, Poinciana-lined verandas, loggia and salt water pool. And its location a mere two blocks from the beach made it a realtor's dream.

At the time of Burkett's death, real estate prices were climbing faster than the wild wisteria on the Cowleys' pergola, so Katie's husband, Parker, agreed with his wife and his mother-in-law that they should buy True's and Burkett's house for its appraised value. For Parker and Katie it was now or never (or so they rationalized), their one chance to live out their lives in the tropical splendor they'd aspired to since the day Parker slipped a two and a half carat symbol of his love and affection on Katie's finger.

After much schedule juggling, the family convened for a Sunday brunch meeting by the Cowley pool. Everyone agreed that True's grandchildren would come for extended visits to Belle Hill. True figured she would see more of them than she did now. The plan had as an added benefit the elimination of thousands of dollars invested in summer camps that the children were growing weary of anyway, thereby easing the financial pressures of the new mortgage Parker and Katie were about to assume.

When True called Maisy Downey to inform her of the whole radical, spontaneous (insane?) plan, the old lady didn't seem at all surprised. As a matter of fact, it was as if she'd known all along that True would be transplanting herself to Belle Hill, Alabama.

"We're beside ourselves to find someone to manage things at Oak View. The woman who Bertie Wallace—he's in charge over there, so to speak—the woman he hired isn't working out and has given notice. You'd be great at it!"

True agreed to take the job then and there. But she'd need some time to get settled, find a place to live and everything, she said.

"Well, now that you mention it, I know of a place that's available—a nice little place that's right near Oak View, come to think of it. Reasonable rent, too. I'll email you some pictures of it."

When True saw the photos of the cottage and learned of the very reasonable rent, she signed a year's lease that would start when her house sold—quite a generous arrangement, to be sure.

She'd rented a house, sight unseen. And taken a job without really knowing a whole lot about it. She was leaving some good friends in Florida, though the transient nature of Vista Palmas kept long-term friendships to a minimum. She was relocating to a place based completely on emotion and some vague intuitive notion that she was going home. Six months after burying her husband, True Cowley signed the ownership of her home over to her children and prepared to head north.

She lay on the leather sectional that was the last piece of furniture she and Burkett had bought together. (Now that she thought about it, he had picked it out, and she had gone along with it.) With her cheek resting on the soft flesh of her inner arm, she comforted her own confused self as she had learned long ago to do. Looking at the honeyed walls of the living room that had been home to her for so many years, she wondered, *Have I lost my mind?*

6.

True Cowley Meets the Marlboro Man

True set her Styrofoam coffee cup on the wooden kitchen counter. Luke-warm latte splashed over the complimentary pamphlet the moving company had given her, partially obscuring the happy yellow lettering of its title, *Stress Free Home Transition.* True shook her head at the oxymoronic title and turned to face what the brochure described as phase five of home transitioning (unpacking) and what True thought of as phase three of her life (widowhood).

She peeked into the nearest cardboard cube. Good. It was filled to the top with books—mostly Juliette Benoit paperbacks. This was an omen, True decided. To her, the books represented reward, leisure, escape. The opposite of what she was feeling at the moment. They were a reminder that time to curl up with a good book—although not "escapist" paperbacks, but good books, she reminded herself—would be hers to enjoy once she'd overcome the tribulations of translocation. Though True had sworn them off, the Juliette Benoit novels of "high-spirited adventure and high-principled romance" had been a mainstay throughout phase two of her life—the last thirty years. The married years. She hadn't had the heart to toss them out. Yet.

She ran her hand over *Hong Kong Hiatus, The Cairo Connection* and *L. A. Layover.* The sight of their dated covers gave True the psychic equivalent of a pat on the arm, and she willed herself not to pick up her all-time favorite, *Marseilles by Monday.* She forced herself not to scan the blurb on the back cover, for she was in desperate need of a hit of Juliette Benoit and her intrepid heroine, Bailey Jones.

True closed her eyes. Ahhh, there was Bailey Jones, Benoit's irrepressible American heroine, in her blue Aston Martin, down-shifting the convertible roadster through the Marseilles traffic before heading down to the Cote d'Azure. True could feel the wind whipping through her hair, and omigod, was that the scent of lavender in the crisp Provencal air?

True knew that the mere flip of a page would transport her to the literary equivalent of an Audrey Hepburn movie, except that besides being merely spunky and beautiful and having great clothes, that "irrepressible adventuress, Bailey Jones" would be saving Cary Grant instead of the other way round—and all while solving several convoluted mysteries with nary a chipped nail!

True sighed again. How long would it take to flip through the chapter headings or read that dreamy final paragraph one more time?

But no, she'd been seduced by the pages too many times. In her present state of mind one taste would surely lead to a two-day Benoit binge, and she was officially on the wagon. The master plan for phase three of the life of True Cowley included a strenuous exercise regimen, low-carb diet and improved reading list. Fast food fiction was out. No more haunting the pages of old favorites unless they were classics, of course. And then there was the biggest challenge of the plan, which was a no-stone-left-unturned (or looked under, a la B True) search into her mother's murky past.

True shook this thought to the recesses of her mind and got back to the problem at hand. There wasn't room for necessities in this little jewel box of a house, much less space for stacks of old paperbacks. With one bare foot she bumped the box over the wooden threshold and out onto the back porch. The stories that had given her so many hours of pleasure were now officially recyclables.

"Sorry, but you have got to go!" she said, louder than she had intended.

"Uh, sure thing. I'll just come back later."

A male voice. Southern accent, very easy on the ears. But definitely irritated.

True looked up in time to see a tall man with thick, salt and pepper hair turning to leave. His hands were pushed into the pockets of his jeans, accentuating narrow hips and broad shoulders beneath a yellow golf shirt.

"Oh, wait! Are you Mr. Bean?"

He couldn't be Mr. Bean, though. Mr. Bean, her cranky new landlord? The one who had only agreed to lease "his father's boyhood home" to True because she knew his Aunt Maisy? The one who the paperboy had referred to as "the shriv with a bad attitude?" Well, now that she thought about it, the kid who looked to be about twelve but was driving so had to be at least sixteen, probably thought of her as a shriv.

"Yeah. I'm Jackson Bean." He stopped, but made no move to enter the porch.

"Sorry, Mr. Bean. I wasn't talking to you. Please come in," she said, pushing the screen door open.

After a brief hesitation, he came into the kitchen and glanced around. He cocked his head at her, a little grin playing at the corners of his mouth. *Obviously, no one else is here*, he seemed to be thinking, *so who were you yelling at?*

The paperboy was right. Jackson Bean was not young. But he wasn't exactly shriveled either. As a matter of fact, he was still something to look at—tall and athletic (did he work out every day?); angular, weathered face (think The Marlboro Man if you're old enough to remember him—True was actually craving a cigarette); clear blue eyes (was it the smile lines around them that made them seem to twinkle?); and an infectious grin (complete with one very deep dimple).

Well, Marlboro Man might be her landlord, but he was the guest here, she reminded herself. Besides, he couldn't change his mind and throw her out. The rental agreement had been signed a week ago.

So True looked into those blue eyes (Mediterranean blue, she decided) and arranged her features to mirror his amused stare.

"I was talking to the books," she said. *Well, that makes no sense.* She felt a perplexed look settle over her face and shook her head.

"Those books?" He nodded toward her paperback friends. The ones who had eased her over so many bumps in the road of her life. "You read that stuff?"

"Not really. Someone gave me those." *Traitor*. "That's the recycling pile."

She threw an apologetic grimace at the dog-eared stack and knew she could never get rid of them now. Which was worse, a pile of old books or a pile of guilt?

"Glad to hear it. That stuff's nothing but pabulum."

"Pabulum?"

"Yeah. You know, for passive types—people who're afraid to have their own adventures, so they get 'em out of books." He obviously viewed passive types with a pile of contempt.

"Well, some people—very good friends of mine—get a lot out of those books," she said. "And Juliette Benoit is a very talented writer. They tell me."

Why do I care if he knows I like—okay, looove Juliette Benoit romance novels?

He grinned at her. "Well, I hear of women getting addicted to that stuff. I wouldn't want that to happen to you."

After a few seconds he raised his eyebrows. Oh, right. It was her turn to speak. *Take the high road*, she told herself. *It's important to get off on the right foot with the sexy, full-of-himself, romance literature-hating landlord.*

"Don't worry about me," she said, flapping one hand at the mess around her. "I'll be far too busy …" She favored him with her sweetest smile. "… getting everything put away. And I start work tomorrow. Over at Oak View. I'm the new events coordinator. It's sort of a homecoming because I was born at Oak View. Lived there until I was four. Coming back for Burkett— that's my husband …" Her voice cracked, surprising her, and tears pricked at the backs of her eyes. She willed herself not to get emotional and continued. "… coming back for his funeral was the first time I've been back since I lived at Oak View."

Okay, now it was his turn. She stood silently, waiting for some response to her verbal meandering. But he just looked at her—not rudely, but as if he were trying to place where he'd seen her or something.

"I'm real sorry about your husband. It was a nice service.

Burkett and I played on the same ball teams in high school," he said as if to explain why he'd attended the funeral.

"Thanks for coming."

He nodded.

Finally he made a sweeping gesture and said, "So, how do you like the place?"

True looked around her. *Let's see,* she thought, *twelve-foot ceilings, eight foot windows, deep crown molding, gleaming pine floors and freshly painted walls the color of pale saffron. Morning sun tumbling across the porches and filling small, elegant rooms with light. Old palms and azaleas nodding in a stirring of rain-freshened air that carries the scent of jasmine and magnolia. All nestled in the woods at the edge of a lovely little college and a five minute walk to my new job.*

"I like it," she said.

A shadow of disappointment passed over his face. He'd expected her to gush.

"My father grew up in this house," he said. "And I spent a lot of time here with my grandparents when my parents were… were traveling. The back bedroom was mine." He looked around, remembering, and for a second or two she saw the house and the boy as they had been.

"It's a wonderful house," she said. "And I'm so glad you decided to rent it to me." She let her eyes sweep over it all again, seeing her treasures—the pine chest that was the first piece of furniture she'd bought for herself, some fine mahogany pieces and a scattering of oriental rugs that had belonged to her beloved aunt, her mother's photograph album—she saw them all warmed by the lovely ambience of the cottage. Her voice softened. "I'll take good care of it," she said.

"I'm glad you're here." He smiled at her. "A house shouldn't be empty for too long. Well, I just stopped to say hello. Call if you need anything. Oh, and the back door handle is loose. I'll come by and fix it." His smile broadened. "I'll call first."

And so after a misstep or two, newly-widowed True Cowley, recently of Vista Palmas, Florida seemed to have gotten off on the right foot with Mr. Bean, The Marlboro Man.

7.

On the Job Training

A man goes to the eye doctor and says, "I think I need glasses."
"You sure do," says the doctor. "This is a gas station."
Pretty funny, huh?
I miss you. Love, Tommy

True pressed the reply key and typed, *Very funny! I miss you, too. Give your sister a big kiss for me. That was not a joke. And keep your fingers crossed. I'm on my way my new job. I'll call tonight. Love, True.*

True turned off the laptop and headed out the door, trying to think of a new joke for her grandson, Tommy.

Minutes later she stood in Oak View's kitchen, thinking that, like the man in the gas station, she might be in the wrong place.

"Your job is kind of like a highway patrolman's—long periods of boredom intersected by short bursts of pandemonium," said Jane Ellen Jackson Jones.

"Pandemonium?"

"Yeah. Like overflowing toilets at the O.O.C mother-daughter tea."

"O.O.C.?"

"Order of the Camellia. Very prestigious."

Jane E actually paused a reverential nanosecond to show just how very prestigious before continuing.

"But like I was saying, most of the time you just order up tables, chairs and microphones, listen to whiney and/or hysterical brides and their mothers and put up with Bertie Wallace who officially has the ultimate say about what's what at Oak View—he's a real piece of work. Mostly, though, the bridal consultants, individual event chairpersons, George and Buster—you know, the flower guys—and me ... well, we've got it down to a science."

Jane Ellen Jackson Jones, owner of Jane Ellen's catering, but known to everyone in Belle Hill as Jane E, suddenly halted this barrage of information, actually took a breath and looked around. "I know you're only here to observe, but hand me that bowl of sauce, will you?"

True was having some trouble following the bouncing ball of Jane E's conversation. She was obviously in the presence of one of those full-out master multi-taskers. They always made her feel inadequate. In an attempt to mask the perplexed expression she felt settling over her features, True raised her eyebrows and adopted an unperturbed smile. This made her look more alert and intelligent. Or so she thought. Actually it made her look frightened and well, a little demented.

Jane E stared at True for a second or two, then said, "But, hey. Don't worry. It's just your first day! You'll get the hang of it. Uh, the bowl? It's right there on the counter next to your arm."

As True passed it over, a citrusy, buttery aroma caressed her nose and reminded her that she had violated her revamped nutritional schedule once again by skipping breakfast.

"Smells great!" she said.

"Thanks. It's an easy recipe. I'll give it to you later if you like." She smiled at True. "But you can't give it out. Professional secret."

Jane Ellen Jackson Jones was a tall, attractive woman about True's age. Her blonde hair was short and sleek, a style that did the most to accent a pair of very large, very blue eyes. Those eyes are definitely her best feature, True decided. As usual, under the strain of excessive sensory overload her mind was beginning to wander. Jane E was oblivious to this, however and continued to lob tidbits of information at True as her nimble fingers arranged tomato and tofu tartlets and miniscule asparagus and sprout sandwiches on sterling silver platters.

"Oh, how pretty," said True, nodding at the sandwiches.

"All made with wheatless bread, no less," Jane E informed her with a slight eye roll, leaving no doubt as to her opinion of wheatless bread.

"Really? Is the honoree allergic or something?"

"Or something," said Jane E, suddenly looking very tired. "The bride-to-be is organic, vegetarian, vegan ..." she looked at True with a little grimace ..." and probably bulimic," she said. "Anyway, it's lucky you're just here to observe because today is a "spa pamper party." You know, facials, pedicures, etc. They're all getting the super seaweed wrap and pore minimizer—a timed-to-the-second skin procedure. Which means we have to time the food and drinks around it, believe it or not. Anyway, the object of the pamper party is to help the female half of the wedding party get themselves—and their pores—ready for the big day. Which is day after tomorrow. The reception is here, too—on Saturday afternoon. I'm catering it. You'll be here, right?"

"Oh, absolutely," said True.

"As I was saying, the house really isn't at its best as a spa—it's just not functional. There's a perfectly good spa area at the country club, but the bride wanted it here. It's one of the few places she feels comfortable. I'm thinking she's a bit on the agoraphobic side, too."

Jane E deftly garnished the trays with pansies and baby romaine as she talked. Although True never touched the stuff, the organic spread was starting to look downright appetizing. And not just because she was starving.

"Mind if I try one of these?" she asked Jane E.

"Sure. I've got plenty."

True popped one of the asparagus and sprout concoctions into her mouth.

"This is delicious!" She tried a tofu tartlet. "Oh, my gosh, Jane E. How'd you make these so tasty?"

"Swear not to tell?"

"I swear."

"Bacon grease."

"Bacon grease? But I thought the bride was ..."

"She'll never know the difference." Jane E dampened tea towels, spread them over the sandwiches and placed the trays into the refrigerator. "Sue Jean Withers—that's the bride— hasn't had a piece of bacon since she was ten years-old, so she won't recognize it. Nobody else would dare tell her, either." She began slicing celery into a hill of ribbon-like stalks. "For the bloodies," she explained, nodding at the celery. "Besides, I've known that girl since she was a baby, and she's not going to keel over at her own wedding if I can help it." She shook her head and paused before going on.

"I know it's sneaky as hell and none of my business, but by God that girl could use some fat in her diet." She patted her stomach, leaving a smear of green on the white canvas of her apron. "Wish I could give her some of mine."

She grinned at True and for some reason True was reminded of her landlord, Jackson Bean.

An hour later the belles of Belle Hill were washing down "vegetarian delights" with Jane E's renowned bloody Marys and mimosas. Each belle was wrapped in a pink terry cloth robe and turban-to-match while a flock of cosmetologists worked magic on every bit of skin and nail likely to be visible on Saturday.

Sue Jean, the bride-to-be (who really did look near starvation) was throwing back the canapés like bacon had never been invented.

"Jane E, these are positively divine. What is that flavor?"

"Secret mix of spices, honey. I'd tell you, but then I'd have to kill you, and we don't want that!"

Sue Jean winked conspiratorially at Jane E, and reached for another tartlet.

Across the room Nita, a pleasantly plump aesthetician, was busy applying the absolute latest thing in seaweed wrap to the pimply forehead of Sue Jean's maid of honor. Nita, who could detect the aroma of frying bacon two counties over, couldn't help a small giggle at Sue Jean's expense.

The giggle was not lost on Sue Jean. Her nerves being what they were, she began yelling, "What are you laughing at? Is it my pores? My pores are closing before they're supposed to, aren't they! Oh, my God, my pores are closing!"

The facialist, in her rush to tend to the hysterical honoree before her pores slammed shut, tripped. The pink plastic container holding the last of the coveted seaweed wrap hit the floor splattering its contents against the wall of Oak View's side parlor. Streaks of green oozed out in all directions—some as high as four feet above the chair railing.

Tears welled in Nita's eyes. Sue Jean began to tremble. After all, her six-tier, fat-free, sugarless wedding cake was to be displayed in this very room in two days! And the poor maid of honor was left with a half-wrapped forehead. A pimply forehead would be bad enough, but a half forehead breakout could be even worse if you think about it.

Jane E took a calming breath and went out to survey the damage. As she left the kitchen she murmured, "More vodka in the bloodies next round. And pick the water chestnuts out of that spinach dip and run it in the microwave for thirty seconds, will ya?"

Soon the unsuspecting belles of Belle Hill were being wrapped in spinach dip—sans water chestnuts. Sue Jean was given a double vodka bloody Mary and complete assurance that not only were her pores responding to the spin … uh, seaweed wrap, but that the entire room would be repainted that very afternoon—and in a superior shade guaranteed to compliment the tea roses in her bridal bouquet as the present hue never could.

A few hours later the bride-to-be and her twenty-two bridesmaids-to-be staggered carefully—lest they smudge their pedicures—out to a waiting bus to be transported home. Each of the nine weary cosmetologists gratefully accepted a leftover bloody Mary before packing up their paints, polishes, waxes and the remaining faux seaweed dip.

"Well, that was just amazing," said True.

She had insisted on helping Jane E and her staff of two teen-age assistants with the clean up and was now being instructed as to which of the many rules and regulations attached to the "Oak View Antebellum Home and Gardens Operational Checklist" she actually need be concerned with.

"Half this stuff is Bertie throwing his weight around. You look up "little man complex" in the dictionary, you'll find Bertie's picture. He's text book."

"Who's Bertie?" asked True.

"Oh, that's what everyone calls your boss. He prefers Dr.

Wallace or even Bertram Wallace, Ph.D. but we all call him
Bertie because he hates it. He's a librarian with the college and
oversees the rare book room. Tenure and Aunt Maisy's influence
are the only reasons he's still here, if you ask me. You'd think he
was guarding the Mona Lisa the way he goes on about those
books. It's such a small job that he was put in charge of Oak
View. In charge in his mind only." Jane E looked at her watch.
"He'll be here in about thirty minutes. He wants to meet you
in person. But don't worry. Lucky for you, our Aunt Maisy
suggested you for the job, and if Maisy asked Bertie to jump off
St. James' roof, he'd do it." She smirked at True. "Unfortunately,
she hasn't asked him yet."

"You said your Aunt Maisy? Then you and Mr. Bean are ..."

"Related. Let's have ourselves a drink on the porch, and I'll
update you on our familial ties."

True was a bit concerned about Dr. Wallace aka Bertie
catching her swigging bloody Marys on the job. Offending Jane
E seemed the greater of the two evils, however, so she accepted
the icy concoction and followed Jane E out onto Oak View's
front porch.

"Jackson is my cousin on my daddy's side," Jane E said,
easing herself into one of the big rocking chairs. "In case you
haven't noticed, just about everybody in Belle Hill is related to
everyone else."

"I'll be careful not to say anything about anyone," joked
True. "Might be talking about their kin folk."

Jane E laughed. "You got the picture." Her face turned
serious. "Your family is one of the exceptions, seeing as how
it only goes back a few generations. Your people always fell in
love with people from somewhere else. That's a plus as far as
I'm concerned."

"Why do you say that?"

"Too much of a good thing always comes to a bad thing. I'm
quoting Maisy." She took a long pull on her drink, and True was
reminded of the old lady. "Maisy says it's like all that European
royalty, marrying cousins and all. Lot of characters ..." Jane E
made little quotation marks with her fingers. "... over there
according to her. And as far as Belle Hill is concerned, just look
at May Dooty and Little May Dooty."

"Who?"

"The Dootys. They're always marrying their cousins. Distant cousins, but still … May and Little May both have those extra pinky toes. Where'd that come from?"

True choked on her drink.

"You okay?"

"Yes, it's just— Wow. Extra toes. Really?"

"I'm not kidding. Little May has never worn a sandal, much less gone bare-footed that anyone knows about. Why she didn't just have it removed is beyond me."

"Wow," True said again.

"Anyway, we were talking about Jackson. I'm younger than he is, but we've always been close. He's been through a lot— most of it his own doing, of course, but still …"

True wasn't sure how to respond to this, so she said, "He seems very nice. And he's certainly attractive."

"That he is," said Jane E. "And it's gotten him into almost as much trouble as it's gotten him out of. He was quite the ladies' man in his younger days, though he's calmed down a good bit now. He's been married twice, you know. I'll tell you about it some time, but tell me a little about yourself before Bertie gets here. Any grandchildren?"

So True spent a few minutes telling Jane E about her precocious five year old granddaughter, Mary Kate and her sweet, funny grandson, Tommy, who (to his mother's horror) wanted to become a comedian. Katie accused True of abetting Tommy's misguided aspirations by trading jokes with the nine year old. She told Jane E the one Tommy had emailed to her that morning.

"By the way, you don't know any good ones, do you?"

"Good kids?"

True laughed. "No, good jokes. It's my turn to send Tommy one."

"I'll think about it, but right now we've got your pea-headed boss to deal with."

She jerked her head to the right in the direction of the parking lot beside the house.

Sure enough, a short, pudgy man wearing a three-piece suit and bow tie was coming up the oyster shell path. In startling contrast to his body, he had the tiniest head True had ever seen on an adult. And from the look on his face, he seemed to be positively wired.

True quickly put her drink on the wicker table next to the rocker and stood, straightening her apron.

"Don't let him stress you out," said Jane E. "Oh, that reminds me of a joke."

"What?"

"A man goes to a psychiatrist and says, 'Doc, I keep thinking I'm a wigwam and a teepee. What's wrong with me? Isn't it obvious? says the psychiatrist. You're two tents.' I have a nephew who likes jokes, too."

"Tommy will love that one. His dad will, too."

About that time, Bertie reached the porch, and True crossed over to him.

"Dr. Wallace? I'm too tense."

True heard Jane E give a snort behind her.

"I mean, I'm True Cowley. It's a pleasure to meet you."

Now that they were eye to eye, she realized that his eyelids didn't cover any part of the pale irises. The exposed white all around the blue gave him that wild-eyed, wired look she had noticed at first glance. She wondered if the personality was a result of people's reaction to what they saw and expected or if coincidentally this physical characteristic simply matched his intense interior make up. True realized that her mind was wandering off on its own again and snapped herself back to attention.

"Thank you. Thank you, and no need to be nervous," Bertie was saying. She had to stop thinking of him as Bertie, or sure enough, one of these days while caught in some mental haze, she would call him Bertie to his face. Dr. Wallace, Dr. Wallace, Dr. Wallace, she reminded herself.

He—Dr. Wallace—took in her dirty apron. "I trust Miz Jackson (he nodded curtly at Jane E who raised her bloody Mary in salutation) has you well-oriented by now, though I don't recall kitchen duty being part of the job description."

"She insisted, Bertie," said Jane E.

"Good. Good. Learning the ropes, eh?" He glanced at True's half-empty glass on the table, pressed his thin lips into a tight line, and said, "Well, well, you come with the highest of recommendations. The very highest. My dear, dear friend, Maisy Downey, is this institution's most beloved benefactress, you know."

"Oh, yes. Yes, I know."

Bertie's echo-speak was contagious, it seemed.

He smoothed his thin comb-over nervously and turned his teeny head in Jane E's direction.

"And how did the party go this afternoon? Oak View still in one piece? Heh, heh, heh."

"Well, we did have one small mishap involving seaweed wrap on the east parlor wall," said Jane E in a bored voice. "It'll have to be painted before Saturday."

"Good Lord," said Bertie, hurrying red-faced into the house to survey the damage.

"Good Lord!" they heard him cry seconds later. "I thought this was a ladies' party. How did this happen?"

"Trust me, Bertie. It was just an unfortunate accident, and the only lady involved was not a guest, but a professional aesthetician who shall remain un-named." Jane E took a sip of her bloody Mary. "Seaweed happens, Bertie."

Jane E went into the kitchen to "finish up" while Bertie and True sat at a desk in the adjoining office. True's duties were much the same as those she had performed on a volunteer basis at the south Florida historic home known as Vispera. She would not be expected to cook or serve or tidy up as she had today except in the event of an extreme emergency, he assured her.

Emergencies happened a lot, she knew. But she didn't mind. The afternoon's "spa party" had been more fun than she'd had in months.

Bertie finished up the meeting with neighborly chit-chat. Had she gotten settled? Was it true that she'd never, never ever returned to Belle Hill until now?

True got the impression that Bertie found this not only peculiar but an affront toward the citizenry of Belle Hill. He did not mention the fact that she had lived in this very house, which was odd since he (along with everyone else in Belle Hill) surely knew her story. Perhaps he was waiting for her to mention it, but Bertie was the last person she wanted to engage in that conversation. Maybe she was letting Jane E's opinion of the little man color her own viewpoint, but True had a feeling that her new friend was dead-on in her estimation of Bertie Wallace, Ph.D.

Bertie placed the keys to Oak View in her hand. True looked at them and felt that she was holding not only the key to her past, but quite possibly the key to that very scary place, phase three of her life—also known as the future.

8.
Psychology 101

After everyone left Oak View, True carefully ticked off the items on her list. Lights and ovens off. Doors locked. *Double-check light switches and locks* had been penciled in. (Due to the strange lights mentioned by the repairman True and Maisy had seen that first day at Oak View?) Thermostat set on seventy-eight for cool and sixty-five for heat. Toilets flushed (who doesn't flush a toilet?) but not running. *Jiggle handles* had been penciled in. Alarm on.

She let herself out of the side door into an afternoon that was unexpectedly cool, the lingering scent of wisteria and the first hints of a blooming jasmine floating in its soft air. True walked around to the rear garden where an endless carpet of lawn blended into the golf course which in turn merged into St. James cemetery on one side and abutted a ribbon of woods on the other.

The cemetery, visible halfway down the hill, beckoned her. The feeling was almost as strong as the pull toward Oak View had been on the day of Burkett's funeral. True stared at the picturesque scene. It was possible that one of those silent markers peeking through the trees was her mother's grave. Which she still had not visited. The longer she put it off, the bigger it loomed and nagged at her nerves. A five minute walk would put her there. After all of the years and miles that separated them, it was right there. *But not today,* True decided and pulled her gaze from the cemetery.

Belle Hill was appropriately named, she decided and in her opinion the "beautiful hill's" crowning glory was St. James

College, the jewels in that crown being St. James Chapel and Oak View. On the spot where True stood, the land fell away toward the edge of the eleventh green where the grounds of newer homes had attached themselves to its expanse. They had not been built when she'd watched the stars and moon and lightning bugs as a child from Oak View's back lawn.

True sat on a wrought-iron bench with an all-over grape design meant to please the eye rather than the bottom. She shifted unproductively and wrapped herself in the hazy memories that were returning with increasing frequency. To soften the process of exhuming her past, True thought of these memory-fragments as so many Monarch butterflies migrating home to light pleasantly here and there, waiting patiently for her to make sense of the pattern they created and thereby provide her with her mother's story. This little exercise also helped her to focus on something besides her widow-ness.

She dreamed of Burkett every night. In the dream, she was trying to talk to him as he attempted to sink a short putt on the eighteenth at the Vista Palmas Golf Club. Everyone was shushing her, but she couldn't or wouldn't stop talking. She wanted to ask him about the money, the betting, how he could have kept it all from her. He missed the putt. Then he was walking away from her into the men's grill—no woman's land. She didn't follow. Night after night the dream dogged her and morning after morning she woke drenched with perspiration and guilt, but with no answers.

But True had a plan. Each night, after supper she either emailed or called her grandchildren. Calling was preferable, of course. Their voices were the sweetest sounds she knew. Mary Kate and Tommy would fill her in on their days for a few minutes (and of course, Tommy would almost always have a new joke) before begging off. But sometimes they felt talkative and True would be on the phone with them for quite a while. One evening she spent over an hour tutoring Tommy on his times tables. He had been reminded by his humorless teacher, Mr. Hudgins that "Math is no joke!" Tommy imitated Mr. Hudgins' hypo-nasal voice, and True had to laugh.

True's daughter, Katie, always wanted to speak to her mother, unlike when she and True had lived minutes from one another in Vista Palmas. Now the bored or even agitated tone in Katie's voice was replaced with the one she adopted when talking to her friends. It seemed that Katie was learning to appreciate her mother, now that True was not so handy. Even Parker took the time to chat with his mother-in-law, inquiring about her finances, her health and most importantly, just what was going on in her life.

Before she went to sleep True would read an uplifting book for awhile. Self-help books and sweet stories of women overcoming great obstacles were stacked on B True's lovely French rosewood work stand that served as her bedside table. But eventually True drifted back to that box of Juliette Benoit paperbacks on the top shelf of her closet. She felt bad about failing one aspect of her grand plan so soon, but the escapades of Bailey Jones always had the most uplifting effect on her. And after all, that was the point, right? To be uplifted?

Part two of the bedtime ritual consisted of closing her eyes and visualizing a happy time in her life with Burkett or family times with Katie and then as grandparents to Mary Kate and Tommy. She figured this habitual focus on the positive would eventually have the desired effect of replacing nightmares with sweet dreams.

She knew she needed to grieve for her husband and she did, yet the process was skewed somehow — first by the suddenness of his death and then by his deception. And as if this big, black heap of sadness and anger weren't enough, True piled on the guilt. She knew it probably wasn't deserved, but she couldn't help it.

How could I not have known what my own husband was up to?

If she'd paid closer attention, could she have helped Burkett, gone to Gamblers Anon or something? Just thinking about the pressure he'd been under made her ache all over. No wonder her husband had had a heart attack. Why did he keep it all from her? *Because he could, that's why.* Could it have been avoided if she'd been paying attention?

The Vista Palmas Funeral Home and Crematorium offered referrals for grief counseling and held meetings for the newly widowed (which Katie signed her up for), but True's feeling that her grief process was out of kilter made her wonder, how do you grieve for someone you didn't really know? She had only attended one session. She did keep the Managing Your Grief manual, however, read it cover to cover twice and referred to it often.

Since her nights were devoted to sweats and nightmares, True was determined to use the daylight hours to move forward — or in the case of the mystery surrounding her mother, move backward. In any case, she was redirecting her emotions like section eleven in her grief book suggested. (Never mind that she hadn't quite followed the suggestions in sections one through ten). As the days since her return to Belle Hill rolled by allowing precious hours alone with Oak View, and True implemented the redirection theory, the more prolific and vibrant her childhood memories became.

She'd had a swing. She recalled a man … a black man, a very dark black man … she didn't remember his name … and he was hanging the swing from a low oak branch. He'd helped her position herself just right on the seat made from a wide pine board he'd sanded smooth as chamois. The man had wrapped her fingers one by one around the ropes at just the right height and given her that first gentle push. True closed her eyes, feeling the long-ago breeze on her face, hearing the man's encouragement. "Now you getting it. Easy now. That's right."

Then the vision was gone. She knew it would return, but only if she didn't try to force it. Experience had taught her that. True stood and stretched before turning in the direction of the woods and home.

Situated here and there in the small patch of pines and palmettos, azaleas and magnolias and dogwood was a cluster of several houses within shouting distance of one another, yet completely hidden from their neighbors' views. Hers—or the one she occupied, was one of the closest to Oak View. Beyond that was Jackson Bean's. There was another cottage where, according to Jane E, two unmarried sisters had lived their entire lives, and a few other houses inhabited by other Belle Hillians whose acquaintance she had yet to make.

So with memories, observations and emotions jitterbugging through her brain, she got up, trying to rub the grapevine imprint from her behind. Not far from the edge of the woods, the path to her new home veered off to the right. It seemed to be well-trodden, so there must be something of interest down there, she figured. What the heck, no one was waiting at home for her. Why not do a little investigating?

The path seemed familiar, somehow, and she knew that just around that clump of scrub oak, there was something … And then there it was. The grotto. She'd been here with her mother. It wasn't that she'd forgotten it exactly, but just didn't remember where she'd seen it. Like something in a book, perhaps … or a movie … But here it was, and it was certainly memorable.

She sat on the stone bench across the path from the structure, which was twenty feet tall and at least as wide. Constructed of stacks of rocks oozing with long-petrified mortar, it was covered in ivy and fig vine. It was divided into the "cave" side with its domed ceiling soaring like a chapel's above the stone floor and the other enclosed side which was solid rock halfway up. Above this was a large niche which held a life-sized white marble statue of the Blessed Mother. Her slender hands were in prayer, holding a string of rosary beads, and she wore an expression of serenity and holiness.

She's still beautiful, after all these years, thought True, walking into the grotto. Just above True's head to the right was an opening that led to the niche where Mary said her endless prayers. True could see her plainly, praying away as if all the years had never happened.

True remembered Nick hoisting her up so that she could crawl through to the statue, and how scary it was, how high it seemed, how sharp the rocks were against her skin. Nick had been disappointed by True's reticence. She could hear her calling—remembered her mother's voice—full of irritation— calling to her lily-livered daughter, "Oh, for heaven's sake, True. I used to love climbing all over this thing when I was little."

But once inside the narrow opening that lead to the statue, True had started to cry. Immobilized by fear, she couldn't move forward or back. Nick had climbed up and snatched her down before sitting on the stone bench, statue-like, herself, intent on her journal. The Blessed Mother had simply gone on with her prayers.

True walked back out onto the path and stared at the bench.

She had felt lonely here that day. They'd been too busy for her, those two mothers—Mary stuck forever reciting the mysteries of her son and Nick forever scribbling in her journal.

The shadows were growing long and the air a bit too cool. The lonely feelings she'd experienced in this place grew on the shadows. True looked at Mary and figured she was praying the sorrowful mysteries, the story of the passion and crucifixion, as the dusk gathered around her. It was time to leave Mary to her sorrows and get on home.

•

The phone was ringing as True crossed through the back porch to her kitchen.

"Ms. Cowley?"

Mr. Bean's deep voice surprised her.

"Yes. Mr. Bean?"

"Jackson."

"Oh, okay. Jackson. Oh, and call me True, of course."

"If it's not too late, I thought I'd take a look at that loose handle on your back door."

"Well, could you give me thirty minutes? I just walked in."

"I'll see you in forty-five."

"Even better," she laughed. "See you then."

True looked around her. Not too bad. A few dirty dishes in the sink. A vase of wilting lilies in the living room.

"Oh, oh," she said aloud, spying the rumpled copy of *New York Nemesis* on the coffee table and remembering her landlord's disdain for her favorite author. She snatched up the Juliette Benoit paperback from the table and stuck it under the sofa cushion, vaguely aware that this was a bad idea. She would probably forget where she put it and not find it until she moved again, if ever. But her mind raced ahead to the dishes in the sink. Rinsing them, she put them in the dishwasher. She picked off the sagging blooms and yellowing leaves from the vase of lilies and fluffed up the bouquet, decided they could use fresh water, then snipped their stems before putting them back in the vase. The time was getting away from her as usual, so she spritzed some lavender air freshener around, turned on the ceiling fan to distribute it and hurried into the shower.

Again Jackson Bean stood at her back door. Only this time he held a battered tool box and wore a pale green golf shirt with his jeans and jogging shoes. True imagined his closet with rows of jeans, khakis and golf shirts in assorted colors. (*Does the man not own any other clothes?* wondered True. *Although he does do a lot for those jeans*).

She had showered, shaved her legs, washed her hair, blown it dry and applied a miniscule amount of make-up—didn't want to give Mr. Bean, er, Jackson—the wrong impression. She did put on her new skirt and a silky tee shirt in that peachy color that people always said looked great on her. Bronzy sandals showed off the pedicure she'd treated herself to the day before. By the time she got to the door, he was already fiddling with its handle.

"You don't happen to have an Allen wrench, do you?" he said in the way of a greeting.

"I doubt it," said True. "What is an Allen wrench?"

"It's a little L-shaped thing. I don't know how people get along without one."

"But you don't have one," she pointed out.

He looked at her, smiled good-naturedly and said, "I have one. I just don't seem to have one with me."

"You know, I saw something like that … Now where …?"

True went to a drawer in the kitchen where some odds and ends had been left by a previous tenant.

"Is this what you're looking for?"

"Yeah. Thanks." Jackson grinned at True. "Now who'd've thought you'd be the one with the correct tools for the job? Here, since you have it, let me show you how to use it. Put it in that little hole by the handle." True leaned down in front of Jackson and a last ray of sunlight played on her hair and released the just-shampooed fragrance.

"Now just tighten it up."

Her fingers deftly turned the wrench and Jackson noticed how pretty her hands were—the olive skin smooth and her nails short and free of polish.

"There," she said and stood up straight almost knocking into Jackson. She didn't notice and handed the wrench over to him.

"You keep it," he said. "It'll come in handy. Sometimes the handle on the outdoor shower gets loose, too."

"Outdoor shower?"

"It's on the other side of the porch."

"Hot water?"

"Yes, ma'am." Jackson smiled at her. "And very private."

"I've never seen that, except at the beach. Well, come to think of it, we had a bathroom attached to the garage at B True's. But that was for Verna, our maid." True made a little face. "I could never figure out if it was a luxury for Verna or a status symbol for B True."

"I'd vote for the status symbol angle if your aunt was anything like the old ladies I grew up with. Anyway, it is odd, but when my great-grandfather built these houses for his children, he added an outdoor shower to each one."

"Which one was your great-grandfather's?"

"Oak View. Only it was called Sunrise back then. Believe it or not, the old man lost it in a poker game. The new owner didn't like the name, changed it to Oak View. My great grandmother insisted that they move to the house closest to Sunrise. It's the smallest, but my great-grandfather was forced to look at the home he'd lost every time he walked out of his front door."

"Wow. That's some story. I guess you really hate gambling, huh?"

"Not really," said Jackson. "Now, is there anything else I can do for you while I'm here?"

True thought about it for a second. There was that burner on the stove that wouldn't light, even though she'd taken it apart and cleaned it.

"No, I think that's it," she said.

With the absurdly low rent Jackson Bean was charging, he shouldn't have to be her personal handyman. Besides, she kind of liked her new landlord and the novelty of his down home persona. There hadn't been too many of those in Vista Palmas, that was for sure.

And True was lonely. She had Maisy, had hit it off right away with Jane E and had met a few other potential friends, but most of her time in her new town had so far been spent in getting settled, learning the lay of the land and soaking up the memories at Oak View.

Though Burkett had squandered their money on his stupid,

inept golf game, had cashed out his life insurance policies without telling her and left his devoted wife in a huge financial lurch, left her to suffer the pain of betrayal on top of the sudden crushing vacuum created by his untimely demise, she missed her husband—at least her naïve perception of who her husband had been.

True craved the sound of a male voice. She missed that straightforward kind of conversation one had with men. She missed the presence of another person sharing her world.

Being around Jackson helped fill—just a tiny bit—the void left by Burkett. So she decided to save the malfunctioning burner for another time—when he might be inclined to stay for awhile. For one of those times when she was feeling a little crazy with the emptiness of the house.

"Well, thanks for fixing the do …"

True was interrupted by the sound of crashing underbrush.

Jackson turned in the direction of the foliage that encroached on the small yard. "JuJu!" he yelled into the bushes. "Sit!"

A large chocolate colored dog scrambled from around the side of the house. It appeared that the animal had underestimated its own speed in taking the corner. As it cleared the house, it noticed True standing on the back steps.

The command to sit and the sight of the stranger vied for the dog's attention and of course a potential new playmate won out. Tripping over its paws, the creature righted itself and lunged at True. True realized JuJu was not a threat what with its tail wagging and its tongue lolling out of its smiling dog face, but she wasn't about to have her new skirt ruined by this undisciplined beast.

Before she could stop herself she heard herself curse the crazy dog as she put out her hands to ward off its attack of affection.

From her advantageous spot on the top step, True caught the dog's paws while attempting to push it away. By some trick of leverage that True could not repeat in a million years, the dog was flipped into the air and landed on its back with a thud.

JuJu, having misunderstood True's expletive, gazed at True for one awe-filled second before scurrying over to Jackson where she did, indeed, sit.

Master and dog stared in amazement at True and she couldn't

help thinking their expressions were strangely similar.

"Man," said Jackson finally. "Where'd you learn to do that?"

"Oh, it was an accident. I hope I didn't hurt him."

"Her."

"What? Oh, I hope she's all right."

"She's fine. Tough as nails. But she got your shirt dirty."

True looked down and sure enough there was a sizable slobber smear on the front.

"That's okay," she said. "I'll just throw it in the wash."

"No, it isn't okay. Let me take her home …" He gave JuJu a stern look, as if to remind her she was still in trouble. "… and I'll be right back. If you don't mind."

Ten minutes later Jackson and True (in a fresh shirt) sat on her front porch with a cold beer and a chilled glass of chardonnay, respectively. Jackson had returned, dogless, with an apology in the form of the wine along with three home-grown tomatoes and a bag of just-filleted fish.

"That damn dog is the worst one I've had yet." Jackson was saying.

It turned out that the topic of their conversation was the latest (and last, vowed Jackson) in a line of female chocolate labs named JuJu he'd owned.

"For some reason though, I've gotten real attached to her, as bad as she is." He grinned at True. "To tell the truth, I am crazy about that crazy dog."

He shook his head and tilted back in the rocking chair across from True. "I don't know what's wrong with her, though. I've trained a lot of dogs. This one's plenty smart, and she wants to mind. It's just that she's …" Jackson shook his head again.

"Distracted?" said True.

"Yeah. It's like she's always distracted."

"She's just a puppy, isn't she? Learning a lot of things? Could be she's a little too smart. Interested in everything at once. She's got personality, that's for sure."

"You know, I think you're exactly right. You don't have some kind of dog psychology degree, do you?"

True laughed. "No, but I've had a lot of dogs, too. Sometimes it's just easier to see things when you're not so close to the problem."

True and Jackson traded dog stories for awhile, decided to have another drink and before True knew it, Jackson was showing her how he pan-fried fish while she sliced tomatoes. It turned out they both liked them with salt and pepper and mayonnaise—a Belle Hill tradition that True had somehow kept with her. It was a nice, companionable meal. Jackson was funny and easy to talk to. He seemed genuinely interested in everything True had to say, which now that she thought about it, Burkett had not. Of course we know he had some big problems vying for her attention.

As Jackson headed down the path to his own house, he thought about what a nice person True Cowley seemed to be. And different. Hard to figure out. Oddly enough, he liked that in a woman.

9.

And Afterward at the Reception

True had been back and forth from her house to Oak View all day. As Jane E had promised, the efficiency of the professionals who spent their weekends toiling away so that others could party care-free was nothing short of amazing. True mostly studied her many check-lists and tried to stay out of their way.

Open tents of clear plastic went up in blessedly cool air, providing practically invisible protection over the various food stations. Tables and chairs were arranged in the garden and bars set up in the most advantageous locations for the efficient dispensing of libations to the thirsty, foot-sore and/or conversationally challenged.

As the last of the lace tablecloths were topped with knotted runners of the palest green voile, the "flower guys," George and Buster, began to work their magic. They were big men, tough and muscular and looked as if the ability to touch a flower without crushing it was beyond them. However, their large hands deftly twisted vines, endless strings of tiny lights, green hydrangeas, baby's breath and delicate lilies around the ugly tent poles transforming them into fabulous cylindrical arrangements. Clouds of baby's breath entwined with more twinkling lights clustered at the tops of the poles.

Complimented by the sumptuous, silky runners, candles nestled in bouquets of lilies, green hydrangeas, and pink roses topped each table. Baskets of corresponding flowers adorned the porch—just a hint of what awaited guests when they entered the back lawn. When the sun went down and the lights and candles came alive, it would be enchanting.

Jane E and her staff performed an intricate dance in Oak View's tiny kitchen, though most of the food came in vans equipped with warming ovens. Chafing dishes of hot seafood dips surrounded by delicate pastry shells, platters of cheeses, elaborate fruit bouquets and a dessert table of downright decadence were only the beginning.

There were delicate lamb chops, bite-sized softshell crabs, a pirogue overflowing with boiled shrimp on a bed of ice. There was a small mountain of beef tenderloin and homemade yeast rolls and horseradish sauce if the guests were inclined to make themselves a sandwich.

Knowing the bride's dietary predilections, True questioned Jane E about the abundance of non-vegetarian fare. It turned out that the FOB (father of the bride) refused to fork over the big bucks for "a bunch of damn sprouts and hummus." If Sue Jean (really Sue Jean's mother, of course) was to have the wedding of her dreams, then "by God, we're having real food and plenty of it," said dear old dad.

The only concession was the aforementioned wedding cake. Its lovely (imitation) fondant-swathed layers had been carried in and assembled atop a bed of cabbage roses and petals and were now enthroned in all of their sugarless glory beneath an ethereal arbor of baby's breath. The new paint color on the walls—as promised by Jane E—was a perfect compliment to the cake's pale green and white icing as well as the bride's bouquet.

An hour before the wedding party was to arrive True dashed home to shower and don a beige silk suit, B True's pearls and a pair of sensible pumps. Appropriately yet subtly attired she walked back through the woods to Oak View, grateful that her presence at most future events would not be required. But for the next few weeks or months she would be observing, helping out when needed, checking things off her lists and "just learning—yes, learning the ropes," as Bertie put it.

She arrived well before the bride and was so glad because Sue Jean made a down-right stunning entrance on the arm of her husband (who was handsome in that linebacker kind of way that afflicted all of the Moore men—and one female cousin).

Sue Jean had opted for the most modern, sophisticated of bridal looks which True had to admit suited her stick-like figure quite well. She wasn't crazy about Sue Jean's headpiece selection, however.

A bouquet of exquisite white feathers (True overheard it described as a plumed fascinator) was somehow attached to one side of the bride's head so that it seemed to sprout from her asymmetrically coiled brown hair. At first glance it appeared that she'd had a disastrous and violent encounter with a snowy egret or maybe a large seagull. True was reminded of Alfred Hitchcock's *The Birds* and gave a little shudder. But then she reminded herself that Sue Jean was quite the style setter in Belle Hill, so the bird-wreck look was probably the latest thing in bridal gear and that she'd better get used to it. True sighed at this unhappy thought and turned her attention to the gathering crowd of well-wishers.

If the spa pamper party gave True a chance to observe a segment of the twenty to thirty-year-old crowd, then the wedding reception of Sue Jean Moore Withers to Withers Watson Moore (yep—fourth cousins on their mothers' and fathers' sides) gave her an opportunity to scope the rest of Belle Hill's social set.

The under-forty group was a gaggle of strapless silk. Everyone in this bunch of beauties wore some variation of the same dress accessorized with dangling earrings and six-inch heels clinging miraculously to their rapidly swelling feet. None carried purses. The only dissimilarity in this demographic was in the hair department. Shoulder-length, swingy-shiny or shoulder-length twisted up and held with an attractive clip were the two variations.

The forty-plus women were uniformly attired in silk suits, pearls and sensible strappy sandals (or pumps for the seventy-pluses). Small, suit-matching purses hung from their shoulders. The occasional rebel sported an actual cocktail dress and/or stilettos.

The most impressive of these "live wires" was a willowy blonde who could have been a time-tested forty or a well-preserved fifty-five. She was engaged in an animated conversation with a couple of strapless-clad bridesmaids (who sported identical up-dos caught in lovely clusters of tiny lilies).

The older woman's laughter and voice (and mid-west accent) rose above the hum-drum of conversation and soft music, and True thought she looked like someone who could be named ... Nick.

Except that her teeth were sooo perfect, flashing blue-white when she smiled. And those professionally arched brows. They remained in perpetual high surprise as the neon smile faded.

The neckline of her silvery frock took a dangerous yet calculated plunge to suspiciously perky breasts. These elements were somewhat un-Nick-esque. Trying too hard, decided True (though True had nothing but admiration for the marvels of plastic surgery, orthodontia and cosmetic dentistry). Though the woman's looks caught everyone's interest, it was her attitude, her confident, cool, I'm-in-charge demeanor that held their attention. That was the Nick-esque part. Yes, she was definitely the kind of person who could carry off a name like Nick.

I wonder what size she wears, mused True. *Probably a six. Maybe even a four!*

True was an eight. And only if spandex was involved.

Her mental ramblings were interrupted by the sight of a familiar figure coming her way, a drink in each hand and a very cute smile on his face.

Good Lord, the Marlboro Man in a tux.

As he got within speaking distance of True, he raised one of the drinks—a pomegranate martini from the looks of it. He cocked his head to one side as if to say, "Here's your drink."

True stepped forward, closing the small distance between them. "Well, I really can't," she said, beaming back at him. She couldn't help herself. He really was something in that tux. "I'm working, but ..."

The blonde was suddenly somehow between them, balancing on the tips of her toes, kissing Jackson's cheek and wrapping one sleek arm around his neck like a boa (constrictor).

"The mystery man returns," she said, taking the drink. She glanced at True as if she were a fly in her martini. "Thanks, darling," she said to Jackson, and turned back to continue her conversation with the bridesmaids.

But Jackson—the mystery man?—was looking past the

blonde at True. And he was looking confused.

"Oh, I thought you were talking to me …," said True. "I mean I was surprised that you were bringing me a drink …" She clamped her lips shut, wisely trying to think before she went on. She stood there staring at Jackson with that ridiculous expression on her face that he found … well, that he found completely charming.

"Would you like a ginger ale or something?" he said, grinning at her, "since you're on duty and everything."

She laughed, mentally thanking him for smoothing over the latest in what she thought of as an endless conga line of her life's embarrassing moments and said, "No, thanks. I'm supposed to check in with the band about something. Nice to see you again."

True turned away but not before noticing the blonde watching her, smiling and pretending to listen to what the bridesmaid was saying. But her eyes followed True, and her eyes were not smiling.

Everyone was very friendly, possibly assuming True was a guest, but probably due to the opportunity to make acquaintance with the keeper of the Oak View calendar. The calendar booked up a year in advance of the peak wedding months of March, April and May. Though the rest of the country may swoon over the thought of a June wedding, many a bride had literally swooned at her June wedding in Belle Hill due to an early onslaught of heat and humidity.

The other desirable month is October when the weather is almost always predictably great—except for the occasional late hurricane that puts the damper of all dampers on things.

Of course big football weekends are never under consideration. If any men actually showed up, they were liable to have the game plugged into their ears during the service. Everyone still talks about Baskin Smith, who stood up at his own niece's wedding and yelled, "touch down, Auburn!" in the middle of the Ave Maria. It happened twelve years ago and some of the female family members are (justifiably) not speaking to him to this day.

So due to her interesting history, new status as keeper of the calendar and the fact that she was just plain likable, True could hardly keep up with her check lists and observations for being introduced around.

"Oh, here you are," trilled one elderly lady. "My name is Olivia Honeychurch, but everybody calls me Poo. I'm your neighbor. Lived there all of my eighty-seven years with my baby sister, Flora. We never miss a wedding." She opened her purse, snagged a couple of softshells from a passing tray and while simultaneously juggling a martini glass, dropped them into her bag. Noting True's shocked expression, she said, "Don't worry, I keep a nice sandwich bag in there so my purse doesn't get greasy."

"Good evening, Miss Poo. Whatcha drinkin' there?" said a man who had approached with an almost comical swagger. He was older than True, probably a nice-looking guy at one time. He had a black eye. He peered at the crabs in the woman's purse as if they were a couple of lipsticks.

"Good evening, Dwayne."

True noticed that the old lady was giving Dwayne what B True referred to as the sideways lizard eye.

"This happens to be what is known as a flirtini," continued Poo Honeychurch primly. "But don't worry, you're safe," she said, adding a smirk to the aforementioned lizard eye. It was obvious that Dwayne was not on her list of favorites. She turned to True and said grudgingly, "Dwayne, this is Mrs. Cowley."

The man put out his hand and True shook it. "The name's Bond," he said. He didn't relinquish True's hand, and making a gun shape with his other hand (which he pointed playfully at her) he winked exaggeratedly. "Dwayne Bond," he said.

It was so ridiculous True had to laugh, but Poo rolled her eyes, grabbed a couple of shrimp rolls from another passing tray, dropped them in with the crabs, and said, "Dwayne, everybody's tired of that." She turned to True. "He thinks he's double-O-seven." Then back to Dwayne. "Where'd you get that shiner, Dwayne?"

But he was spared the embarrassment of an explanation by the rather hurried approach of Maisy Downy.

After brief hellos to Poo and Dwayne, she said, "You know True is our new director here at Oak View. I hate to deprive you of her delightful company, but she's needed at the fruit table."

As they walked away, Maisy said, "Thank me because A—you're not really needed at the fruit table and B—I just saved you from the infamous Dwayne Bond."

"So he told me. What's with the double-o-seven routine?"

"I don't know." Maisy shook her head and blew out a breath of exasperation. "The name Bond and he thinks he looks like Sean Connery—which he did sort of—thirty years ago. But like they say, he's been riding it hard for a long time. Now he's paying the price. Lost his looks. Never could measure up to that brother of his, either—Reverend Wayne over at Big Welcome Baptist. On top of that, he came from nothing, never got over it. You know how it is.

"People call him the car wash king because he's got these big car wash things all over the state and makes a load of money at it. He drives a black Hummer, wears a lot of gold jewelry, chases every skirt he sees—young, old, single, married—it doesn't matter. Testosterone and insecurity—a terrible combination if there ever was one."

"That was some black eye he had," said True.

"My bet is that old Dwayne parked that hummer of his in the wrong garage once too often, if you get my meaning," said Maisy, her old eyes twinkling.

True laughed. The old lady always cracked her up. "Okay, now tell me about Poo Honeychurch."

"What about her?"

"Well, for one thing, she has a couple of pounds of hot seafood in her purse."

"Oh, that. I'm surprised Jane E didn't warn you about the Honeychurch girls. They live in that cottage near you with the ugliest dog you ever saw—a bad-humored pug named Faulkner. The girls have lived there their entire lives, never married. They are what people used to refer to as genteel poverty. They exist on a small, fixed income, but have a house full of fine antiques, art, china, crystal, jewelry, you name it. They sell a piece every few months to supplement."

"But a guest stealing food from a wedding …"

"Well, they don't think of it as stealing, just as taking home a few leftovers. And they're not officially guests. They probably weren't invited. To them, everything that happens at Oak View is just a neighborhood party, and it's their neighborhood. But they're terrible snobs, and if the people involved aren't up to their standards, they won't go—no matter how good the food is."

"So everybody just goes along with it?"

"They do. As a matter of fact, it's gotten to be kind of a status symbol to have them at your function. Nobody even bothers to send them wedding invitations because they will insist on bringing a gift—could be an old jelly jar or a priceless piece of porcelain. Either way, no one wants it."

"You said functions. They show up for other things, too?"

"Oh, yes. Especially if it's free and there's food and alcohol involved—serve sherry and they'll be the first ones there and the last to leave."

"Well, that's the craziest thing I ever heard of," said True. "But sweet, when you think about it."

All things considered, the evening had gone well. One bridesmaid who'd been "over-served" was "barfing in the boxwood by the patio" according to an unsympathetic usher, when she lost her balance and got herself wedged, head first in the prickly hedge.

It took two waiters quite some time to get her out. True figured the lengthy extrication had something to do with the fact that the girl's dress was up to her armpits and she was wearing thong undies. At least they matched her dress.

True overheard Poo Honeychurch remark to Maisy, "Good heavens, did you see those underpants?"

"Who didn't?" said Maisy. "By the way, they're Victoria's Secret. I have them in fuschia."

A nostalgic feeling came over True as she remembered B True's time-honored advice to always wear nice underwear because you never know when you might be involved in an accident. Taking a drunken header into the boxwood probably wasn't what she had in mind, but still …

Another couple was reported missing, having last been seen staggering off toward the eleventh green, full bottle of champagne in hand. Once it was established that both parties were well past the age of consent, Jane E shrugged and deemed it the sign of a successful party.

Soon Mr. and Ms. Withers Moore were exiting through a shower of rose petals into an idling white limousine. True wished them a silent good luck, figuring they would need it. Having witnessed the groom scarfing down the beef tenderloin and knowing of the bride's dietary dysfunctions, there was bound to be some unpleasantness on the horizon. True sighed. She just hoped they made it through the honeymoon without a food fight.

10.

Things in Common

The next morning True attended the early service at St. James Chapel. A church of architectural precision, it was one of the oldest and most photographed in the south. The mere mention of this venerable spot was enough to throw a prospective bride into a fit of nuptial bliss. As you can imagine, there was hardly a Saturday that three (the maximum allowed) couples didn't tie the knot at St. James.

On this particular Sunday morning, True found an empty seat next to Maisy, who was dressed in varying shades of pink from her silvery blonde head to her crooked little toes. She gave True an approving smile and patted the younger woman's hand as she slid into the pew. The chapel's spectacular windows stood open, admitting the glories of spring weather on the gulf coast — a true testament to the Almighty. The flowers from the previous day's ceremony still adorned the altar and window sills. The choir was in top form and Fr. Baker, his vestments radiant in the morning rays of sun, his radio announcer voice echoing off the hallowed surfaces of mahogany and marble, plaster and stained glass, kept the sermon mercifully short. True's Sunday was off to a fine start.

There was a good turn-out considering the previous evening's liquor consumption. Even the bridesmaid who'd literally and figuratively showed her you-know-what at the reception made the walk of shame as far as the second-to-last row.

Dr. Bertie sat alone toward the front. The dozen or so hairs atop his tiny cranium had come unplastered and they waltzed upright in the slight breeze, making him seem vulnerable and sad. True almost wished she had joined him in his empty pew.

True noticed Jackson in a back row on the opposite side from her. Next to him was Jane E. Next to her was the blonde from the night before. Whereas the hedge-diving bridesmaid was perspiring and had taken on a greenish tinge, the blonde merely looked a bit haggard. Still, it was enough to add to True's general feeling that all was right with the world.

After the service, True waved to them all from a distance, and Jackson started toward her. But the blonde grabbed a passing man, and Jackson was forced to change course and speak to him. Jane E, however, excused herself and approached True.

After exchanging pleasantries and the obligatory observations as to the amount of humidity present (this is part of practically every conversation that takes place along the gulf coast), True said in her most blasé manner, "By the way, Jane E, who was that attractive woman with y'all? The blonde? I think I met her last night, but I seem to have forgotten her name."

For some reason, Jane E looked at True a bit quizzically before answering.

"Oh, that's Holly Varjak. Teaches history at the college."

"Holly Varjak," True repeated. "Unusual name."

"It is for these parts. Anyway, she's been in town about a year. Transferred from another college out west somewhere, I think. Odd she ended up here, but I understand she's a fairly recent divorcee, has no children. I guess she wanted to make a fresh start or maybe the job appealed to her. Who knows? She certainly didn't come to St. James for the salary. Anyway, Jackson has been passing the time with her, as we say, but she's just a clone of every woman he's dated. I can hardly keep them straight." She laughed. "I don't think he can, either."

Conversation predictably segued into commentary on the previous night's soiree. The women agreed that it had been a resounding success. Both also concurred that the presence of the party-crashing, hors d'ourves-hoarding Honeychurches and the bridesmaid's spectacular dive into the boxwood added just the right amount of spice, thereby insuring that the party would remain firmly and highly placed in the town's collective memory for decades. (This achievement runs a frighteningly close second in importance to the success of the marriage itself as far as some brides and their mothers are concerned.)

"That reminds me," said Jane E, "I hate to ruin a beautiful Sunday morning by bringing up Bertie, but he likes for us to double-check—yes, even triple-check, if need be …" she mimicked the little man … "things in the house after each event. He's especially on edge because of the malfunctioning lights— they keep flickering at night, according to him, even though the electrician can't find anything wrong." She looked over her shoulder, checking to make sure the little man hadn't sneaked up on her. "Personally, I think it's Bertie's wiring that could use some professional help," she muttered.

At first True figured Jane E was kidding as usual about her nemesis, but there was something serious in her tone.

"What makes you say that?" asked True.

Jane E shook her head. "His personality has gone from irritating and eccentric to neurotic and downright unpleasant. Anyway, it's easier and quicker to pacify him than to argue with him."

They agreed to meet that afternoon at Oak View to go over Bertie's all-important post-party checklist. "And if you're not exhausted from last night, would you like to come by my house for supper?" asked Jane E. "I have some cold tomato soup I want to try."

"I'd love to," said True. "As a matter of fact, any time you want to try out a recipe, you can count on me. Your food is fabulous."

The caterer waved a hand dismissively.

"No, I mean it," True insisted. "Your food is the best I've tasted. And I went to some pretty swanky parties in Vista Palmas. There's always a little surprise in each of your dishes." True's eyes got big and she grinned. "Don't tell me it's bacon grease!" she teased.

Jane E laughed. "No, but never underestimate the culinary importance of pig fat. Come around seven, if that suits. My family will be cleared out by then—a baseball game. Oh, and I live two doors down from Maisy—the only yellow house on the street. Come through the side gate, if you don't mind. I'll probably be out on the back porch."

•

Before leaving for Jane E's, True sat on her front porch, thinking about her grandchildren, wondering what they were up to and second-guessing her decision to put so much space between them. Dusk was closing in. It was that homesick time of day according to B True—the time when birds are getting back to their roosts, families settling in before dark. True had to agree with her old aunt. It was the time she felt the loneliness like an ache. A year ago, Burkett would have been fixing them drinks, expounding on extractions and sand traps, firing up the grill, swapping jokes with Tommy on the cell phone.

True smiled in the twilight. What would B True have thought of Katie and her family and their sixteen-hour days, late-night soccer games and pre-dawn swim practices? Katie appeared to be missing the roosting instinct altogether, but maybe it was just a sign of the times.

True heard herself sigh in the silence. The old cottage felt like it was closing in on her. She opened every window in the place, hoping to air out not only the small rooms, but her spirit before going out for the evening.

•

True found Jane E's house easily enough. Its small front garden was bursting with shrubbery. A brick walkway snaked its way to the front steps then veered off toward a narrow driveway. True located an arbored gate at the end of the drive and found her hostess lounging in a cushioned swing on the back porch. The smell of tomatoes and baking bread floated through the open French doors leading to the kitchen.

"Great timing," said Jane E. "I've just opened a bottle of wine I'm trying for the first time. I need to get an objective opinion. I'm afraid my judgment is being swayed by the great price I'm getting. If you like it, I'll order some for you."

True took a sip, then another. *Wow, very tasty.*

"I'm no connoisseur, but I think it's great. In a neutral sort of way. It should appeal to a variety of tastes, is what I'm trying to say."

"That's exactly what I thought. It's nice to make a friend who shares my taste in wine."

"It's just nice to make a friend," said True.

To her horror, tears pricked at the backs of her eyeballs. She felt her face flush, saw the look of concern on Jane E's face.

Oh, great. A potential friend and I'm going to scare her off. I don't believe I'm doing this!

But the tears came.

Jane E handed her a cocktail napkin, and True dabbed at her eyes.

"I am so sorry," she sniffed. "I don't know where that came from."

"Well, I do," said Jane E.

"You do?"

"You're in a new place, learning a new job. And you lost your husband less than a year ago. You need friends, people to talk to. Just let me get the bread out of the oven. I'm all ears if you're in the mood."

It turned out that True was not only in the mood but in desperate need to purge herself of what Maisy referred to as the pent-up miseries. So Jane E refilled their glasses, sat back in the swing and set it moving with her foot.

True told her about Burkett's death and the strangeness of trying to negotiate the grieving process under a different set of rules. What were the rules for simultaneous grieving, forgiving and understanding?

She told her of the sudden, inexplicable need to know her mother's story and to flesh out the shadows of her early childhood, how that need was the basis of True's seemingly irrational decision to return to Belle Hill—and to Oak View. She confided her urge to escape Vista Palmas and her daughter's obsessive-compulsive lifestyle. She confessed that she was terrified of facing old age under her present financial circumstances, of being dependent on her daughter, Katie and Katie's husband, Parker.

"I certainly understand about children and guilt," said Jane E. "I've always worked, and like most working moms, felt guilty about time away from the kiddies."

"I bet they were well fed, though," said True.

"Well, yes." Jane E grinned at True and again True was reminded of Jackson Bean. "If leftover party food for breakfast is your idea of well fed. And I did always send the best goodies for class parties. I missed a lot, though. Weekends are family time for most folks. My weekends are Monday and Tuesday. I'm lucky to have so much family around, though. Not to mention great neighbors and life long friends. Belle Hill can be suffocating at times, but it has its high points."

"The town I grew up in was like that, but Vista Palmas—where I've lived most of my adult life—well, it's just more transient by nature. A place to visit." True sighed. "People move in and out like the tides." True had a sudden thought. "You know, you and I might have been lifelong friends if not for my mother's death."

"True, have you ever thought that maybe you've had the best of both worlds?" Jane E shook her head. "Like I said, this town can be suffocating. I understand your interest in your mother's past, but sometimes I wonder if it's not best to ..." Jane E frowned, searching for the best, the kindest words. "Sometimes it's best not to dwell on what might have been. Maybe just let it all rest in peace. Besides, we're friends now. That's what counts."

Was Jane E of the "let sleeping dogs lie" philosophy in general or was she specifically—like B True and Katie, trying to dissuade her from finding out about her mother?

"As far as your conflicted feelings of grief," Jane E was saying, "I think I know a little of what you're going through." True's new friend pressed her lips together for a second or two before going on. "We lost a cousin's child. He was just a teenager."

"Oh, I'm sorry, Jane E," said True. "As hard as this has been, the death of a young person is always so difficult."

"Yes, that was it, but then I never really got to know him. He was a toddler when his mother took him away with her. Luckily I had a summer with him the year before he died. His death left us all ... what? Furious is as good a word as any, I guess."

"Furious more than sad?"

"No, but furiously sad." Jane E twisted in her seat. "It's terrible, but I kept asking myself, 'Would we have been better off not having had that summer?' Of course not, but ... Should we have done more to keep in touch with him so that we could have had more than a measly summer? Of course we should have. I guess we thought we had all the time in the world. And it was never the right time." She sighed. "So many emotions. The suddenness of his death and all of those questions I kept beating myself over the head with … well, it made me feel the same things you're describing. I couldn't get through the process, as you put it."

"So how did you, finally? Please tell me you did."

Jane E's laugh was quiet, rueful. She looked down at her hands and said, "Well, never completely, in some ways, but I finally reconciled myself to the idea that life just doesn't make sense a lot of the time, that human beings are flawed and that grief is an individual thing. You just have to face it, give in to it some days, not give into it some days and eventually, as they say, time does heal."

"Obviously," agreed True. "There are so many people walking around with seriously sad stories and amazingly positive outlooks. Incredible people."

"Yes, but some don't adjust as well as others, that's for sure. Like Jackson."

"My landlord?"

"One and the same."

"I've been wondering about him. I like him."

"And he likes you. I can tell."

"So what's his story?"

"The boy who died—the one I was telling you about. He was Jackson's son." Then Jane E was standing. As if knowing how abrupt the motion was, she smiled at True and said gently, "Let's get our soup first. I'll tell you after we eat."

The soup was chilled tomato—made with a basket of heirloom tomatoes from tart green to sweet yellow. Jane E's son, Jay, had inadvertently thrown his gym bag on the little treasures as they rested in the back of her SUV.

"I couldn't believe it!" she laughed. "He walked in with this dripping basket and said, 'Mom, I think I just made instant soup out of your tomatoes.' And I thought, soup—what a good idea. I never would have wasted those beauties on soup, but, I swear it's the best I ever made. See what you think."

True agreed. It was fabulous.

The bread had cooled so Jane E sliced it, toasted it and spread it with leftover pesto.

"You're very resourceful," True complimented her. "I could take lessons from you."

"Well, unfortunately it's born of experience, but I have learned to be a lemons-to-lemonade kind of girl," she laughed. "Being in my line of work, I had no choice."

She got up and put their dishes in the sink, waved off True's offers of help, and busied herself in the fridge.

"Speaking of lemons …" she said, setting a plate of lemon squares on the table. "These are left over from a party. Don't want them to go to waste."

True sunk her teeth into the crisp crust and jellied filling. That wonderful tart sweetness that makes the lemon square a perennial southern favorite filled her mouth.

"Jane E, this is delicious. I'm surprised you're not as big as a house with all this wonderful food around you."

"It's hard. I've been trying to lose ten pounds." She sighed. "But I'm constantly tasting." She grinned at True and popped a lemon square into her mouth. Powdered sugar floated onto her blouse. "Another occupational hazard in my line of work, I guess."

"Speaking of lines of work, how did you get into the catering business?"

"I've always been a foodie—loved to cook, loved to garden." She patted her stomach. "Loved to eat. But it was my cousin, your landlord, Jackson, whose story I intend to tell you—who hired me for functions at the paper, invested start-up money that he would never let me repay because with the kids and my husband, Andrew, on a college professor's salary, he knew we didn't really have it. The last time we sent him a check we received it back, torn to shreds."

"So Jackson has always worked at the paper?"

"Always. Are you're wondering how he lives as well as he does on what must be a pitiful income?"

"That wasn't exactly what I was thinking, but now that you mention it, how does he?"

"Everyone around here wonders that—including me. My cousin is not exactly an open book." She sighed. "I think he likes being mysterious, if you want to know the truth. The gossips around here have always driven him crazy, and he likes to egg them on, is my opinion." She popped another lemon square into her mouth, chewed it thoughtfully. Finally she said, "But I worry. I can't imagine that he would be into anything illegal, yet … look, I'll be honest here because … well, because I've noticed how he looks at you." She smiled at True, but her eyes grew serious. "I know that look. It's been quite a while since I've seen it, but it's unmistakable."

Jane E seemed to consider her words. "I love my cousin, but he's always been a wild card. In his youth, he was a mess! Too handsome for his own good, Mr. Personality, a great dancer—the total dream-guy package—and he's always loved women—I mean really loves their company. Understands them. The girls found him pretty irresistible, as you can imagine. But he's also one of those sporty types—hunting, fishing, football—all that, so guys like him, too."

She sighed again and continued. "But I don't know that he's really all that close to anyone. He's an enigma, is what he is. And probably one not worth trying to solve in my opinion. He's one of those guys who's just too damn much work." Jane E threw up her hands. "I mean, who needs it?"

"But he was married you said."

"Oh, yes. And that goes back to what you were saying. I think he's one of those people who didn't get over the trauma of it all." Jane E pushed her chair back. "If you're still interested, let's go back out on the porch and I'll tell you about it."

Still interested? True almost tripped over her own feet getting out onto the porch.

Jane E took her place on the swing and True settled herself on a chaise. The night air was cool and soft and alive with crickets talking as B True used to say. Through an old stand of river birches at the back of Jane E's garden, the house beyond was visible, its balconied rooms glowing like lanterns through the rustle of the trees. Bats darted high above them, hopefully gorging themselves on mosquitoes.

True settled back and was reminded of the physical and emotional comfort of B True's back porch on those first frightening nights after her life took its initial crazy turn. She could almost hear her great aunt's quivery voice with its old-south accent as B True read the happiest stories she could find to True from her place on the glider. It was the best she knew to do for a traumatized four-year-old. This porch—like B True's—

was a great spot for a story.

11.

Broke Back Mountain of Baggage

Jane E told True how Jackson had come to meet Barbara his second summer after college. A year had been all Jackson could take working for his Uncle Billy at the First Bank of Belle Hill, and besides, he'd always wanted to see Montana, find out for himself what all the "big sky" talk was about. So he turned in his notice to a remarkably understanding Uncle Billy and headed west.

The combination of his easiness with boats and Barbara's dad's desperate need for summer help landed Jackson a job taking thrill-seeking tourists through mid-level rapids on a rubber raft.

Barbara, a spunky beauty itching to see life on the other side of the mountain, was no match for the laid-back southern charm of Jackson Bean. His stories of life on the coast set her dark eyes dancing and the chemistry between them set both their hearts racing. For all of his past history with women, Jackson had never really been in love and when he fell, it was with an awesome severity.

Jackson taught his young bride to hunt, water ski, fish, and party like a native. Barbara had even learned to handle Jackson's boat, backing it into the slip as well as anybody. She taught herself to cook as well as, but never better than his own mother.

His friends and family never came close to understanding her with her "cool, yankee ways," but they opened their hearts to her and treated her like one of them. It was as if she was a cousin who was a little on the peculiar side. You overlooked it because she was family.

When the babies came—a boy they called Jack and a girl named Evelyn after Barbara's mother—Jackson kept right on playing, never looking back. If he had, he'd have noticed that Barbara was growing up and that he'd left her alone on too many August nights. That she'd started dreaming of mountains and dry air.

October is a beauty on the gulf coast, but it's still just summer all freshened up, and Barbara began going "home to show the kids what a real autumn was all about." December got to her the worst, though—too much rain, no chance of snow. On their last Christmas together, Jackson's mother served fried fish, turnip greens, cornbread and iced tea. The day had turned out so pleasant, they'd eaten on the back porch. It was just too much. The next day, Barbara told him she was taking the children and going back to Montana for good. She'd known it the day before, she said, but didn't have the heart to tell him on Christmas.

"Yessir, that Barb, she's all heart, ain't she?" said Uncle Billy, the sarcasm twisting his old face.

They'd all agreed with Billy—what with Barbara running back to whatever Yankee planet she'd come from taking little Jack and Evelyn with her—she'd effectively ruined Jackson's life.

Jackson remarried a "salt-of-the-earth Alabama girl this time" and they'd had high expectations. But it didn't take, and Jackson began referring to the woman as the ex-wife, to Barbara as "my wife, divorced now." That should have told them all something. But it didn't. As they saw it, Barbara had spoiled him for any chance at happiness. In that closed up part of their minds, she would remain the sole culprit in the demise of both marriages.

Jackson's Uncle Billy had summed up the general consensus. "Barb. They named that woman right." He said it often, spitting the words out, putting an end to any possible further speculation on the matter.

Jackson rode the wave of their sympathy as far as it would carry him, but by the time it dumped him on the beach of reality, the wide, open spaces of indifference and apathy had formed between him and his children. His half-hearted attempts at establishing a relationship became little more than insulting, and for the second time in his life, someone important to him wanted nothing to do with Jackson Bean.

"Wow," said True when Jane E was through. "That's some story. But did he eventually reconnect with his children?"

"Well, as you know, there's always more to the tale," said Jane E. She shook her head. "In this case, the awful part about Jack."

"Jane E, you don't have to tell me."

"No, I want to." She took a deep breath and went on. "One day when he was sixteen or seventeen—something like that—Jack showed up at Jackson's door." Jane E shook her head again, then smiled, remembering. "He was pale and awkward, with short, flat hair that was already losing the battle with humidity. 'There was no life in his eyes,' is how Jackson put it. 'And dressed for canoeing or bird-watching or some damn thing,' Jackson said. 'But I swear,' he said, 'He could've been standing there in a tutu, and I wouldn't have cared. I've never been so happy to see another person in my life.'"

Three months later the young man who hugged his daddy good-bye was tan, muscular and at ease with himself and everyone else. His speech and dark hair had loosened up with the climate, and it suited him. Jackson looked into his son's face, saw the dark eyes dancing, and was in love all over again.

The next winter Jack called his dad, said how he missed being able to smell the earth and the gulf, how he'd gotten used to the softness in the air and the women's voices. Jackson wasn't used to such talk from a male, but realized that his son had put his own feelings into words for him. Jack told his dad that he wanted to come and spend the following summer with him and was even thinking about attending St. James College."

"So the mother—Barbara—she was okay with that?"

Jane E nodded. "His mother understood, Jack said, but she'd told him—and I imagine it was with tears shining in her eyes—'I just hope the place doesn't break your heart like it did mine.'"

"Oh, how sad," said True. The same small town she was counting on to mend her heart had broken Barbara's.

In the end, all their hearts would be broken, Jane E told

her. "Jack died alone on an icy Montana road not far from his mother's house. Barbara and Jackson hardly spoke to one another at Jack's funeral, though I don't think it was hard feelings as much as they were just too bewildered by it all.

"Jack's sister, Evelyn, didn't understand any of it, which is not surprising, and when she married and moved to Denver, Jackson got wind of it from a relative who brought him an old newspaper clipping.

"'When did life get so messy?' he asked me that day. That was almost fifteen years ago, and I'll never forget how he looked when he said it. I remember wondering if he would ever be able to get himself through it. I don't know that he has."

"And Barbara?"

"I heard she'd remarried several years later, and is doing well. She had a strong faith, I remember. That helped, I'm sure. And I think she had had the practice of working out the trauma of her failed marriage. She was a resilient person. Faced things down." Jane E made a face. "Unlike my charismatic cousin. Unlike most males, I guess. They tend to keep it all in, or at least our generation of men was like that."

True thought of Burkett and his secret demons. She certainly agreed with Jane E's assessment of the males of their generation and their lack of coping mechanisms.

"Jackson's daughter has a daughter herself now," Jane E continued. "But Evelyn won't have anything to do with any of us—including Jackson. And God bless him, he's tried. He really has. She won't forgive him, though. He's never seen his only grandchild."

"Good Lord," said True.

"So you see what I mean. A lot of emotional baggage comes with Jackson Bean." Jane E shook her head. "A back-breaking mountain of baggage."

The rest of the evening, the new friends talked about Oak View, the best places to buy this and that in Belle Hill and movies and books they'd enjoyed. As they talked and laughed, their acquaintanceship morphed into friendship. True stayed later than she'd intended and hated to leave. Jane E sent her home with leftovers, a hug and a promise to let True return the hospitality the following week.

12.

A Light in the Darkness

A word to the wise. Man who pass gas in church must sit in own pew. Hope you had a nice Sunday. I miss you. Love, Tommy.

Why did little boys think jokes about bodily functions were so hilarious? But True had to admit it, farts are funny. Especially in church. Mother Nature's little practical joke was how True thought of it.

She thanked her grandson for his words of wisdom, assured him that she missed him, too, and went off to brush her teeth, but found herself thinking about her evening with Jane E.

Who doesn't have baggage? True pondered the question as she flossed. *I can't even visit my mother's grave—which I have been curious about my entire life! I mean, how many people have more baggage than I do?* True washed her face and wondered. *Well, a lot of people, I guess—Jackson Bean being one of them.*

True slipped into bed and looked over at the empty pillow next to her. At least she wasn't sleeping single in their old king. When she'd married Burkett, he had immediately purchased a king-sized bed. True agreed that the four-poster of her childhood was not built for two people of modern proportions, and moved the old mahogany creaker to a guest room, but whenever Burkett was out of town on dental meetings and/or golf weekends, she would leave the luxurious expanse of the king for the womb-like coziness awaiting her in the guest room. And when she moved to Belle Hill, the mahogany four-poster was one of the "treasures" that came with her. As she explained to Katie, there would be no room for a king-sized anything where she was going.

Now, in response to the smell of rain in the air, True got out of her bed and proceeded through the darkened house lowering windows. Then she remembered she'd left the sun roof open on her car. She grabbed her keys, found a sweater and slipped it over her nightgown, put on her rubber clogs that stayed by the back door and dashed into the yard. A damp wind was kicking clouds across the moon, threatening a downpour.

True hopped into the car, turned the key, and watched the glass slowly slide to a close. She sat staring up into the cloud-diffused moonlight, her thoughts drifting as they so often did, on the breeze. Sounds—a short, defiant bark, a crashing of underbrush, a thud on the ground, a muttered expletive or two—jolted her from her reverie. *What on earth?*

True got out of her car, shutting its door as quietly as she could, and crept to the edge of the woods to see what her landlord and his dog were up to now. She was careful to keep in the shadows, glad that the sweater she'd grabbed was the gray of smoke and night. Of course, her white, cotton nightgown fluttered around the space between her hips and knees like a free-floating, ruffled ghost.

While she tried to make out what she was seeing on the path to Oak View, the clouds parted briefly, illuminating a bizarre scene. It was Jackson and JuJu, all right. The man was back to muttering curses in the direction of the lab as he untangled the dog's leash from one of his long legs.

"Why in the hell … Damn dog …"

True caught snatches of this verbal lashing of poor JuJu as Jackson maneuvered himself into a standing position and began dusting off his khaki pants with his free hand. The dog periodically answered her master's comments with a sharp, cheeky bark. It occurred to True that JuJu was probably cussing right back at her master in dogspeak.

As clouds closed in on the moon once more, Jackson leaned over and picked up a flashlight from the ground, pointed it randomly at True and clicked it on and off, testing that it still functioned.

"Aaag!"

He had seen her in that burst of illumination, and it had

scared him enough that he dropped the flashlight again. True heard him clicking and banging it, trying to get it going again.

"Who is that? True? Is that you?"

True suddenly remembered her ensemble. Short sweater, short, translucent nightie, and those green rubber clogs. (Was she wearing black bikini undies? She couldn't exactly recall, but she thought so.) The wind gusted, and an updraft caught her nightgown. She pushed it down a la Marilyn Monroe in *Some Like it Hot* and prayed Jackson's light would continue to malfunction.

"Yes, it's True. It's me, True."

"You scared me to death. What are you doing out here?" he yelled into the darkness. "JuJu, come back here. Damn dog."

A second later she felt JuJu's cold, wet nose on her thigh and heard Jackson's approaching footsteps.

True absent-mindedly massaged that spot behind the dog's ear—the one they love to have rubbed—thereby taking JuJu's mind off True's thigh and settling her down.

"Well, I came out to close my sun roof and heard something in the bushes. I was trying to see what it was."

As Jackson made his way to where she was standing, his flashlight came to life, its beam directed at her see-through nightgown. True could only imagine what Jackson thought of her sweater, nightgown and clogs get-up, though as he quickly aimed the light away, she caught the remains of a surprised, amused look on his face.

"What are you doing out here?" she asked.

"Oh, I'm just walking JuJu. Come on. I'll walk you back to your house."

He directed the light out in the direction of True's cottage.

"JuJu sure takes to you," he said. "You have a way with her."

"She's a beautiful dog," said True. "She has a good personality, a lot of spirit. I like that …" She smiled down at the dog. "And I guess she senses it or something."

When they got to the edge of the yard, which was somewhat illuminated by the back porch light, Jackson extinguished the flashlight. He looked into her eyes for a few seconds, careful to avoid glancing at her weird but racy ensemble. But she knew he was thinking about it because that little grin was playing at the corners of his mouth.

"Good night, True," he said softly. "Sweet dreams." Heading off toward the woods, he added off-handedly, "Oh, and don't forget to lock up."

"Thanks," she said, but something in his tone had changed, and it belied the casualness of his advice.

When she slipped into bed—for the last time—the linens were crisp and cool. Thunder sounded in soft, distant rumbles just before its promised rain began falling in muffled thumps on emerging banana leaves, in whispers in the azaleas.

True slid her well-worn paperback, *Destination Dubrovnik* by Juliette Benoit from beneath two hardback copies—*The Hours* by Michael Cunningham and *The Power of Positive Thinking* by Norman Vincent Peale. She had just finished the first chapter in Bailey Jones' fast-paced Adriatic adventure when her eyes began to close.

True dropped the book and her reading glasses to the unused pillow next to her. Her mind wandered to the banana trees in Vista Palmas. She imagined how tall they would be, dwarfing the ones that were forced to begin anew each year in the subtropical climate that claimed Belle Hill. Soon the thoughts were darting like bats through her brain. She remembered reading to her grandchildren in the hammock as raindrops pelted the huge leaves. Had anyone fertilized them yet? She recalled how the sun made the great leaves translucent, how their soft thickness felt in hands, how the bananas started out as an impossibly small version of the future stalk and how she had taught her child and her grandchildren to appreciate all of these things. Such amazing beauty in one plant.

Thoughts of her grandchildren had her off and counting the days since she'd last seen them. Then, remembering Dr. Peale's book on her bedside table and reminding herself that positive thinking was part of her new and improved regimen, she counted the days until summer vacation instead. She smiled to herself. (There really was something to this positive thinking.) Summer would be here before she knew it. The wedding "season" would be over. She would have lots of time with Mary Kate and Tommy.

It had been months since Burkett's death, weeks since her relocation to Belle Hill, and though loneliness was still an ever-present threat, there had been a shift in her. Crossing some tiny psychic bridge to an infinitesimally better place, she'd found a resting place in her climb up the hill.

True thought about her mother and brought her arm up to her face as the rhythm of a train blended with the sound of the rain. She waited. Yep, there it was—the whistle. As always, it seemed to be calling to her. Tonight it was telling her that it was time. Tomorrow she would start her search for Nick's story in earnest, and it would begin with Maisy Downy. She heard Jackson Bean's voice, softly wishing her sweet dreams. The train whistle sounded again, leaving town, and lulling her to sleep.

13.

If it Ain't Aunts it's B's

Two cannibals are eating a clown. One says to the other, "Does this taste funny to you?"

True pressed reply.

I can hardly type, I'm laughing so hard, she lied. *How do you make a cream puff?* She'd gotten this one via Jane E's nephew. *Okay, give up? Chase it around the block a few times. Love you. True.*

That one was pretty lame, even for a nine-year-old—or a grandmother, but it was the best she could come up with. Tommy would have fun teasing her about how bad it was. True smiled and turned off the laptop.

She decided to call Maisy as soon as she returned from her now almost-habitual daily run/walk around St. James campus. But as she came into the house, the phone was ringing. It was Poo Honeychurch.

"Sorry for the short notice, but I'm feeling pretty good today, and I have to strike while the iron is hot. My sister, Flora, and I would like for you to join us for dinner tonight. Is seven thirty okay?"

"Uh, yes. That would be lovely," said True. "What can I—" But the line was dead.

As soon as she turned the phone off it rang again. This time it was a frantic Bertie. Could True meet Al the electrician at Oak View in thirty minutes? And call him (Dr. Wallace) back immediately after the meeting with Al. That would be Al the electrician. He (Bertram Wallace) wanted a full, yes, full report.

"From Al? The electrician?" asked True sweetly. She couldn't help herself.

The man True remembered from her first visit to the house introduced himself as Al from Al's Electric. Though they met on the house's front porch as they had months earlier, he didn't seem to remember her.

"Yep, thought we was done with all this," he said scratching at his ear. "I got plenty to do without runnin' over here every time Dr. Bertie gets worked up. I swear if it ain't ants it's bees." He shook his head, disgusted. "I done checked the wirin', checked the switches, checked the alarm, the locks, everything I can think of. If somebody was in here last night, they got that alarm code."

"What happened exactly?" asked True. As usual, Bertie had neglected to fill her in on the most important details.

"Somebody reported seein' lights flickerin' in here again."

Of course, the vision of Jackson Bean and his flashlight darted through her mind.

"Who reported it?" she asked.

"You'd have ask Dr. Bertie about that. He wouldn't tell me. Probably some kid, rattin' out another kid. Who knows? People tell me it's haunted in there. Wooo." His eyes grew big and he waved his fingers around. True thought she remembered him performing the same routine at their first meeting. Either that or she was having a serious bout of déjà vu.

Whatever, True found it just as funny the second time around and couldn't help but laugh.

"Wooo," he said again, blowing tobacco breath in True's face. Leaning alarmingly close, Al looked over first one shoulder and then the other and said out of the corner of his mouth, "Wouldn't surprise me if it wadn't ol' Bean."

"Jackson Bean?"

"Yeah." Al stood up straight and stared ahead as a thought came to him. "Heh! He's your neighbor. Hell, he's your landlord, ain't he? Don't you live in Jackson Bean's house over yonder?" He threw an arm in the general direction of her house.

"Yes, I do." *Does everybody know everything that goes on around here?*

As if to answer her question, Al added, "Heard you got a pret-ty sweet deal on your rent. Be nice to have a moneymaker like that and not have to worry about what you git for it. Between me and you, it's a lit-tle suspicious as to where Bean gets his where-with-all, if you get my drift."

What is he talking about? "Actually, Al, I don't get it," she said.

"I'm talking about how me and everybody else in town wonders how Jackson Bean affords his Hollywood lifestyle with no discern-o-bill income. I figure he's got a in with bookies—he's a sportswriter, you know."

"Bookies?" True croaked the word out. *Oh, my God! My world is overrun with gamblers!*

"Well, I ain't sayin' for sure. Could be somethin' else. He spends time up in the delta with some dudes could scare the gators off, if you get me. Lord knows what they're up to."

"Good grief," said True. "But why would you think he's behind whatever is going on in Oak View?"

Al might've decided he'd gone a lit-tle too far with this latest scandal-spreading tirade because he stopped talking, clamped his lips together and gazed up at the ceiling, suddenly knee-deep in some mental calisthenics or other.

He snapped his attention back to True. "Now what was we talkin' about?"

We? thought True.

"Oh, right," he answered himself. "Bean. Well, Bean, like I say, I heard he's out and about all hours. All hours." He cocked his head and raised an eyebrow at True before continuing.

"And like I say, livin' above his means and all. Probly nuthin' to it. Heh! Must be nice, though. We all need to take lessons from Mr. Bean on how to put in a few hours a week and pull the big bucks."

He glanced back at the house. "Anyway, like I was tellin' ya, folks say a woman used to live here long time ago, say she met a untimely death, that she might still be around, guardin' somethin' in there." His eyebrows rose over eyes grown wide with implication. "Well, I don't hold much with all that haunted sh— uh, stuff, but I got to say, this place is startin' to give ol' Al the heebies. My advice to Dr. Bertie and you, Miz True, is let the sleepin' dog lie, else somebody's gone git bit." Al bobbed his head for emphasis, paused a second and then, being the space invader that he was, leaned in close to True. It was all she could do not to lean back herself. "My meanin' on that is, don't go pokin' into things — you know, the past and such."

"Well, thanks for the advice, but …"

The sarcasm in True's tone was evidently lost on Al because he leaned in once more, glancing over first one shoulder then the other.

"And here's a freebie," he said. "You just might want to talk to old Carver."

"Carver?"

"Calls himself the caretaker over to the cemetery. You probably seen him slippin' around here. Real old guy, too old to do any real work, you ask me. Black as that railing there. Hair white as them walls." He jerked his head in the direction of Oak View's front wall. "Spooky old dude." He straightened up, eyes wide as yet another thought occurred to him. "Hell, he's your neighbor, too. Lives free-o-charge in that little, bitty house closest to Oak View. On the auspices of Miz Maisy Downy. Whadya think of that? Nice work if you can git it, is all I say."

A beeping noise came from a phone clipped to his belt.

"Okay, okay," he yelled to the general direction of his hip. Then, smiling at True, he said, "Gotta be goin', but you just holla, you need anything."

Using every muscle in his face, he winked at True, distorting his whole countenance. As he headed off to his truck, it occurred to True that she'd gotten yet another suggestion to leave her past alone. It also occurred to her that Al might just be the spookiest thing at Oak View.

A call to Bertie confirmed that electrically speaking, the house was okay and that it was "someone who requests anonymity" who had called "Dr. Bertie" about the strange lights in Oak View.

"How many people have the alarm code?" asked True.

"A very, very trusted few," was his answer. "And they are above reproach. Above reproach. Just you ask Maisy Downy."

True figured that Bertie would stick up for Jack the Ripper if he thought Maisy trusted him, but had to admit that Maisy's character assessment went a long way with her, too. If Maisy was okay with the "trusted few," then that was good enough for her.

Putting the problem out of her mind, True moved on to more pressing matters. These included setting up an alumni reunion weekend, giving a tour to out-of-towners who would be hosting an after-rehearsal party on a distant October Friday, double-checking that chairs, podium and microphone were awaiting the bi-annual Belle Hill Belles Beautification Committee Awards ceremony that very afternoon, ordering fourteen tables, twenty-eight decks of cards and matching tallies for a bridge luncheon and, as it turned out, rescuing a box turtle that had somehow gotten trapped in one of Oak View's bathrooms.

"How did you get in here?" she asked the turtle. But Ms. Turtle (there was something a bit feminine about her) wasn't receiving, as one of the "belles" might have put it, and disappeared into her shell. "I know just how you feel," True said.

Deciding that her new friend might decide to make an appearance while one of the "belles" was seated on the convenience, True carried the reptile (or amphibian—she couldn't remember to which group it had been assigned) down the path toward home. After a few minutes, she walked into the woods and put it down.

"Now you stay here where you belong," she reprimanded it.

I've got to stop talking to this turtle, she thought, feeling the tiniest bit sorry for herself. Talking to one's self and/or animals other than pets is what comes from being alone too much. So far today, an unresponsive reptile had been her only non-business related interaction.

True watched the turtle until it peeked its ugly little head out and ambled into the underbrush. Oh, who was she kidding? She'd been alone plenty. And liked it for the most part. What she was, was lonely.

As if to prove the point, she caught herself wondering if the turtle had a mate back at Oak View wondering where in the heck his or her other half had wandered off to.

As she turned back toward the path, something big and brown shot through the bushes ahead, startling her. JuJu. She blew out a sigh, realized that Al the Electrician's ghost talk— especially the part about the woman (her very own mother?)—

and her untimely death had True on edge.

JuJu started to bark, probably at the turtle True had supposedly saved from starvation beneath the claw-footed tub at Oak View. Was JuJu supposed to be running loose?

Hunger and her conversation with the peculiar electrician had True's mind jumping all over the place, so she hurried back to the path and focused on lunch. Besides, one animal rescue per day is plenty, she told herself.

•

Jackson Bean got up from his computer, stretched, and realized he had not seen his dog in a couple of hours. He walked onto the porch and whistled. Nothing. He started out into the yard, but returned, unplugged the laptop, put it in the top drawer of the walnut desk that had belonged to his daddy. It wouldn't do to start being sloppy now. The key was where he'd left it atop the door frame. Jackson locked the drawer and returned the key.

The day was pleasant, and he was creaky from sitting for hours. That was the good thing about dogs. They made you get up and move. Pain in the neck, but heck, what wasn't?

He wandered in the direction of Oak View, taking his time. There was something in the woods just off the path. Lately JuJu had gotten in the habit of taking off when he called her name so he crept quietly into the trees, ready to grab the dog when he got close. But it wasn't JuJu.

It was True Cowley and she was holding a good-sized box turtle. She shifted a bag that hung on her shoulder and set the animal down. She stood there watching it, talking to it like it was a disobedient child. Jackson listened. Not to the words so much but to the sound. Her voice was light, almost musical, always on the verge of a smile.

Now True was shaking her head as if reminding herself that it was silly to be talking to a turtle.

But Jackson didn't think it was silly. He had only known a few women who had such an easy way with animals. In each case it had turned out to be a real good sign.

His thoughts on this were interrupted by a blur of brown through the bushes. It was JuJu alright, heading for home. He turned around to follow her.

•

True's stomach was growling non-stop by the time she entered her kitchen. She found some of Jane E's leftovers— smoked chicken salad and Creole coleslaw, fixed a glass of iced tea, got her mother's photograph album and placed it all on the coffee table. Al's ramblings about Jackson Bean and bookies and dudes in the delta together with his gossip of ghosts guarding the valuables (but really, what valuables?) in Oak View had True in a major muddle.

The album smelled like a combination of B True's house and B True herself. A bit musty, like old wood and kind of fresh, like B True's lavender cologne. True inhaled the aroma of her past and started in on the chicken salad. She sipped iced tea, closed her eyes and was back at B True's, going through her mother's picture album for the zillionth time. True's favorites were the ones from her mother's high school years that held her cheerleading and tennis and dance pictures. Although the photographs were all black and white, due to Nick's personality and True's adoration of her mother, to her they were in living color.

Nick was always smiling, even laughing in some—especially in the prom and Christmas Soiree pictures that were supposed to be the most formal. In one she was sticking her tongue out at the camera or the photographer or maybe the world. But in every one of them her date looked like it was the happiest night of his life just to be there with Nick Hunter on his arm.

True sighed. Though there was a similarity in the shape of the face and the smile, True had evidently inherited everything else from mystery dad—the one, if you remember, B True said should be left under his rock.

She hated having her picture taken or reading in front of the class or anything that fell into the "center of attention" category. Hence her assumption that she was nothing like her beautiful, laughing mother who would think nothing of sticking her tongue out in a formal picture taken at the Christmas Dance.

One day B True sat on the sofa next to True as she finished up with the few pictures of her mother and herself together. As always, True attempted to conjure up the memory that went with each photo, trying to put herself in there with Nick, imagining the cold air sneaking beneath her crocheted hat or the warmth of the sun that caused her to squint into the camera lens. She couldn't do it, though, and on this particular day, even the softness of True's arm couldn't block the tears filling her eyes. That's when B True let out one of her shaky sighs, dabbed at her own eyes, and finally told True an abbreviated version of her mother's story.

The high points were how Nick would never tell anyone who True's father was and "so it's just one of those mysteries we have to live with," and how when True was three-and-three-quarters years old and in the care of her grandparents, Nick fell off a boat during a party and drowned.

"I've heard that drowning is not a bad way to go," said B True. "Very floaty, you know." This was meant to make True feel better.

True remembered asking why she hadn't been invited to the funeral. B True blew her nose into her already soggy hanky and said there hadn't been one. They had never found Nick, though everyone did their best, searching for days on end.

"We had a lovely memorial and you were there," she said. "You just don't remember because you were so young."

"I don't guess y'all took any pictures?" True had asked.

"Of the memorial service?" B True laughed though she was still crying. "No. We didn't take any pictures, True."

B True kissed the little girl's cheek and headed off to the kitchen. True could hear her alternately sniffling and chuckling as she scrubbed potatoes for their supper.

In spite of True's preoccupation with trains, addiction to the feel of the inside of her arm against her face, and her unusual family situation, she'd managed to accumulate a small group of friends. Good girls from nice families with uneventful pasts, they had been instructed by their well-meaning mothers not to mention True's deceased one, and they didn't. So except for B True's photo albums, the teary, ten-minute revelation about B True's long-lost niece's untimely demise, and True's one mother-memory with the trains, it was as if Nick Hunter never existed.

A few of True's small group of friends married right out of high school, but most went to girls' schools up east. True headed to Florida where she made new friends but sadly lost touch with the old ones. B True died just after True graduated, snipping the last tie to the last twenty years of True's conventional yet unconventional little life.

The sadness True felt at her great aunt's passing was tempered by the feeling that B True had made a deal with "the good Lord" as she always referred to Him. He'd given her a chance at motherhood—a dream she believed could never be realized—and let her live long enough to get the job done. It had been a good bargain, well-kept by both parties.

B True left True her house and everything in it including the mahogany four-poster bed. B True's younger brother, Henry, took care of all the legal details for True, selling the house and putting the money away for her future. (It came in handy as a thirty percent down payment on the Cowleys' first home in Vista Palmas, Florida.)

Henry and True put on a lovely service for B True, which True had videotaped.

14.

The Thousand-word Picture

True finished the last forkful of Jane E's Creole slaw as she turned the final page of the album. This page held one of her favorite snapshots. Nick was bent over what looked to be that journal of hers which was fairly large and leather-bound with a clasp. She held a pen poised over the book, her face thoughtful, but amused as if the perfect words to add to the paper had suddenly come to her.

She appeared oblivious to anything or anyone else.

What is she writing? What thought has just occurred to her? wondered True as she always did when seeing the picture. *And where is that journal?*

When she'd asked B True about it, her aunt had shaken her head wearily.

"I've looked everywhere for that book, asked everybody about it … I knew you'd want it one day. It might… explain some things." She let out one of her shakier sighs and dabbed at her eyes with the hem of her apron. "I think we have to face facts that it's gone."

True had not brought up the subject of her mother's journal again (B True's tears were not worth it), but figured that the book had to have been left at Oak View. Overlooked somehow. And according to B True, anything left in Oak View after Nick's death had become the property of St. James College and would have been removed from the house by whoever was in charge of such things at the time.

True closed the album resting on her lap. She could ask

Bertie if he'd ever heard anything about it being found in the house. But True was a woman who navigated on instinct, and her instincts were telling her to hold off on mentioning Nick's journal to her boss. There was something about Dr. Bertram Wallace ... something she didn't trust.

True raised and lowered her shoulders, then stretched her head from side to side as if to rearrange the jumble of her thoughts into some kind of order. It was not working, so she picked up the phone and called Maisy Downy.

True explained that she was ready to begin the search for her mother's story. Maisy offered her help. When True mentioned her dinner date with the Honeychurch sisters, Maisy let out a slow whistle and said she would be at True's by five-thirty.

"Gives us time for a long chat—and a short drink—before you go," said Maisy.

True felt her face register shock when she opened the door, but she simply could not help herself. Maisy was wearing cut-off jeans so tiny they must have come from the children's department. Her little stick legs ended in yellow platform sandals. A silver tote bag was thrown over a yellow tee shirt that said, *You'd be smiling too if you looked this good at eighty.* Her platinum hair was pulled into a high pony tail.

True attempted to replace her astounded expression with a non-committal one, but it was too late.

"Some shirt, huh?" said Maisy, letting her off the hook. "Got it for my birthday a few years ago. Jackson gave it to me."

"Jackson Bean?"

True thought back to her last encounter with her landlord, the way he'd looked at her and wished her sweet dreams—as if he knew what her nights and her dreams were like, as if he really meant those clichéd words.

"True?"

The sound of Maisy's voice brought her back to the present.

"Oh, I was just thinking ... uh, I can't believe you're over eighty."

Maisy was wearing a self-satisfied smile, but all she said was, "Yep. I can hardly believe it myself."

They drifted out to the rocking chairs on True's front porch. True handed her a glass of red wine over lots of ice, per Maisy's instructions. She set a bowl of mixed nuts and her own un-iced cabernet on the bamboo table between them then settled into an unoccupied rocker.

"So, what do you want to know?" asked Maisy.

"Everything," said True. "For instance, who was Nick, really? How is it that nobody knows the identity of my father? Is it possible that Nick didn't know? What happened the night she died? Was it really an accident? Where are the people who knew her, who can tell me about her? And, Maisy, this might be the most important. Where is her journal?"

Earrings in the form of dangling bunches of miniature lemons were set swaying. Their back and forth motion was mesmerizing, but True managed to pay close attention to Maisy's words.

"B True didn't have it?"

True filled her in.

Maisy sipped her watery wine and thought. "I'll tell you what I remember about your mother—and it's not much. But before I do, tell me what you think of her gravestone?"

"Well, actually, I haven't seen it."

Maisy stopped rocking, but made no comment.

"Every time I head over there ... Oh, Maisy, I don't know. It's silly, but I just can't seem to make myself go there."

"And that's the very place you should begin." She started the rocker going again. "There's a man, Mr. George Washington Carver Jenkins, but everyone just calls him Carver, and he used to work for the Hunters, takes care of the cemetery now."

"You know, I think I remember Carver. He built me a swing when I was little and taught me how to use it. I can't recall his face, but I remember his voice—very patient and kind."

"That's Carver, alright. And he'll be at the cemetery tomorrow. Why don't I meet you both over there?" Without waiting for an answer, she added, "I'll call Carver and arrange it. You need to see it, sweetie," she added softly.

And so it was decided. They would meet right after True's morning meeting at Oak View.

"Now where were we?" said Maisy.

True told her about her gossip-laden meeting with Al the electrician, careful to leave out the part about Jackson Bean. He was Maisy's nephew, after all.

"That man gossips worse than a gaggle of church women," said Maisy. "As a matter of fact, I think that's where he gets most of his misinformation." She smiled at True and there was mischief in her eyes. "Still … Where there's smoke, sometimes there is a little fire."

"You mean you think Oak View is haunted? By my mother?"

Maisy slowed her rocker down and took a thoughtful sip of her wine before she answered. "I think you—all of us who knew her, really—are haunted by your mother. Her life was too short, her death … well, it was out of order, if you know what I mean. And as far as Oak View is concerned, I'm not too concerned about those lights—we'll get to the bottom of that eventually. But tell me, True, don't you think houses—especially old houses that have seen a lot of life? Don't you think they keep the spirit of the people who have lived there?"

"I don't think I've ever thought about it."

True let herself wander back in time to B True's house then to Oak View and the memories it released the day she had returned to it. She thought about the warm feelings she'd had the minute she'd stepped into Jackson Bean's cottage.

"I would like to think that something of the inhabitants remains after they've left a place," True said. "I mean, it's certainly a nice thought." She smiled at Maisy. "Depending on the inhabitants, of course. But that's not really the same thing as being haunted, is it?"

"I wouldn't know the answer to that," said Maisy, in unexpected reply to True's rhetorical musings. But the lightness in her tone and the steady look in her eyes made True wonder if the old lady did indeed know the answer to this and many other things, as well.

They were quiet for awhile, sipping their wine and thinking. Finally Maisy leaned her head back, started the rocker going again with a push of her foot. The look in her eyes said she was going back, remembering things, putting them all in order.

"As I told you, Nick didn't seem to be part of your grandparents at all. She was always so … unsettled. Always into something—the wilder the better, to tell the truth. She had a big heart, though, and everyone loved being around her. But no one really knew her very well, I'm afraid. When she turned up pregnant and refused to name your father and then refused to go quietly away and give you up to some nice couple, your grandfather and Nick had quite a set-to. Your grandfather threatened to disinherit Nick. She threatened to never speak to him again."

"Wow. I caused a lot of trouble, didn't I?"

Maisy smiled at True. "Oh, it was bound to happen. Not the pregnancy, but the big falling out is what I mean. Now listen to the rest of the story. We were talking about your grandfather. You were his only child's only child, named for his dead wife's beloved only sister, and so he came around. Nick, for once seeing the practicality of things, apologized. By the time you were born, it was one little happy group living back in Oak View. You were a wonderful influence on Nick. You just brought out the best in your mother as well as in your grandfather. Truth be told, I think life had gotten downright stale for that man.

"Things clicked along until you were about three, I think. That's when the car crash happened, killing your grandfather. We all knew that your grandfather had Oak View in a trust to be enjoyed by Nick, but to go to the college upon her death. This had always seemed right, Oak View being on the campus and your grandparents loving St. James like they did.

"On the other hand, things had changed. Folks couldn't imagine him not leaving his only real asset to Nick outright, what with her having you to look after. There were rumors— not so reliable—of another will that superseded the first one. We all knew the old man would want to provide for his beloved grandchild. And Nick seemed unconcerned about the future, though she wasn't one to worry too much about tomorrow, you know.

"Then, of course, the second accident—the drowning— happened." Maisy was shaking her head, rocker going, agitated by the memory. "There was no second will, or if there was, no one could find it. And believe me, B True and your Uncle Henry tried everything to locate it—as well as your mother's journal. So when B True came to the rescue, we all knew it was for the best—for you to be raised away from here. Away from all the sadness."

"And speculation," added True.

"That, too," said Maisy. "That's why B True cut all ties to Belle Hill. She wanted you to grow up free of your past." Maisy smiled at True. "Her intentions were the best, you know."

Maisy had another glass of icy merlot and looked through Nick's pictures. When she got to the last page she smiled at the photo of Nick on the porch of Oak View and said, "Now there's your proverbial thousand-word picture." She drained her glass, put the album aside and stood to go.

"I almost forgot," she said. "I brought you something."

Foraging around in the silver tote, she eventually found what she was looking for. "Aha," she said, and brought out a present. Its shape told True that it was a book. The wrapping was silver and yellow — like Maisy's outfit.

Surely a coincidence, thought True, untying the sunny ribbon.

"Maisy, you've done so much al— Oh, my gosh, how did you know?"

Peril in Portofino. Maisy read the title. "It's the first one she's written in quite a while. You just seem like a Juliette Benoit fan to me." She leaned in to True. "So am I." She thumped the book in True's hand. "This is a good one."

True gave Maisy a hug, careful not to make it a tight one. The tiny old body felt so fragile, she was afraid of breaking it.

At the door, Maisy said good-bye, then turned. "Oh, a piece of advice. I'd eat a little something before you head over to the Honeychurches."

Before True could ask her why, Maisy was down the steps and halfway to her car. Which just happened to match her purse.

15.

The Match-makers

Remembering Maisy's advice to eat a little something before going to dinner at the Honeychurches, True found the remains of Jane E's fabulous chicken salad, rolled it in a piece of sandwich bread and ate it with a handful of strawberries. She brushed her teeth, reapplied lipstick and realizing that she had a few minutes to spare, picked up the book Maisy brought her. *Peril in Portofino.* The cover, an impressionist's rendering of blue sea, green mountains, and technicolor houses was splashed over with *Bailey's Back!* and *Benoit fans celebrate her return!*

Its edgy but nostalgic appearance was funky and appealing and True turned to the back cover. A black and white photo of the author, an attractive woman, in her twenties, True guessed, topped the blurbs and reviews. It was the same dated picture that graced all of Benoit's books.

True stared at the photo. "Juliette, you remind me of someone," she said aloud. "But who?"

B True's mama's clock chimed.

"Oh, Lord. Now I'm late." She tossed the book onto the kitchen counter, grabbed her purse and headed into the woods toward the Honeychurch sisters' house.

The house was like something out of a faded story book, luminous in the evening's afterglow. It sat in a patch of overgrown yard ringed by the ever-present camellia bushes. True imagined them covered with delicate blossoms, each bloom a cloud of alabaster petals broken by a sunny yellow cluster of stamens. *Elegans,* thought True, remembering the name. *Now how in the heck did I know that?*

Her thoughts and the enchanted setting were marred by the sudden growl of a pug dog who sat in the middle of the Honeychurches' crumbling brick pathway. As True approached the wheezy old thing, it began barking at her. She did her best to ignore it. (True had learned from B True that it doesn't do to acknowledge rudeness—even that of geriatric pug dogs.)

There were two birdbaths, humming-bird feeders, tiny statues—elves and toad stools, mostly—a life-sized cement alligator and an upright tombstone with a time-obscured inscription. Clematis vines had long ago woven themselves into natural swags and jabots atop the generous porches. "I bet this place is a hit on Halloween," True murmured to herself.

As she side-stepped the yapping pug, she heard laughter and the unmistakable voice of Jackson Bean (the gambling, alligator-scaring, light-wielding, Oak View prowling Jackson Bean, True reminded herself) coming from somewhere beyond the clematis.

"Hello!" True called.

"We're out here on the back porch," Poo Honeychurch called.

"Hey, there." It was the Marlboro Man himself, walking toward her through the overgrown landscape, smiling that lovely smile of his, and True decided that there was no way he could be a gambling, womanizing, gator-scaring prowler. Could he?

"I've come to lead you to the porch."

The dog started up again at the sound of Jackson's voice.

"Shut up, Faulkner," Jackson snarled at the hound. He might just be able to scare a gator, True decided.

"Thank you," laughed True. "I don't think I could have found it without help."

"So glad you could join us," said Poo when they'd made their way to the porch. "I don't think you've met my little sister, Flora."

"Nice to meet you," said Flora, who was a smaller, prettier version of her older sister, and handed True an attractive drink full of lime slices and mint. "Mojito," she said.

"It's so last year," said Poo, "But like Flora says, 'If it was good enough for Hemingway …" To punctuate her remark, she paused and took a jaunty swig. "… it's good enough for me."

"What's that?" said Flora, giving her sister the sideways lizard eye.

"I said Flora makes the best mojitos. Doesn't she Jackson?"

"Yes, ma'am, she does. He grinned at True. "Try it."

Unfortunately, True was thirsty and took a greedy swallow. *Oh, my God! I've been poisoned!* she thought.

"I'd go easy," said Jackson. "Flo makes 'em pretty strong."

"That's right," said Flora proudly. "I only use the best for my high-balls. One hundred and fifty-one proof rum. And I double it. I say if you're going to have a drink, you should be able to taste the damn thing."

Good Lord. The old lady must not have a taste bud left, thought True. Her eyes were watering so much that she could barely see, but she was pretty sure Flora was lighting a cigarette — with one of those barbeque grill lighters.

"Whoa, Flo," said Jackson as the flame jumped out. "That one fifty one is flammable, you know. You don't want to set your hair on fire again."

"It never did grow back over on the side," said Poo. She gave her sister the lizard eye, but she was smiling. "She has a comb-over."

Flora waved their comments away, but chuckled before taking a lung-shuddering drag of her cigarette. She looked at True and said, "My sister lies like a rug, you know. We've tried to break her of it, but …" She shrugged and rolled her eyes up to the ceiling. "Smoke?" She waved her cigarette pack in True's general direction.

"No, thanks. I quit." *Thirty years ago.*

"Good for you," said Flora and took another drag.

True noticed that the old ladies were dressed alike and if she wasn't mistaken, it was the same outfit she'd seen Poo in at the wedding reception — long blouse of yellowed white silk, black polyester slacks and black leather pumps. And lots of diamonds. And the biggest, creamiest pearls True had ever seen.

True took her deadly cocktail and looked for a place to sit. The single unoccupied chair was stacked with books. Odd. So she sat in the only spot left on the porch, which was next to

Jackson on a wicker loveseat.

That's when she noticed the hors d'ourves. A silver tray bigger than the coffee table on which it sat held a bag of potato chips and a plastic container of onion dip. The last time True had onion dip her hair was in brush rollers and she was wearing shorty pajamas. Not wanting to offend the Honeychurches, however, she found a big chip and scooped up the fattening glop. The salty, oniony, creamy, crunchy combination was like one big delicious nostalgia bomb on her tongue.

"Omigod!" she said. "I had forgotten how much I love this stuff."

She had another chip and even a tiny taste of the mojito. The second sip didn't seem as strong. Perhaps the ice had melted, cutting the one-fifty-one a little.

Jackson laughed and tried a chip. "This is good. Salty, but good." He took a swig of his drink, turned a bit red in the face (which only made the Mediterranean blue of his eyes that much more intense, True noted), and grinned at True. She took another tentative sip of mojito and grinned back.

Faulkner, the pug dog, walked out onto the porch. He sauntered up to the settee, turned his bug-eyed, wrinkled countenance on Jackson and True and growled.

"Shame on you, Faulkner," said Poo. "Flora, you've been giving him onion dip again, haven't you?"

"Oh, I just gave him a few chips."

True noticed that she was looking like a guilty, shriveled up little girl.

"Maybe I went a little heavy with the dip."

Jackson and True, who had mouths full of said dip, looked at each other, both thinking the same thing. Surely she didn't double dip when feeding the snarly hound!

"Onion dip gives him the wind," explained Poo, "And puts him in an ill humor."

"Though he does love it so," Flora added wistfully.

Faulkner sniffed at the hors d'ourves, but thankfully turned on his twisted little excuse for a tail and settled himself on the floor next to Poo.

Jackson leaned over to True and murmured, "I don't know if that dog is uglier coming or going."

True laughed and had another sip of her drink, which was getting to be downright palatable.

Encouraged by her giggling response to his little joke, Jackson leaned over again and said, "You know where that name came from?"

"Faulkner? Well, yes, he was ..."

"No, not Faulkner, Pug!" Jackson mumbled, obviously enjoying the whole ridiculous miscommunication.

"Okay," whispered True, "Where does Pug come from?"

"Short for repugnant."

"What's that, Jackson?" asked Flora, giving him a dose of the evil eye—sans the smile.

"I said Faulkner's a pug dog." But he was looking at True, grinning at her with that dimple and those incredible blue eyes of his.

When True realized she was staring (and probably adoringly) at the Marlboro Man, she managed to tear her gaze away and noticed Poo and Flora smiling at Jackson and her as if they were a couple of kittens. That's when the blinding flash of the obvious hit her. This was a major fix-up. The drinks, the loooveseat, for heaven's sake—it was all some misguided matchmaking attempt by the Honeychurches!

But then True surprised herself. Instead of being dutifully mortified (poor Burkett had not even been gone a year!) for some reason (one hundred and fifty-one reasons, actually), she found the whole thing hilarious. Besides, as phase three of her life plan dictated, old-lady antics didn't fall into the "worth worrying about" category.

So she settled back and decided to make the most of the situation, enjoying Jackson's aftershave and the idle conversation, which, as she tuned back in, she realized was centered on the best place to get blueberries, strawberries and tomatoes. Johnson's Quick Mart or the road-side stand out on the old bay road. Of course, if you could get on Kitty Fitzpatrick's good side, she might share her famous home-growns with you. The chit-chat continued in this vein for a while until True took a sip of her drink and heard a slurping sound. Her mojito had vanished.

"Pretty good, huh?" said Jackson, who had already polished his off.

Before True could stop her, Poo was refreshing their glasses. "Thanks. They really are delicious," she said. What she was thinking was, *If y'all think I'm touching another drop of this stuff, you're crazy.*

But the Honeychurches are a bit crazy, and before she knew it, True was sipping on her second mojito and smiling sweetly at everyone with bits of mint stuck in her teeth.

Dinner was served by Poo and Flora in the dining room, which looked like a stage set from The Haunted Mansion and smelled like one of B True's old atomizers (which smelled like narcissus that had been in an over-heated house too long). To describe the atmosphere as cloying was an understatement.

The menu consisted of three coconut shrimp apiece with mango sauce, accompanied by a chunk of smoked salmon roughly the size of True's thumb. There was also one very large sweet potato per plate. Everyone was given a fresh mojito in an elaborately engraved sterling silver goblet.

Except for the sweet potato and the mojito, it was Jane E's menu from the Belle Hill Bibliophiles' luncheon two days prior. Actually, it was Jane E's food from the Belle Hill Bibliophiles' luncheon.

As True was digesting this realization and attempting, through her rum fog, to figure out, date-wise if dinner could safely be eaten, a whimper and a rumble came from beneath Jackson's chair. She glanced over to see Faulkner on his back, stubby legs in the air, snoozing off his overindulgence in onion dip. True considered that in this position, the old pooch was even more repugnant than he had been either coming or going. Jackson wrinkled his nose and said, "Good God, Flo. How do you tolerate that animal?"

The guilty little girl expression returned to Flora's face.

Poo merely smiled and said, "Why don't we take our plates out onto the porch?"

A lady never notices an odor, you know.

They gathered up silver and linens, plates and goblets and headed back outside. Faulkner snorted contentedly now that he had rid himself of "the wind."

True tried a shrimp. Soggy but still tasty. The mouthful of salmon was also tasty, but dry, having been heated up several times. The sweet potato was perfect.

She was starting to feel somewhat better about things (ptomaine poisoning no longer seemed imminent) when Flora said, "So True, I guess you're here to dig into the past. That's never a good idea, in my humble opinion."

"That's right, honey," said Poo. "Everything was settled long ago. There's not another will or anything. Your grandparents were wonderful people, but they didn't have anything."

"Well, there was that Sheraton sideboard," said Flora. "It was a beautiful piece."

"B True took that," Poo reminded her. She looked at True. "It's all gone, dear. Best just forget about it."

True didn't know how to respond to this, so she said, "Okay."

The sisters looked at one another and—what else could they do? They dropped the subject like a hot yam.

Jackson had been looking at the old ladies with what B True would have called a "suspicious humor about him" as they talked, but True's simple response had not only silenced Poo and Flora but restored Jackson's "positive humor."

He smiled at True, and she saw that admiration had replaced the steely glint of wariness in those amazing, twinkling, Mediterranean-at-sunset blue eyes of his. She couldn't fathom why he was responding in such a positive manner to what she considered her ridiculous reply, but the fact that he did made her feel quite light-hearted.

Dessert consisted of slightly smushed petit-fours decorated with someone's (not the Honeychurches' True would lay big odds) coat of arms. True declined the stale, pretentious delicacies with the excuse that though the temptation was mighty strong, her desire to lose five pounds was stronger.

"And besides, she said, "I couldn't eat another thing."

That part was the truth.

16.
Moonlight Madness

Though instructed to "leave it for the housekeeper," True and Jackson cleared the dishes and put them in the kitchen sink to soak. There was no dishwasher. Poo and Flora and Faulkner saw them out. When they got to the porch, Flora threw her cigarette into the yard and retrieved an industrial-looking flashlight from behind a pair of wellies stashed in the corner. Everyone said their "good-nights" as Flora struggled into the boots and walked into the yard.

She turned a narrow beam of light onto the path and said, "I never walk out here at night without my boots and light. Snakes."

True looked down at her own bare ankles, took Jackson's arm and headed toward the woods. They were half way through the Honeychurch garden when the light was extinguished.

After the brightness of the flashlight, everything was like pitch.

"Let your eyes adjust for a minute," advised Jackson. "And don't worry about snakes." True could just make out his grin in the darkness. "Faulkner's wind has probably driven them all off," he said.

Sure enough, True began to see that there was plenty of moonlight. What a relief! It was the total darkness that was getting to her—not the night time, per se. She actually found it exhilarating to be in the woods at night. And really, she didn't mind snakes all that much—if she could see them.

"That was some evening," she said as they started walking.

"Of course, Maisy warned me."

"Aunt Maisy?"

"She stopped by this afternoon."

"Well I guess you've just about had your fill of eccentric old ladies," said Jackson.

"I used to live in South Florida, remember?" said True. "At least here, they're not wearing bikinis."

"I hate to tell you, but my Aunt Maisy showed up at the country club in a stunning little red, white and blue number last Fourth of July."

"She didn't!"

"Oh, yeah," said Jackson. "It was something to behold."

True was still laughing when they got to her front door.

"It's early yet," said Jackson. "Want to keep walking? Get the mojitos out of your system?"

The moon and a breeze were throwing shadows around, bathing even mundane things in a silvery iridescence. It was not a night to waste.

"Sure," said True. "Where to?"

"Oak View. I promised Maisy I'd keep an eye on things over there."

"I've never seen the house by the light of a full moon," said True, feeling very relieved that instead of prowling around Oak View, Jackson had actually been protecting her birth place the night she'd surprised him in the woods. She grinned at her landlord. "I'd love to walk over there," she said with way more enthusiasm than she'd intended. She was absolutely, mystifyingly delighted at the idea of a moonlight stroll with Jackson Bean.

She blamed this on the mojitos.

True and Jackson headed back through her garden toward the path to Oak View. As they approached the woods, Jackson said, "I guess you've heard about the strange lights in there at night."

"Yes. The electrician told Maisy and me about it the first day I visited the house."

"You mean Al?" She could tell from his tone that Al was obviously not a pal.

"Yes, Al from Al's Electric," True said, mimicking Bertie.

"Why?"

"I didn't realize the light show's been going on for so long. It's odd that Aunt Maisy didn't mention it to me right away."

"Yes. And that first day—when Al told us about the lights—Maisy didn't seem surprised at all. It's very confusing. There must've been other … sightings, but the next time I heard about it was just before the night of the storm—the night I saw you and JuJu in the woods."

"And you still went out in the dark to investigate?" He grinned at her. "You're pretty tough, aren't you?"

"Well … not really," stammered True, feeling a bit proud of herself before realizing the question was rhetorical.

Jackson went on. "Seriously, True. Be careful. Until the big mystery is solved, I wouldn't spend too much time there alone if I were you. Just to be on the safe side." They walked in silence for a minute or two before he added, "There's probably nothing to it. Actually, I'm starting to wonder if the whole thing isn't just a case of local mass hysteria."

"Why do you say that?"

"For one thing, the locals are kind of prone to mass hysteria around here. The other thing is, I don't sleep all that well, so sometimes JuJu and I go over there during the night—as you know. I've gone at all hours, and never seen anything. Well… no lights, anyway."

True stopped walking. "But something else? Besides lights?" she said.

Jackson sighed. "Foot prints. And they could've been made by someone curious about the lights, which goes back to the local hysteria theory. Anyway, as you know, the porches at Oak View are hosed off regularly, always early in the morning. But I've gone over there after it's closed and then again later and seen muddy prints that weren't there on my first visit. They were on the porch and the back steps. And I swear they're a match for those snake stompers of Flora's."

"You're kidding," said True.

She started to walk again, running her hand over the needles of a small pine. Its crisp scent mingled with wisteria and the masculine, soapy-clean smell of Jackson. What with Flora's one-fifty-one rum still pumping through her veins, True was becoming downright re-intoxicated by it all. She closed her eyes and inhaled deeply, losing all track of the conversation for a moment or two.

"I wish I was kidding," Jackson was saying. "I know I'm starting to sound like one of the resident gossips, but I'm telling you, those old ladies are up to something."

Once True was able to tear herself away from the heady aroma of pine and wisteria and Jackson Bean and reconcile the picture of Flora in her snake stompers, flashlight in hand, creeping around Oak View in the middle of the night, she said, "It was strange how Flora and Poo warned me against looking into the past… into my past. I mean, why do they care? It's my past. And all of that talk about how my grandparents didn't have anything, insisting that they didn't leave a will. That was just too strange."

"Yeah. I think they protested a little too much. Makes you wonder if there isn't another will somewhere."

Could there really be another will? Though Maisy had told her of the rumor, she hadn't given it much credence until now. She was turning this development over in her mind as they took a familiar turn in the path and stood in the still, dark thicket at the edge of Oak View's side yard.

The house was glorious in the moonlight, framed by the ancient oaks and the airy expanse behind it from which it took its name. But windows that winked invitingly in reflected sunlight now lay in shadows, discouraging visitors.

"It looks like it's sleeping," said True. "Like it doesn't want to be disturbed."

"It does, doesn't it?" agreed Jackson. "Well, we won't disturb it, we'll just …"

"What? Oh, I see it," she added in a whisper. "There's a light inside." She watched it flash in an arc across the windows. "Somehow it doesn't look like a flashlight, though."

"You're right," Jackson said, pulling her farther into the shadows next to one of the big oaks.

And then he was gone. Jackson disappeared into the proverbial thin air! But she could hear him cursing in whispers. Peering into the darkness, she could see that he'd tripped over a wisteria vine as big around as her arm. She tried to stifle a drunken giggle, but it came out as a snort.

Oh, my gosh, I sound like Faulkner, she thought.

"Why I let myself drink those damn drinks of Flora's …" Jackson was muttering as he got to his feet.

True was startled by a creaking sound.

"What was that?" she said.

"Just my knees," grumbled Jackson.

"Oh," she said and was spared from further comment on her dinner companion's creaking joints by a flash of light across the front windows. "Look. There it is again. Exactly the same as before. And it's definitely not a flashlight."

Jackson smiled at True. "You up for a little investigating, Nancy Drew?"

"Sure thing, Clouseau," said True.

"Oh, so you're a funny detective, huh?" he said. But even in that dim light, True could see that he was smiling. "Okay. Now unless you have a better idea—and I'm open to suggestions. After all, you're the only one who hasn't fallen down yet. We'll scout it out first, then go in the back door. Element of surprise and all that."

True could tell that it was Jackson who wanted to play detective. She figured there was some logical explanation for the lights in the house, but it was kind of fun playing Nancy Drew - gosh, or even Bailey Jones, so she merely nodded, tried to adopt a serious expression, and followed Jackson's lead deeper into the breezy shadows playing at the edge of Oak View's lawn. They covered the entire perimeter of the property, stopping now and then to look and listen, at which point Jackson would whisper instructions as to their next location for surveillance and they would dash to the designated spot. The whole thing was totally silly, but True was having more fun than she had in ages.

When they'd made it around the border of the grounds, Jackson instructed her to "remember to stay out of the moonlight."

"It's a good thing we happen to be wearing dark colors," he added, looking her up and down with that little smile of his.

"Yes, it is," True said, taking in Jackson's black polo shirt and jeans. He looked very good in black she decided and realized that she too was smiling. She reminded herself that she was still under the influence of demon rum and said, "I think we should check out the interior."

Jackson chuckled softly and said, "I agree, Agent Cowley."

He dug a key from the pocket of his jeans and waved it in front of her. "Let's go."

Does everyone in this town have a key to Oak View? True wondered briefly, but quickly got her thoughts back on an "investigative" track.

When they got to the side door, however, True could see that not only was it not locked, it wasn't even closed completely. Jackson's face grew serious as he pushed the door open. They crept across the near-empty room until they got to the main hall. Walking to its center, they were afforded at least a partial view of most of the other rooms. They stood motionless until the sound of their own breathing scraped the silence. There didn't seem to be anything out of order. If anyone was there, they were being extraordinarily still.

True relaxed a little and had just opened her mouth to speak when a muffled thud sounded from below them. True and Jackson looked at one another, their eyes wide. Each put a finger to lips to warn the other to keep quiet. True had to concentrate on the possible seriousness of their circumstances to keep from giggling, but it was apparent that Jackson, probably seeing himself in the role of male defender (and one hampered by mojito over-indulgence) failed to recognize the situation was rife with humor.

Another thud told them that someone or something was on the tight stairway that snaked its way from a small hall near the kitchen down to what had been the potting shed but now served as a storage space.

As a child, True had been afraid of the twisting, cave-like stairway and had ventured down there only once—and that was during the day when sunlight illuminated the peeling plaster and narrow, tapered steps. She wouldn't want to try it in the dark, even with a flashlight—the splintery potting cabinets and rows of white, wooden folding chairs would make for tough going. She actually felt a small wave of compassion for the hapless prowler.

True looked around and realized there was nowhere to hide. No closets. No cabinets. No large upholstered pieces of furniture. She glanced at the heavy drapes in the ballroom. They might work, but whoever was coming up the stairs would see them as they made their way down the hall. There were a few chests, but they had been placed against walls. The great pocket doors rumbled like thunder when moved. And True remembered that the hall floors near the ballroom creaked like a broken accordion.

Jackson was coming to a similar conclusion. He gently took True's arm and nodded toward the second room back from Oak View's porch on the same side of the house as the stairway. This did not seem like a great plan to True. There was not an exit to the outside from there. They would be trapped by … by what? Her mother's ghost? Flora Honeychurch? A curious raccoon?

She let Jackson lead her out of the hall, but as she left it she saw the lights again, just out of the corner of her eye. They arced across the front of the room, and she was reminded of Casa Vispera, the historic house and museum where she had volunteered in Vista Palmas. She saw herself putting a final stem of heliconia in an arrangement in the house's fabulous Ponce de Leon room. *Why am I thinking of Casa Vispera now?* she wondered.

Another thud on the stairs and then another. Not a raccoon.

"Wait here," whispered Jackson.

He tiptoed to the doorway and peeked around the frame then jerked back as if he had indeed seen the spirit of True's mother. But she could tell by the relaxing of his shoulders and the lessening tension in his muscles that whatever he'd seen was nothing to be afraid of. This was a good thing because it was coming their way.

Jackson stepped back into the room, and True could see a little smile playing at the corners of his mouth, causing a dimple to appear. She sighed rather loudly before she realized what she was doing, and the footsteps stopped. She clamped her lips shut. Jackson looked at her and shook his head, but he was still smiling.

A small figure in a black stocking cap stepped into the room. Was it Flora? No. Too big. Besides, it was wearing a bow tie.

"Hello, Bertie," said Jackson, as if addressing him after a church service at St. James'.

Bertie let go a girlie-scream that scared the heck out of True. So she screamed, too. Jackson obviously had anticipated Bertie's reaction and possibly True's because he remained totally calm. Like Cary Grant in *To Catch a Thief* or *Charade*, thought True, feeling the tiniest bit like Grace Kelly or even her all-time favorite, Audrey Hepburn.

Bertie was now looking from True to Jackson like a cornered, over-dressed mouse. True figured his brain was tripping over itself in duplicate trying to decide on a plausible excuse as to why he was creeping around Oak View dressed like a sissy cat burglar. True and Jackson said nothing.

Finally it seemed that Bertie decided on the old "offense is the best defense" plan.

Puffing himself up and snatching the stocking cap from his head, he said in a low, authoritative tone, "Just what, may I ask, just what in God's name, are the two of you doing in this house after hours?"

Bertie's comb-over had been seriously disturbed by the removal of his cap, and his ten or twelve remaining hairs stood on end, seemingly undecided as to which way to fall. But Bertie was unaware of this as he raised his eyebrows and attempted to stare down Jackson who was at least a foot taller than he was.

"We saw a light," said True, "And came to investigate. If you remember, you told me that we needed to get to the bottom of this thing."

Jackson pushed himself from the wall upon which he had been leaning in exaggerated nonchalance.

"So Bertie," he said, "Tell us what you were doing stumbling around the basement in a stocking cap."

Bertie appeared to become aware of his hairs floating comically above his head and plastered them down with his free hand.

"Just the same as you. Investigating. Investigating the very apparition that brought you in here, of course. You know this house is dear to me. Dear to my heart. I have spent the last decades taking care of her, as if she were my own. Why shouldn't I take an interest—a personal interest in her well-being?"

He seemed to have persuaded himself, at least, that his snooping around the house was innocent. However, he was the only one convinced. True's eyes started an upward roll, but she caught them just in time. Bertie was her boss, after all.

"Well, thank you for being good neighbors, but I'll take over from here," he continued, now somewhat in control of himself and the situation. "I'll just lock the door behind you." He hurried toward the front door and they followed. "Good night, good night," he said, pushing them out onto the porch and locking the door.

True looked at Jackson who looked slightly confused and thoroughly irritated.

"Wow," she said. "First Flora and now Bertie. No wonder the house looks tired." She glanced at Jackson. "You don't believe him, do you? That all he was doing was investigating the lights?"

"Not for a second. But what was he doing?"

"Looking for something. That's obvious. But what?"

They headed down the steps, crossed the oyster shell drive and approached the woods, each lost in their own thoughts.

"This is just off of the top of my head," said Jackson, "But you don't suppose he was looking for the alleged second will, do you? I didn't want to tell you, but it's been a hot gossip topic since you came back. Since Flora and Poo brought it up, well … you might as well know."

"Why would Bertie care enough to go poking around?"

But she knew the answer as soon as she'd asked the question. Bertie's job as steward of Oak View was all he had, all he cared about as far as True could tell. It would kill him if the house ended up in the hands of a private owner. If he was searching for the will, it was likely in order to destroy it.

Jackson was a few steps ahead before he realized that True had stopped, lost in this miasma of new information. He turned and was unprepared for his reaction to the sight of her. The moonlight caught in her hair and settled in the deep brown of her eyes. It also illuminated the confusion and dismay in her pretty features.

The warm, protective feeling he'd had the first time he'd seen her at Burkett's funeral returned. As always, any unbidden feelings of tenderness toward the opposite sex that reared their pesky, little heads in Jackson Bean were accompanied by a reflexive wariness. Yet the sight of her there, so pretty in the moonlight, chewing her lip, upset.

He was definitely, disconcertingly moved, but instead of throwing up his defenses … He decided to blame it on the mojitos.

And by doing so, Jackson Bean not only opened a long-fastened door. He walked right through it.

Before he could stop himself, he had turned back to True and folded her in his arms.

17.
Meanwhile, Back on Eighteen

True's brain was spinning even more than usual as she locked her back door. She watched the lanky figure of Jackson Bean, who really should have been riding a horse into the woods (the Marlboro Man image still floated across her mind's eye fairly frequently) until he disappeared from view. The crazy quilt of an evening had generated so many new problems. And most of it had transpired while she and Jackson were both drunk! She might as well admit it. They had both gotten loaded at the Honeychurches'. Of course that was central to the old ladies' matchmaking scheme. Now her head hurt and her overindulgence in Flora's onion dip was coming back to haunt her in the form of severe acid reflux. She took two Advil with a tall glass of water, chased it with a couple of Rolaids and hoped for the best.

As late as it was, True knew she wouldn't be able to sleep, so she emailed her family in Vista Palmas, describing her strange night out. She wisely omitted the landlord-hug part, though her mind kept returning to this—to how comforting it was, how sweet, how … *Good Lord, it felt good.* The feel of Jackson's arms around her, there in the moonlight and his words … He'd told her not to worry, to give everything time to work itself out. It would happen, he promised her, and he would help however he could.

True shook her head and thoughts of Jackson Bean from her mind. Wisely, she clicked the "send later" key—saving the long narrative to be edited by a soberer eye the following morning.

The distant call of a train and the soft inside of her arm against her cheek worked its magic, and True quickly fell into a sleep so deep that she didn't even hear JuJu scrambling after a rabbit just outside her window. And Jackson's whispered curses at his beloved chocolate lab? They simply worked their way into her dreams.

In the familiar nocturnal scenario, Burkett stood on the eighteenth green, wearing plaid plus fours and his favorite saddle golf shoes. True was trying to get his attention, but was being shushed by the other golfers.

Burkett missed the putt, and True felt a tidal wave of guilt wash over her as her husband made his way to the men's grill. She'd distracted him, causing him to miss the putt and lose the bet—a very large bet based on the low whistles and slow head-shakes of Burkett's buddies.

But now like a rewound film, the dream began again. This time there were new dimensions to the nightmare. Golf carts adorned with wreaths and purple bows drove silently up their designated path behind the green, the shiny metal of stilled putters and drivers and wedges reflecting in the sunlight— reflecting across Burkett's face as he squinted at the small white orb lying innocently on the its carpet of unnaturally vivid green.

In addition, new characters had been added to the scenario's main cast. Jackson Bean was at the back of the gallery that had assembled to watch Burkett's disastrous sixteen-inch putt. True longed for Jackson to come to her, to wrap her in his strong arms and console her, but he simply sat there on a black horse, whispering curses at JuJu, who barked as Burkett drew his putter back with such precision. In the dream, True saw the sun reflecting in her husband's eyes, heard the bark echoing in his ears, and the wave of guilt that had washed over her began to subside. The missed putt wasn't all her fault.

Next to Jackson on a lovely palomino, sat Holly Varjak, the blonde history professor who had been with him at the Withers/ Moore reception. Had been his date.

True sat up in bed. Holly Varjak. How could she have forgotten about Dr. Holly Varjak, the sophisticated, brainy, tall blonde who dated Jackson? Why had she let Jackson Bean, a suspicious character with more than his share of emotional baggage by all accounts, and a man with whom she had a business relationship, and who obviously had a girlfriend, hug her like that?

Like what? He was just trying to be nice and really, he was operating under the same alcohol influence as she. But that hug... remarkably, that simple (yet complex?) gesture had taken her to another plateau in her climb out of the valley of grief and confusion. And that was a very good thing. True knew that. What she didn't know, she reminded herself, was Jackson Bean.

And what about the rest of the dream? The funereal procession of golf carts, the golf clubs reflecting the Florida sunshine into Burkett's eyes. JuJu barking just as Burkett was making that costly putt. It wasn't all her fault.

If she had known that Burkett's gambling had reached addiction proportions, she would have intervened. And she had tried to involve herself with their finances, but Burkett had discouraged her at every turn. If she had handled things perfectly, maybe the outcome would have been different, but no one is perfect, right? *Right. No one,* she reminded herself. It wasn't all her fault.

The wisdom crammed in that stack of self-help books on the bedside table, channeled by the spirit and daring of Bailey Jones (and fueled by the attentions of Jackson Bean?)—well, it all started to coalesce in True Cowley that night. And for a few minutes, her brain emptied itself of the maddening swirl of thoughts and images. Just before she fell asleep for the second time, the blessedly blank slate of her mind lit up with a single picture. True saw the lights reflecting across Oak View's sleepy windows. And she smiled to herself in the darkness because she knew what they were.

18.

Conjugal Trepidation, and an Implausible Explanation.

The next morning True slept later than she'd planned. No surprise there. But the shocker was that she felt great. The hangover she'd taken to bed with her was gone. The usual initial waking seconds of disorientation simply didn't occur. There was no sickening realization that Burkett was gone forever, no anger at him or herself for his weakness and deception. Could she still be drunk? The aforementioned hangover had come and gone, so that wasn't it.

Determined to enjoy the all-is-well sensation before it deserted her, True opened the doors to a morning lazy with balmy warmth, fixed herself a cup of coffee, made herself comfortable at the kitchen table and fired up the laptop. There was an email from True's daughter, Katie, brimming with A-type over-organization concerning the children's forthcoming visit. Schedules (bedtimes, mealtimes, amount of TV-viewing time), nutritional information (preferred foods, forbidden foods, vitamin intake) and reading lists (with books and study sheets) would be provided.

"When did summer vacation get so complicated?" True asked her computer. She shook her head remembering Katie's daily application of organic sunscreen and ingestion of vitamin D. Seeking the logic in that particular regimen gave True a headache, so she'd fallen back on B True's time-honored advice on such matters and "just tried not to think about it."

But surprisingly, the brittle efficiency of Katie's email was softened with a chatty report on the good health of True's garden. Katie had even included a detailed description of True's beloved royal Poinciana tree. She asked about Oak View and Maisy and Jane E and believe it or not, requested the recipe for Jane E's asparagus quiche (which True had raved about in a prior email).

"You're cooking now?" True said to the computer.

But she was smiling. The softer tone playing through Katie's email gave True reason to hope that her daughter was beginning to appreciate if not adopt her mother's more relaxed view of the world. The change in the dynamic between True Cowley and her daughter was what B True called a lagniappe—a little something extra and unexpected. True hadn't in her wildest dreams considered this bonus when she'd made the impetuous move to Alabama. Could it be that the decision to leave Vista Palmas was the right one not only for her, but for her daughter as well?

True's son-in-law sent a hello and there were emails from Tommy and Mary Kate as well. They seemed as excited as ever about their impending visit and sent short reports on their school's end-of-the-year events. A final addition to the joint email read, *Hey, True, What do you give an elephant for Christmas?*

True was surprised to find that the email she had composed the night before was remarkably coherent, so in response to Tommy's riddle, she added, *Hey, Tommy, Anything he wants!* and hit the send key.

After a "heart healthy" bowl of cereal and fruit, True grabbed a back pack and jogged to the nearby grocery store. It was small and expensive, a delightful place brimming with gourmet delights, but today she would throw budgetary concerns to the wind and indulge herself. It was funny how so many of the things she'd taken for granted as an everyday occurrence in Vista Palmas were now so appreciated. *Is this a good thing or a bad thing?* she wondered as she put her purchases away.

Back at the computer, True easily pulled up her mother's obituary. It was predictably factual, mentioning only that Gertrude Nicholson Hunter's death was unexpected and accidental, and that she was loved by all who knew her. More delving found the newspaper account of Nick's death. There had been no witnesses to her fall from the party boat of Marcel Johnson Boudreaux of Jefferson Parish. The other partiers had retired. When they awoke the next morning all that remained of Nick was an overturned martini glass and a sandal dangling ominously from a cleat. These were found on the boat's bow where her friends surmised Nick had gone for a last look at the stars. *Last look, indeed*, thought True.

A thorough search had not turned up a body. Presumed death by drowning. Presumed. What if Nick had slipped away somehow? Faked her death to escape … what? Her responsibilities to her little daughter? This line of conjecture was the stuff of B movies and bad novels. And the thought that Nick would purposely leave True was unthinkable. No, she would not go down that path, True decided as she printed out the obituary and the article and slipped them into a pocket folder.

A quick shower, clean skirt and blouse and she was ready for her first meeting of the day. It was bound to be a doozie since it involved planning a reception with the down-home-and-proud-of-it-by-God Bakers and the prickly, uptight-and-always-right Baxters at Oak View. Mrs. Baker bowled, window shopped at Dinette World and was known to drop the F-bomb without a whole lot of provocation. She lived in a blue vinyl house. Mrs. Baxter played golf and bridge. She only shopped at a few select stores in Atlanta and NYC. Smelling salts had to be administered the last time someone used the big expletive in her presence. Her home was old, pretentiously unpretentious and furnished to perfection down to the last lamp finial in the laundry room.

But as Maisy had once pointed out, perfection can be damned tedious. "Once you've reached perfection, what's there to look forward to?" she'd said. True was in agreement with this philosophy, of course.

True was determined to squeeze these polar-opposite, prospective in-laws into her "not worth worrying about" column, but not surprisingly they kept popping out.

I mean what is the worst that could happen? They'll choose another site for the reception? It's not as if there aren't three or four other laid-back, mild-mannered (well, there's no such thing, really) brides waiting to top off the day of all days at Oak View.

True continued giving herself this pep talk until she realized she was wearing herself out. She tried a different tack.

Not worth worrying about. Not worth worrying about.

The mantra had a minimal effect as she made her way down the path to Oak View. Yet it did keep her from visualizing all sorts of catastrophic scenarios.

On the plus side, the morning was sunny and warm. Budding flowers lazed in the breeze. Fresh smells and the dazzling green of spring popped out of every twig and branch and patch of earth.

Mother Nature's excellent humor couldn't help but elevate the Bakers' and Baxters' moods, True told herself. Their petty differences would pale in the warm sunshine. Harsh feelings would soften in the sleepy beauty of Oak View, which was made for a day such as this.

But as True came through the woods, Mother Nature's momentary boost vanished. A shining, blue, bad omen in the guise of a pick-up truck with orange paw prints and an assortment of Auburn University bumper stickers adorning its rear end was parked in front of Oak View. The Bakers. The truck sat nose to nose with a very large, black, bad omen in the form of large Mercedes sedan, which sported a subtle University of Alabama license plate. The Baxters.

True hurried toward the confrontationally parked vehicles. Good grief. Suddenly things were looking downright stormy. The Baxters and the Bakers were on opposite sides of the football rivalry of all football rivalries. And they were early! If there was one thing True couldn't abide, it was early arrivers. It was just the thing to throw her already jumbled cognitive processes into full tilt.

But True recalled section eleven of her *Managing Your Grief* manual, the section that dealt with redirecting emotions, as well as section thirteen's advice to accept things one is unable to change. And of course there was Bailey Jones' cavalier attitude while enjoying cocktails with opposing political forces in Dubrovnik. Would Bailey let anything as minor as prospective in-laws who also happened to be feuding football fanatics give her the tiniest pause? *Of course not!* True stopped herself halfway up the front steps. Inhaling as deeply as she was able, she closed her eyes, pictured Bailey handling the political foes with a smile and a martini, and turned her face to the sun.

Putting worries of forgotten sunscreen along with rationalizations about increased vitamin D out of her mind, she simply let the sun warm her skin while she concentrated on the breeze playing in her hair. Soon she was right there on that terrace in Dubrovnik with Bailey Jones, sipping a carefree cocktail and laughing at life's little practical jokes.

The sound of a man clearing his throat interrupted her reverie. She turned to find the rather formally clad Baxters and the denim wearing (though elaborately coiffed) Bakers staring at her.

Not worth worrying about. Not worth worrying about.

Mr. Baxter glanced at his watch. True glanced at hers. Ten-twenty.

Hoping that her watch wasn't slow, she said to the unhappy assemblage, "I'm True Cowley. Please enjoy the garden until I get things opened up inside—say ten minutes?"

She smiled her most disarming smile (exactly like the one she imagined Bailey Jones used to defuse those politicos on the coast of the Adriatic) and unlocked the front door. The house held the previous night's damp and chill, so she went about opening every door and window and shade and shutter. Sunshine and morning air tumbled into the tall rooms, and quickly dissolved all remnants of the night.

True exited the side door and saw that there were now six people in the garden. The prospective bride, Tracie Ann Baker and groom, Sansford Smythe Baxter had joined their parents, lightening the general mood of their elders to the extent that they almost looked as if they could stand the sight of one another.

Tracie Ann and Ford … due to a lisp that lingered into grammar school, the long version of his name had not survived kindergarten. Talk about your blessing in disguise! Anyway, Tracie Ann and Ford seemed oblivious to the cloud of parental dissension threatening the blue skies of their relationship.

As it turned out, the future Baxter couple was a refreshing

example of complimentary opposites. The elder Baxters, Ford's parents, were a merger of two wealthy and prominent Catholic families; the Bakers—Tracie Ann's mother and father—were non-Catholic, non-prominent/wealthy and non-social. The disparities in their backgrounds didn't seem to bother either Tracie Ann or Ford who could be found most Sunday mornings at Belle Hill Presbyterian pretty much doing their own denominational thing.

Tracie Ann possessed an easy laugh and sense of the ridiculous that softened the crispness of the more reserved Ford. Ford's respectful attention to his fiancée's ideas gave the less secure Tracie Ann a needed boost in the confidence department. Despite their dissimilar upbringings, they possessed an abundance of mutual attraction and respect that made them a very good fit.

As True approached the group, Ford was smiling at his fiancée as if he'd just won first place in the love lottery.

You're a lucky girl, Tracie Ann, thought True.

And then it dawned on her that she had seen the same look in another pair of eyes—eyes that reflected all the sparkle and depth and mystery of the Mediterranean. And that look had been directed at her.

But of course she wouldn't let herself believe it.

True tried to shake highly implausible though lovely thoughts of Jackson Bean from her mind and focus on the tasks at hand. But every time she looked at Tracie Ann and Ford, she saw herself and Jackson Bean! She gave the young couple one last friendly smile, determined not to look their way again and turned her attention to the prospective in-laws.

While the Bakers discussed the placement of the beer kegs, Mother Baxter sought out an "island of elegant repose" for the Baker Heirloom Punchbowl. This was the intended receptacle for some type of innocuous fruit punch, the recipe for which was another in the ever-lengthening list of Baxter matrimonial traditions.

As Ms. Baxter launched into a protracted description of The Heirloom, True realized that as far as Mother Baxter was concerned, the Baxter Bowl had taken precedence above everything (including the bride-to-be). Ms. Baxter's insensitivity was not lost on the Bakers, either. Ms. Baker was attempting to run her fingers through her heavily lacquered hair and Mr. Baker was getting himself all bowed up, as if readying for a physical confrontation. True hoped it wouldn't come to that because Mother Baxter would have him tied in a knot before you can say War Eagle (War Eagle is the Auburn University football team's war cry, in case anybody doesn't know).

True took the Bakers and the future Ford and Tracie Ann Baxter on an extended tour of the garden, leaving Mother Baxter and the watch-watching Mr. Baxter to look for a suitable spot for the punchbowl of all punchbowls. Once the beer keg and country/western/gospel singer placements were secured, True got a quick signature and a hefty deposit. She then sent the Bakers on their way and a prayer of thanks to the Almighty.

The prayer of gratitude was due to the Bakers' choices of Jane Ellen's Catering (Jane E wouldn't bat an eye at the post-nuptial country/western theme); George and Buster, the flower guys (they could pull off anything); the best photographer in town (the pictures should be priceless!) and Zola, an iron-willed, mono-monikered bridal consultant (she would have the Baxters and the Bakers trembling in her presence long before Tracie Ann's special day). Yes, if anyone was up to the challenge of a fruit-punch-and-beer, hoe-down reception wrapped around a two-hundred-year-old, hand-painted punchbowl, it was this little band of party geniuses.

There was one tiny fly in this pie of optimism, however. The Baxter Bowl was currently being held hostage by an elderly, somewhat … okay, by a totally senile aunt who had claimed title as the blackest of the Baxter black sheep when she was still at M.S.C.W. (Mississippi State College for Women, also fondly known as The Dubyuh). And that was when she was young and still retained relative control of her faculties. Sadly, age had not softened the murky heart nor dulled the conniving machinations of the soulless Aunt Tudie. She cast a shadow so long it was capable of souring the sweetest of celebrations. And she had let Mother Baxter know in the most certain terms that if she wasn't at the reception, then the Baxter Punchbowl wouldn't be attending either.

Mr. Baxter, weary of heirloom squabbles and squandered

minutes, hustled his wife out of Oak View, but not before Mother Baxter, her voice quivering with emotion, assured True that Sansford was "not about to be the first Baxter in five generations to celebrate his nuptials with the Baxter Bowl in absentia."

True closed her eyes and luxuriated in the sudden, sublime silence for a full minute before locking up. She decided to leave the windows open since the D.A.R. (Daughters of the American Revolution—but then, you know that) ladies would be in to decorate for their bi-annual meeting and tea. She would check in with them later that day, but in the meantime was determined to get to the cemetery and visit her mother's final resting place.

As she approached the side door closest to the cemetery, a familiar figure approached. It was Holly Varjak, Jackson Bean's girl de jour, True reminded herself , looking for all the world like Grace Kelly playing Bailey Jones in *The Avignon Adventure.*

Holly's hair hung—no, cascaded—in lovely, pale waves, setting off her lovely, pale skin and eyes. She wore a creamy blouse and tan slacks. True watched Holly head straight to the small door leading from the garden to the storage area beneath the house. Besides being camouflaged by a covering of lattice that blended perfectly with the wall into which it was set, the door was well-hidden by a pair of those amazing, tree-sized camellias. This was very handy for workers during the many outdoor festivities held on Oak View's grounds. It was also a way of getting up to the kitchen without having to walk through guests in the house. And it was supposed to be kept locked at all times.

But how would Holly even know of its existence? And why would she want to expose her pastel duds to the dank, dusty, dirty storage room beneath the house? True decided to find out.

She crept down the twisting stairway as far as she dared and crouched down so she could see into the expanse beneath Oak View. Holly had closed the garden door behind her, but a row of short windows lining the curved wall allowed sunlight to penetrate the space.

Holly maneuvered around the stacks of chairs and other party accoutrements to get to an interior wall that supported the very cabinets and shelves that had held Grandmother Hunter's gardening supplies. True imagined her grandmother puttering in the filtered sunlight, her trays of seedlings and gardening catalogs spread around her.

The imaginary scene dissolved as Holly bumped her slender hip on something and murmured a very unladylike response. She was in deep shadow now. Taking a pen light from her pocket, she ran the beam down the back edges of the cabinet, pressing here and there with well-manicured fingers.

True was forced to lean down and forward to keep Holly in view. By this time her knees and ankles screamed for relief, so she raised up just a tad to lessen the strain in her joints. Unfortunately it was just enough to throw her off balance. Thanks to a firm grip on the railing, she only crashed down a couple of steps. Of course this was enough to alert Holly Varjak that she was not alone.

"What the— Who's there? Who is that?" Holly sounded more irritated than alarmed or embarrassed or guilty or any of the responses one might expect from a caught-in-the-act trespasser.

It took True a few seconds to get herself back to an upright position.

When she was able, she straightened her hair and clothes as best she could, limped down the remaining stairs and said, "It's True Cowley. Can I help you?"

"Oh, hello. I'm Dr. Varjak. I teach at the college. History. I have a professional interest in Oak View."

"Really. Well, I would be glad to arrange a tour for you, Dr. Varjak. Um, is there something in particular you were looking for down here?"

"Oh, I'm interested in every aspect of the house. Top to bottom. And thanks, but a tour won't be necessary. I like poking around on my own."

The professor looked at her watch, which True doubted was even visible in the dim light. "I'm afraid I have to run. Nice meeting you Trudy," she said, making her way to the door.

"It's True …" began True, but Holly was already on her way out.

True went back up the stairs and watched Holly through the parlor windows. It seemed that she didn't have to run, after all.

She was standing in the front yard, lost in thought as she gazed at the fountain. Minutes later Holly shook her head in disgust and strode confidently back onto St. James' campus.

19.

Grave Implications

Why bother? True wondered as she locked Oak View's side door behind her. *They should just install a revolving door and be done with it!*

True felt a flutter of irritation when she thought of the pompous Bertie and that affected, self-absorbed Holly Varjak! They had their nerve snooping around. Both under the house. Both of them looking for something under the house. But what? What was down there that could be of interest to both Bertie and Holly? And Flora Honeychurch? And maybe even Jackson Bean? This last possibility was especially upsetting.

The first idea that popped into True's head was to call Jackson Bean—even though he was still on the suspect list. But what if he was totally innocent? He had offered to help, and if the previous night's adventure was any indication, he would get a major kick out of it. But his girlfriend was now a headliner on the list of suspects, True reminded herself. Oh, it was all giving her a headache!

When the flurry of disjointed thoughts and half-formed ideas finally settled in her brain, True was convinced that there was only one person she could go to with her dilemma. Under normal circumstances, Bertie would be the logical one to approach. But then these weren't normal circumstances. Her boss was a midnight prowler himself! Maisy Downy was the only one she could talk to.

With great difficulty True put the strange happenings at the house out of her mind. Having two trains of thought roaring through her head at once was counterproductive at best, maddening at the least. She was determined to stay on one track for the time being—the track that led to her mother's grave side.

She had been back to the cemetery only once since Burkett's funeral—to check on his grave and marker. Her husband's final resting place was in a prime spot, oak-shaded and close to a marble bench that blended in nicely with the grave stones. This bench overlooked Belle Hill's downtown and the bay beyond. The ever-present oaks and Spanish moss, camellias, bridal wreath, and azaleas were interspersed with the occasional cabbage palm and low palmetto. The same English, Spanish and French names appeared again and again on the markers.

True found it all very comforting. And though Burkett might have been happier interred in a glitzy mausoleum shaded by the majesty of a royal palm, True reassured herself with the fact that he was surrounded by generations of Cowleys and Burketts and near enough to a golf course that he was hopefully resting or putting in peace.

True heard the rattle of metal tools, and the man from one of her gauzier childhood memories—the man described so aptly by Maisy as having panther-black skin and hair like cotton—came into view pushing a red wheelbarrow loaded with gardening implements. Carver wore pants faded to gray and a long-sleeved shirt of well-washed, pale blue denim. He stood before the startling green of a hedge of yew. It made True want to paint the scene.

"Oh, hello, Carver. I'm True Cowley. True Hunter. I think you knew me when I was a little girl."

"Yes, ma'am, Miz Cowley, I remember. How can I help you?"

True hadn't expected such a cool greeting.

"Well, I wanted to ask you about my mother, Nick Hunter. I believe you worked for my grandparents when we all lived at Oak View?"

"Yes, ma'am, I did. What is it you would like to know?"

"Uh, would you like to sit here on the bench?"

A small frown passed over his face then the impassive expression returned. "No, ma'am. I'm fine."

"Well, as you know, my mother died when I was around four, and I never knew my father."

"Yes, ma'am. Lots of folks never knowed they fathers. I never knowed mine."

"Oh, I'm sorry. Well, I really would like to know my mother. No one will tell me anything about her, though. Maisy said I should talk to you."

He stood silently for a few awkward seconds, then said, "Nobody knowed Miz Nick. She was 'bout like that camellia bush over there. Everybody wanted to be 'round her, couldn't get enough of her. But who can know a camellia?"

Now True was confused. She slumped to the bench.

"But you knew her, didn't you?"

"Your mama and me was close to the same age. She treated me better than anybody ever treated black folks back then. Gave me books, got me jobs. But she was hard to know. Real happy one day, real low the next. Up for days, sleep for days. They got names for all that now, but nobody could understand it back then. What I'm trying to say is, your mama had a good heart, but a nervous mind. She was afflicted with a nervous mind."

Carver ended this description with a little nod. True knew he would say no more. At least not that day.

"Well, thank you Carver, for speaking with me. And Carver. Thank you for teaching me how to swing."

He almost smiled. "You're welcome, Miz Cowley. Miz Maisy asked if I would show you the Hunter plots, then if you don't need anything else, I guess I'd better get back to work."

"Oh, of course."

Good grief, thought True, following the old man. *Could that have gone any worse?* She felt like she'd been in a southern time warp, held captive in *Gone With the Wind* or something. Or returned to those good/bad old days at B True's when even stalwart Christians like B True and Uncle Henry accepted, even expected, such groveling.

Carver stopped and motioned to Maisy who was sitting quietly on an iron bench. Her shirt was black and sleeveless and sported a Harley-Davidson emblem beneath the words, Born to Ride. It topped off one of her ruffled gypsy skirts and a pair of tiny running shoes. She was very still, eyes closed beneath a wide-brimmed hat. She was so still, in fact that True wondered if she— But then the old lady turned stiffly and smiled at True.

Oh, thank goodness! True thought. A wave of relief swept over her, and she realized just how much the old lady meant to her.

Her thoughts were interrupted by Maisy, still very much among the living.

"Beautiful spot, isn't it?" The old lady said. "Hello, Carver. Good to see you, as always."

"And you," said Carver with an unexpected smile.

Maisy turned back to True. "I come here a lot. Might as well get used to it." She winked at Carver and his smile grew bigger.

True was more confused than ever. Because in Maisy's presence he seemed a different person.

The Hunter section of the cemetery was relatively small with only three graves, but it was a beautiful, secluded spot, encircled by camellias on one side and a wide ribbon of daylilies planted to catch the morning sun. There was the iron bench, splashed with shadows. Leaning against it was a push mower, its twisted blades covered with grass clippings that saturated the air with their crisp smell.

"It's lovely, Maisy. Really lovely."

"Your grandmother had a thing for camellias, as you know. Loved daylilies, too. Your grandfather did all this after she died, tended those daylilies himself." She smiled at Carver. "With a little help."

True walked over to the flat stones denoting the departures of the little Hunter family. The elder Hunters' markers were engraved with names and dates. A medallion of some sort was beneath Mr. Hunter's name and a flower that was probably a camellia graced his wife's stone.

Nick's marker, however, was large enough to hold a poem. True read the words aloud.

> *He who binds to himself a joy*
> *Doth the winged life destroy;*
> *But he who kisses the joy as it flies*
> *Lives in eternity's sunrise.*

"William Blake wrote that," said Maisy.

"I know, and I've always loved it. I guess my mother did,

too."

"Well, it was certainly how she lived her life. Always in the moment, you know. Made the most of the good days because like I told you, she was prone to moods."

Before True could respond, a rustle in the shrubbery announced the always-spectacular arrival of JuJu, whose leash trailed behind her like the line of a lost skiff. Clearly overjoyed at the sight of True and Maisy, she raced to True, started to jump up, then changed her mind. Instead, she wiggled every part of her body and a short bark escaped her. She licked True's hand, and as if to be sure she didn't slight anyone, she bestowed a slobbery symbol of her affection on Maisy before racing to Carver. Finally losing the self-control battle, she lunged at the old man. He grabbed her paws and pushed her gently away. When she sat, he leaned down to rub her ears.

"JuJu!" From somewhere in the bushes, Jackson Bean called the name of his beloved canine companion, adding a few minor curses for emphasis.

JuJu froze for a millisecond, then almost shrugged as if to say, Oh, it's only Jackson, and went back to alternately licking everyone and barking.

Carver laughed. "I swear, Maisy, Bean brings out the worst in this dog."

"JuJu!"

True thought she detected a resigned quality to the deep, breathless voice of Jackson Bean, and suspected that the Marlboro Man was in imminent danger of losing his alpha status in the master/pet relationship. Maisy was smiling and shaking her head. True figured she was of the same opinion.

"JuJu!" Jackson yelled again, finally coming into view, sweating and frowning.

He glanced in the general direction of his unexpected audience, but a sharp bark drew his attention to JuJu who now dropped submissively at Maisy's feet and smiled sweetly at her master. Jackson stuck his hands in his pockets and looked down at his dusty running shoes, obviously and rightly embarrassed to have been caught cursing at his dog in a cemetery of all places. But when he looked up, he was wearing that bad boy grin of his, and True couldn't help thinking that it was just about the cutest smile she'd ever seen.

"Jackson, when are you gonna show this dog who's boss?" said Carver.

"I'm trying," Jackson said. "She's the toughest one I've ever had, though."

He walked over and kissed Maisy's cheek.

"Thanks for intercepting the hound from hell. I'd still be chasing her if she hadn't run into y'all."

He looked in True's direction. "And good morning to you, True," he said, the smile back on his handsome face. "Always a pleasure."

His eyes held hers for a few seconds, and she grinned back at him like a demented school girl. She couldn't help herself. The enigmatic Jackson Bean … well, there was just something about him that brightened her day.

He reached down and scratched JuJu behind her ears, his irritation with the dog all but forgotten.

"So what's this, a meeting of the cemetery committee?" he asked.

"Maisy has been telling me about my mother and grandparents." True gestured to the graves.

"Oh, sorry to interrupt," said Jackson. "I guess I kind of forgot where I was."

"That's okay," said True. "It happens to me all the time."

Jackson bent down to scratch the dog's ears again. JuJu answered in contented murmurs and sighs, then closed her eyes for a quick nap, the morning's chase having temporarily exhausted her.

"Well, I got plenty of work to do," said Carver. "Best be moving on. We still on for fishing, Jackson? My freezer's looking pretty poor."

"Still on," Jackson said. "Bring a big cooler."

"Will do," said Carver. He grabbed the handles of his wheelbarrow, nodded to Maisy and True and rattled off.

Jackson turned his attention to Nick's grave. He read the poem aloud. "That's nice." He gave True a rather grim little smile and said, "If everyone could live like that, I guess we'd all be better off."

"Yes, we would," said True. "But it's one of those easier-said-than-done things, I'm afraid.

"Right you are, Ms. Cowley," he said, his happy countenance restored. "Right you are."

"But this means a lot to me—that Nick is buried here in this lovely place with her parents with that wonderful marker. From what I know about her, it sums up her best qualities. The camellia on her mother's stone is a nice touch, too, don't you think?"

"Very nice," said Jackson. "It's a shame people have gotten out of the habit of epitaphs and individualized tombstones. You used to see them all the time."

"Umm," agreed True, nodding and staring at the smaller stones. "I wonder what that medallion on my grandfather's marker is."

"Oh, that's not a medallion," said Jackson. "It's a coin." He squatted down to get a closer look, and his knees creaked loud enough that JuJu woke with a start. She ran over, nudging her master, trying to get him to play.

"He must've been a collector or something," Jackson said, pushing JuJu away and attempting to get a better look at the coin.

"Yes, that's right," said Maisy who had been watching the interaction between Jackson and True and JuJu with detached bemusement and more than a little satisfaction. "I thought it was stamps he collected, but now that I think about it, it was coins."

"If I'm not mistaken, that's a 1927-D Double Eagle," said Jackson.

"How on earth do you know that?" asked True.

"I had a coin collection when I was a kid, and not too long ago I did a piece on a retired professor who had gotten into coin collecting. This professor is an interesting old guy. We hit it off, and he kind of renewed my interest. He had a framed picture of the double-eagle over his desk. It's one of the rarest coins around. Probably as beautiful to a numismatist as that Purple Dawn camellia was to your grandmother."

True bent down beside Jackson. JuJu began poking her head between True's legs.

True took the dog's muzzle in her hand gently but firmly.

"No," she said in a low, firm tone.

The dog looked at True and cocked her head to one side as if to say, "What's the problem?"

True stared her down, and JuJu went back to bothering her master. With a bit of groaning and creaking, Jackson stood with the dog's leash firmly in hand, but wrapped around one leg.

Jackson managed to disengage himself from the leash and said to True, "This is kind of last-minute, but we have a group that gets together for canasta every now and then. It's at Jane E's tomorrow night, and I told her I would round up another player. Maisy will be there, won't you Maisy?"

"Wouldn't miss it."

"We call her the canasta masta—she always wins."

He winked at Maisy, who waved a hand, dismissing her elevated card status.

"Like I said, it's always an impromptu kind of a thing. And just an excuse to get together …"

"Gosh, I haven't played canasta since I was a girl playing with B True. I'll have to brush up."

"It's not rocket science." Jackson grinned at her. "Why don't you ride with me, and I'll brush you up on the way over."

True found herself grinning back at Jackson.

"Okay," she said. "It's a date!"

A tiny shadow passed through the Mediterranean depths of his eyes, and True realized what she'd said.

"Oh, that's just an expression."

Jackson looked confused.

Maisy rolled her eyes.

And as if to change a sticky subject, JuJu gave True one of her quick barks. But True was not to be dissuaded from digging herself into a conversational hole.

"You know, when people say, 'It's a date.' It's just an expression. Like we've agreed on a time, like …"

"That's exactly how I took it," Jackson lied.

Having had enough of this strange, human interaction, JuJu began pulling him toward home. He shook his head good-naturedly.

"Looks like I'm leaving. Why don't you walk over to my house about six tomorrow evening? We'll ride to Jane E's together. She's fixing dinner, trying out some new casserole or something," he called over his shoulder as the "hound from hell" jerked Jackson from view.

True turned her attention to Maisy, who had been uncharacteristically quiet. Oblivious to Maisy's close observation of the interaction between True and Jackson and misinterpreting her silence as fatigue, she said, "Maisy, why don't we sit for a while. I want to talk to you about Oak View."

"And I've been wondering how the little soiree at Flora and Poo's turned out," said Maisy. "I can't wait to hear about that."

True had Maisy laughing and rolling her eyes as she shared the lurid details of dinner at "Honeychurch Manor" with the two sisters—and Faulkner. Maisy was especially interested in all aspects of the two inebriated detectives and their adventure at Oak View.

"So you figured out the source of the mysterious lights in Oak View, huh?" said Maisy with an astonishing lack of curiosity.

"You know, too, don't you?"

"I think so. It's the mirrors. It started happening about the time they hung those twin gilded mirrors in the hall. And the college finally took down that building on the golf course—it was full of termites. Now, if you're driving out on the highway, you notice you have a good view of the house."

"And at night, the car lights reflect on the mirrors."

"Yes. They reflect from mirror to mirror, in sort of an arc. Very spooky, but too repetitive to be the aura of a restless spirit."

True leaned back on the iron bench and let out a sigh. "It's kind of disappointing, though," she said.

"What is?"

"Ghosts are a lot more fun than car lights. But if you had it figured out, why didn't you tell anyone?"

"Well, I wasn't sure. And there's more going on over there than lights or apparitions, True." Maisy turned to look at her, her crinkly face all seriousness. "I want you to be careful over there. Something is going on," she said again. "Sometimes the only way to get to the bottom of things is to just let them play out. So let's keep the solution to the lights to ourselves for a while."

True agreed and proceeded to tell Maisy about Holly Varjak's visit to Oak View. She didn't tell Maisy she was suspicious of Jackson since the old lady's affection for her nephew was so apparent, but she did tell Maisy she was conflicted about filling Jackson in on Holly's actions—her being his girlfriend and all.

"Somebody said that discretion is the better part of valor, and they were dead on, sweetie. There's too much big talk in this little town of ours, and it's gonna come back to bite 'em where it hurts if they're not careful." She looked at True, who was mulling it all over and biting her lip.

Maisy's voice took on a soft tone and she said, "And as far as Holly being Jackson's girlfriend, well, let's just say that Jackson doesn't know it, but he's been looking for the right girl in the wrong places since he and Barbara were divorced."

"Jane E told me about that. And about the death of his son. Such a terrible thing."

"Yes, it was. But that summer we all got to know him was a gift I'll always be grateful for. I've learned to think of it that way. I don't know that Jackson has, though."

The two women sat enjoying the sun and a breeze that played through the daylilies and camellias. Finally True broached the subject of Carver and his "split personality."

"Oh, it's a protectiveness of a sort. Old habits die hard, you know, dear. He'll warm up to you. He was very sweet to you when you were little. You and Nick—and the Hunters, too, were all good to Carver. He just feels funny, I'd guess, it being all these years later."

"Getting information about my mother was like pulling teeth," said True.

"It's hard to know how much to say sometimes." She smiled at True. "Don't worry, though. Like I said, he'll warm up to you. Like we all have."

They were each lost in their own thoughts again until True said, "Jackson is an interesting man. I mean, it's interesting how he knew what that coin is."

"Yes," agreed Maisy.

"But how could he possibly know that the camellia on my grandmother's stone is a Purple Dawn?"

"A lot of unanswered questions, hon" said Maisy, getting up from the bench. "The answers will come in time. You'll figure it out."

"Me?"

"Yes, you." Maisy smiled at her. "You have a nimble mind, True.

"That's one way to put it, I guess," said True.

"I know it doesn't always seem so, but it's a great gift." Heading off down the path, she added, "See you at canasta."

At the mention of canasta, the memory of True's latest faux pas came roaring back to her.

It's a date!? What is wrong with me?

It seemed to True that she had been asking herself that question since she was old enough to think.

As Carver had pointed out, there had been no neat categories like attention deficit disorder when she was growing up. Something you could label and even take a pill for. There were no articles on how to survive a parentless childhood or books pointing out the joys of non-traditional families such as the one she'd had with B True. No school counselors to dissect dreams of trains and explain away the fear that B True might be the next to vanish. Asking questions and searching out one's past were not only not in vogue, but chasing down these dark paths had the high probability of illuminating nothing more than what True perceived as her "oddness."

True looked at her family's graves—the graves of her childhood, is how she was thinking of it, giving in to the melodrama of it all.

Who were you people? And how can I get to know you? And the most unsettling question of all: Do I really want to?

20.

Camellias and Coins

After a light lunch, True made needed wardrobe and attitude adjustments, taking her leave from the self-pity party brought on by the visit to her mother's grave and recriminations over her *It's a date!* statement to Jackson. Now that she had snitched on the various trespassing Belle Hillians to Maisy, she felt better. Like they say, a shared burden is a lighter burden.

She tossed her slacks into the hamper and retrieved the penlight she kept in her bedside drawer for emergencies. Next she located some batteries, got said penlight working again, and headed back to Oak View.

She had a few hours to kill before setting up for the Daughters of the American Revolution. Surely in that amount of time she would be able to uncover some clue or other that would help her figure out what everyone was looking for in Oak View.

After a stab at reconstructing the movements of Holly Varjak in the back garden, True entered the door to the storage room. She went directly to the cabinet in the corner and placed her fingers along the edge as Holly had. The only revelation this produced was that she could use a manicure.

True looked back toward the low windows and the sunlight playing on the bushes beyond. She closed her eyes and like Alice after consuming one of her wonderland potions, became small again, her head not much higher than the flat work surface of the long cabinet. There were stacks of camellia books—red ones with blue writing in a pink square on each cover. Inside the text was interspersed with color pictures of perfect camellia blooms.

"Professor Sargent, Debutante, Purple Dawn." True heard her child's voice naming each one.

"Purple Dawn is my favorite," she could hear Nick say. "Your grandmother's favorite, too. Mama said that sunrise in eternity is always a purple dawn. Repeat that, True. Sunrise in eternity is always a purple dawn."

Again True heard her own child's voice repeating the words to her mother.

"Good," said Nick, shaking the last cigarette out the pack. "Now don't forget that. It might come in handy one day."

That's when True realized that the answers to her own, personal questions as well as to the puzzling activities at Oak View lay not with Holly Varjak or Bertie Wallace or Flora and Poo Honeychurch, or even True Cowley, but with True Hunter. She was the one who knew Oak View with the intimacy and fascination of a child. And soon—if she didn't try too hard, didn't bind the memories to herself with a heavy heart—the secrets locked in her childhood would eventually fly free.

Caught up in this rapture of optimism, True went upstairs and into the wide hall where she heard her mother's laughter echoing off the curved walls of the ballroom. She entered the spacious bathroom where she had stood trembling in a draft until Nick wrapped her in terry cloth and carried her into the parlor. Nick had sat with True by the fire, rubbing her daughter's hair with the towel. True followed the memory into that parlor and saw her grandfather's desk piled high with papers and large, flat albums and coins and the big magnifying glass she was not allowed to touch. She remembered the desk finally cleared of its clutter after her grandfather's death, the coins and books all stowed away or sold, she supposed.

True took in the fourteen-foot ceilings and simple moldings and remembered something else. Each of the room's high corners had been decorated with a trompe l'oeil design of the beloved Purple Dawns in vases atop shelves. The artistry had indeed tricked her eye as trompe l'oeil promises to do. The three-dimensional effect had been so realistic that True had wondered if the vases might topple from their shelves, as a real vase of camellias had done once when a screaming, cursing Nick had slammed Oak View's heavy front door.

True squinted up into the corners of the room, but layers of paint had long since covered over any trace of the short-lived whimsy of the trompe l'oeil. At least the great chandelier remained, with its crystals and ornate medallion of curlicues and acanthus leaves.

As she stood gazing at the chandelier and the medallion from which it was suspended, it occurred to her that those curlicues weren't just random clusters of circles. They were coins. Camellias and coins were everywhere!

True let herself out into the back garden, found a spot on the patio and tried to go to that place of "non-striving and peace" that the final, uplifting chapter of her grief manual described. But the whole coin and camellia thing kept bouncing around in her brain.

"Weird," she said aloud.

And face it, she thought, my relatives are sounding weirder by the day. Who gets so obsessed by Purple Dawns and Double Birds or whatever that coin was that they put them everywhere? And no one wants to talk much about Nick. Who had no close friends and from the sounds of it, was at the least, very moody and most probably manic-depressive or bi-polar. Or is that the same thing?

"Some stones are best left unturned." Wasn't that what B True said? Something like that, but the message was clear.

As the first carload of Daughters of the American Revolution crunched over the oyster shells in Oak View's driveway, True had a revolutionary thought.

I might be the sanest person in my entire family!

21.

Canasta Masta

My friend has adopted a dog with mange. He named him Bald Spot. Love, Tommy. PS—I miss you.

   Hi True. This Mary Kate. I lov u. Ihate Tommys jokes.

True smiled. To think—a five-year-old typing and emailing on the computer! Could True even print when she was five?

Getting into bed, True picked up the novel Maisy had given her and turned to page one of *Peril in Portofino*. She could tell right away it was going to be a good one—maybe even as good as her all-time favorite, *Marseilles by Monday*. Juliet Benoit had the knack of throwing the reader into the story's exotic locale from the first paragraph. And having found oneself in a place such as Portofino, the reader was reluctant to leave until that final page was closed.

In this case, our intrepid sleuth, Bailey Jones is watching dolphins play in the clear, placid depths of Tigulian Bay when a young man jogs by her and snatches her bag. Never mind that it was a gift from the very grateful diplomat whose life she had saved in *The Adriatic Adventure*, it also held her passport and the Modigliani Papers!

Oh, good. An art theft, thought True, snuggling herself into her covers.

Mysteries about art thefts were her favorites.

If she let herself, True would stay up all night reading and finish the book, but she was determined not to gorge herself on the words. Instant gratification paled in comparison to the delicious pleasure and increased psychic benefits of a chapter—

well, maybe on occasion two chapters—per night.

At the end of chapter three, she reluctantly put the book on her bedside table and turned off the lamp. She lay in the dark and imagined herself walking along Portofino's quaint harbor, enjoying colorful fishing boats and frolicking dolphins. She would be on her way to lunch … at an outside table where she would be meeting … who? In the past, whenever she indulged in these dream jaunts (invariably brought on by a Benoit novel) she had pictured herself with Burkett.

In the world of orthodontia, however, the dollars to hour ratio is hard and fast. "If I don't work, I don't get paid," was Burkett's mantra. And besides, one never knew when the next maloccluded preteen would come skulking into the office with the promise of years of income for Vista Palmas Orthodontics. No, there was only time and frequent flyer miles enough for three or four guy-only golf junkets a year and the occasional dental convention which was invariably held at a golf resort in Florida. So True's travels consisted of flights of fancy for the most part.

Changing cognitive gears, True got herself back among the fishing boats and dolphins. She saw herself walking—no, make that sauntering up to the weathered, cloth-draped table. It was occupied by three women—two old friends from Vista Palmas and her new friend, Jane E. Perfect. The women were having wine and laughing, all waving and happy to see True. True put her face against the soft inner side of her arm and in her imagination, took her seat at the table by the bay.

As she floated into unconsciousness, True found herself in the middle of the golf course dream. The one she'd had so many times that it was like a tired rerun of a sad, little TV episode. She was trying to get her husband's attention, was shushed by the other men. Burkett missed the putt and strode away into the men's grill, leaving her alone by the green. The tedium of it was beginning to overtake the sadness of it. And even in her sleep, True knew that this was a good thing.

Later, she dreamed of that seaside table in Portofino. Now Jackson was seated there. He held up a glass of red wine, an inviting, questioning smile on his handsome face. How nice it would be to sit there in the sun sharing conversation and wine with funny, handsome Jackson Bean. But someone had stolen her purse. She had to see about that.

True found herself running away from Jackson Bean, running down the beach in hot pursuit of the purse snatcher, who was suddenly on a train, leaving Portofino. The train's whistle blew, and True knew she would never see him or her purse with its valuable contents again.

She awoke to the fading hum of a real train, leaving Belle Hill. Its sounds had invaded her dream, awakened her then left her drifting in that midnight silence when thoughts grow loud and insistent.

The next morning she could not shake off the dream. It visited her as she cleaned house and attempted to remove the dirt stains from the knee of her damaged pants. It followed her to her meeting with the Belle Hill Bibliophiles summer murders committee.

In an effort to outdo the previous year's successful murder mystery party (where folks pay good money to pretend to commit or solve a murder) and possibly to capitalize on the spooky goings-on at Oak View, the bibliophiles had expanded the event into a series of murder parties to be held during the coming summer at the house. Due to the bibliophiles' exuberance about it all, the meeting had gone into overtime. True had just enough time to shower and wash her hair before her canasta date.

Not a date. Do not say the D-word, she reminded herself.

At six o'clock that evening, True headed out of the door in the direction of Jackson Bean's. She was running late after all because she couldn't find one of the three or four pairs of reading glasses she owned. Straining to see the tiny numerals on her watch, she decided she would have to ask Jackson to stop by the drugstore so she could buy yet another pair of cheaters, as Maisy referred to them. Squinting at cards all night would insure not only a headache and wrinkles but a canasta disaster.

The doors and windows of Jackson's house were open. As she approached, music (reggae?) drifted her way and she could see Jackson at his desk working away on his laptop. There were books. Lots of books. On shelves lining a wall. In small stacks on tables. On the desk. On the floor next to the desk. JuJu dozed at his feet. True wondered if she had the wrong night (it had happened before), but no, it was yesterday when he'd said tomorrow evening, which was now tonight. Right?

As she got almost to the porch, Jackson closed the laptop and stood up. She was close enough to hear his knees creak loudly and him curse softly. Something made her look down, and good grief, it was her friend, the turtle—the one she rescued from the bathroom at Oak View. It looked like the same one, anyway. The poor thing was on its back. Stuck. True would bet JuJu was somehow involved in this. She leaned low over the unlucky reptile (or was it an amphibian?) and first checked to see if it was alive. She couldn't tell, so she turned it over and watched for any sign of consciousness.

Just as True bent down to check on the turtle, Jackson Bean went through his routine, looking out of the open doors and windows, searching the surrounding yard to make sure he was unobserved. Thus reassured, he crossed over to the blue marlin painting and slid it to one side, turned the combination and opened the door to the safe. He stowed the laptop, reversed the procedure and turned to find True Crowley staring at him. There was a good-sized turtle in her hands and a very suspicious look on her face. What was it with this woman and turtles? He checked the big ship's clock that hung over his desk. Ten after five. He had told her six, hadn't he?

Jackson walked to the door and took the turtle from her hands.

"Oh, you shouldn't have," he said, a smile playing at the corners of his mouth.

He put the turtle down in the flower bed. It stuck its ugly head out. But only for a second. JuJu's nap had evidently been quite an energizing one because she raced out of the open door, past Jackson, past the terrified terrapin, past True and off into the woods.

"Damn it, JuJu!" Jackson yelled.

JuJu kept right on going.

"Oh, I'm sorry," True began, but when she turned her attention back to Jackson, she also caught sight of the clock above his desk and its large numerals, which she could clearly read. "Oh, and I'm early. I didn't have my glasses, couldn't see my watch."

"That's okay," said Jackson. "I can use the extra time to catch JuJu."

But he was still smiling.

True remembered his creaking knees and said, "You take your time. I'll find the dog and be back at six. It's the least I can do."

He hesitated for a few seconds before agreeing.

At exactly six o'clock True returned with JuJu (who she'd enticed with a sharp whistle and a piece of hot, aromatic microwave bacon). Instead of a turtle, she was now holding her reading glasses (which she'd found in the fridge when searching for the bacon—scary!) and a bottle of white wine. They left JuJu happily snoozing on the kitchen floor and slipped carefully out of Jackson's back door.

After some small talk about the weather, True said, "Jackson, it's none of my business, but why do you keep your computer and books in a safe?"

Jackson, having had the better part of an hour to concoct a plausible explanation, said, "Well, I had my laptop stolen once."

True was still wearing that dubious expression, so he added, "It had the only interview with a coach who'd just won the championship—all the quotes were on the computer. It was for my column. Due the next day."

He sneaked a glance at True, who was obviously still unconvinced, so he went on. "Only deadline I ever missed—just about lost my job over it."

Concern, maybe even sympathy was now playing in those pretty brown eyes of hers.

"And the books belonged to my mother. They're a collection. Might be worth a little something, so why not keep them in there? I sure don't have anything else worth putting in a safe, and it's convenient being next to the desk."

She seemed to have taken him at his word, so with only the tiniest bit of remorse at having lied to this sweet woman who saved turtles and had managed to return his dog to him, he changed the subject to cards, giving her a quick run through of what he referred to as Canasta 101. As he was finishing up the subtleties of the all-important discard, they arrived at Jane E's.

They were met at the door by Maisy who was attired in a gypsy costume.

"Had a fortune-telling gig at Milton Walker's seventy-fifth birthday party," she explained, taking off a lustrous, black wig and fluffing up her own platinum tresses.

She tossed the wig onto the sofa and asked Jane E for a drink.

"Putting a light spin on some pretty dark futures can work up a thirst," she explained.

Jane E's husband, Dave, together with an elderly history professor from the college by the name of Jonathan and a neighborhood couple called Bobbie and Bob Roberts rounded out the group.

Before attacking the cards, they joined Maisy for Jane E's famous frozen wine coolers and appetizers in the form of avocado salsa and homemade chips. The conversation was light and enjoyable and when the subject of the Honeychurch sisters came up Maisy insisted that True and Jackson describe their recent evening with "the girls."

Jackson's description of Faulkner and his digestive problems had everyone cracking up. Finally Maisy, gasping for air, said, "Stop. I'm about to spurt this wine cooler out of my nose! That's not good for a person of my advanced age."

Canasta was lots of fun. True and Jackson ended up as partners, and he pretended to be annoyed at being stuck with the "newbie." She forgot most of what he had taught her and was forced to devise an off-the-wall strategy of her own. She won two out of three rounds, earning the nickname "Canasta Masta, Jr." Jane E's shrimp and artichoke recipe was a hit, as was True's dinner wine, which had come with her from Vista Palmas and which no one had tasted before.

It turned out Bobbie and True had quite a bit in common, and as the two women scooped Jane E's homemade caramel ice cream into pecan-crusted pastry shells, Bobbie invited True to join her book club. When True accepted, Bobbie promised to send the book list to her the next day.

True couldn't help but wonder if all of Jackson's canasta partners were extended the same invitation. She pictured herself in the midst of a clutch of Holly clones trying to make intelligent remarks about the latest Pulitzer Prize winning tome. Suddenly she wasn't so sure this was the club for her.

"Is Professor Varjak in the book club?" True asked in an off-hand tone.

"Why, no," said Bobbie. She hesitated, then smiled at True. "Professor Varjak would never stoop to our literary level." She hesitated again and then, lowering her voice conspiratorially, she added, "Listen, we had an Audrey Hepburn movie festival when the old downtown theater was renovated. Holly said she refused to waste her time on sappy romantic comedies."

True gasped. "No, she didn't!"

"Yep," said Bobbie, equally incensed at this blasphemy. "I mean, really! Since when is *Breakfast at Tiffany's* a waste of time?"

"Good Lord," said True, equally aghast at the idea, as Jackson came into the kitchen.

Bobbie cleared her throat (a bit theatrically, True thought) and said loudly, "Hi, Jackson. I was just telling True about our book club." She turned to True. "We alternate heavy and light reads. Our next meeting is in three weeks. We'll be discussing the new Juliette Benoit novel, *Peril in Portofino*." She chuckled and said, "I wasn't kidding when I said light."

"*Peril in Portofino*! Oh, I've just started that," True said, the rapture of a new Benoit book flooding her features. But then she noticed Jackson looking at her curiously and flashed back to the day they'd met. He had caught her talking to the box of books and advised her against getting addicted to them. She remembered how she'd disavowed her vicarious enjoyment of Bailey Jones and her globe-trotting exploits.

So she added primly, "I like to read something light once in a while, too."

"Great," said Bobbie. "Write down your email address and I'll send you our calendar and all the pertinent information tomorrow. You can ride with me for the first few meetings—until you feel comfortable with the group. It won't take long, though. They're easy."

When the dessert dishes were done, Maisy announced it was past her bedtime and headed for the door. Jackson and True said their good-byes, True promising everyone a rematch.

"Aren't you embarrassed?" asked Jackson as they ambled down Jane E's front walkway toward his truck.

"Always," said True. "But about what, exactly?"

Jackson laughed and True thought he had the nicest laugh, so deep and easy and …

"About beating everyone when you've never played before," he said, interrupting her thoughts.

She waved a hand dismissively. "I used to play with B True. Besides, ever hear of beginner's luck?"

"Yeah, only we refer to it as newbie luck around here. Guess I'll have to hold you to that rematch to find out."

True laughed. "You're on," she said.

"You know, it's early yet," said Jackson. "How about an after-dinner drink? Or just a walk around downtown? I'm not ready to go home yet."

Ten minutes later they were strolling along Trinidad Street—the trendiest of the surprisingly trendy nine block area that in the last ten years had seen warehouses shake off their dust and grime to become restaurants and shops. Upper stories had been transformed into balconied apartments or condos that were favored by young urban-dwelling lawyers and artists and bankers. Due to the pleasant weather and a delightfully sultry breeze floating in from the bay, French doors were thrown open affording brief glimpses into softly-lit, high-ceilinged interiors furnished in the latest of the latest décor.

In one, a crystal chandelier illuminated Beidermeier and post-modern furniture alongside an enormous mahogany armoire. Abstract art graced its distressed walls. Music, conversation and laughter drifted from the whole eclectic scene into the narrow street. This small slice of Belle Hill was a low-key version of the French Quarter or Key West—or even the old town section of Vista Palmas, thought True.

Every few minutes, someone called hello to Jackson or stopped to be introduced to True. Two of the women they met turned out to be members of the very book club that Bobbie Roberts (wife of Bob, from the night's canasta party) had invited True to join.

From art galleries and book stores, to restaurants and bars

and ice cream/candy parlors to a bandstand in the town square, downtown Belle Hill had something for everyone, it seemed. True was reminded of what she missed about Vista Palmas and why her family felt so at home there.

"… and ten years ago this was just warehouses and junk stores," Jackson was saying. He stopped, realizing that the only one listening to him was himself.

"What? I'm sorry. I'm afraid my mind wandered back to Vista Palmas for a few minutes. That's where I used to live, in Florida. We also have a renewed downtown area. We call it old town. It reminds me of this a little."

"So tell me about Vista Palmas. Pretty good bill-fishing there?"

True laughed. "As a matter of fact, there is."

"I'll have to check it out one of these days. Now tell me about True Cowley's life in Vista Palmas."

He seemed genuinely interested so she described the area and how it had changed over the years from a drowsy fishing village with one golf course to a glitzy sprawl of condo/golf-mania. In True's opinion, the only real improvement was in the original downtown area, which, like Belle Hill, had been retooled without losing its quaint personality.

She told him about her work at Casa Vispera, about her precocious granddaughter, Mary Kate, and her jokester grandson, Tommy. He asked if she had any pictures, and she showed him the mini photo album that went everywhere with her.

"Cute kids," he said. "I can see you in them."

Since his interest still hadn't waned, she told him of her daughter and son-in-law and her worries about their frantic, costly lifestyle. He asked delicately about Burkett, and she found herself confiding in him about the circumstances Burkett had left her in—financially, that is. She didn't mention that her dear, departed husband had left her pretty broke emotionally, too.

"So what about Jackson Bean?" she asked.

"Married twice, divorced twice, a long time ago."

"And you've lived here in Belle Hill ever since?"

"Yes and no. Always had my home here, but did a lot of

traveling—for the column, mostly. Fishing and hunting and sports events. That kind of thing."

She wanted to know more, like how the Belle Hill Courier could send its sportswriter trotting off to who knew where, but one look at his face told her he'd closed the door on any additional personal information. Knowing the story of his son's death and the estrangement from his daughter, she didn't blame him.

They walked on in silence. It was a full two blocks before he regained his usual, laid-back persona and they found themselves back where he'd parked the truck.

True was determined to rid the evening of any remnants of the temporary melancholy that had seeped into their happy rapport, so as she climbed into the truck she smiled and said, "Thanks, Jackson. This has really been a fun evening. It's helped me feel at home here."

"Good," he said, "But hey, it's not over yet. JuJu and I are going to walk you home." He grinned at her and added, "You never know what that'll lead to."

22.

Dysfunction Junction

It was after eleven when they turned into Jackson's driveway. True had agreed to come in for a minute so that Jackson could put JuJu on a leash before walking True home. As the dog howled and danced around the kitchen trying her darndest not to jump on True, Jackson looked for the leash.

"Damn dog hides her leash," Jackson snarled. "Most dogs bring it to you," he said more to JuJu than True, "They're grateful to have someone walk them."

JuJu responded with one of her more impudent barks.

Jackson went off in search of the missing leash as JuJu lost the battle with self-control and lunged at True.

"Sit," True said firmly, taking the dog's big paws in her hands. They stared at each other for a few seconds before JuJu, possibly due to some vague memory of the time True had flipped her over, gave in and dropped to the floor, every muscle quivering with self-restraint.

True looked around the kitchen. The room was a bit spare in the way of culinary accoutrements. A few well-used cookbooks sat atop a wine rack which held three bottles of red, but there were no pots of herbs, bowls of fruit or canisters. A blackened, cast iron frying pan sat on the stove top. Three ripe tomatoes graced the window sill above the sink. It was a man's kitchen. A man more at home with a frying pan and a grill than an oven.

There was a wide opening that led into the study and Jackson's desk. True went to the bookshelf. Books on sports. Biographies, mostly. Expected. There were classics, too.

Fitzgerald. Hemingway. Not surprising. Neither were Grisham, Clancy or even the collection of Shakespeare's plays, when she thought about it. But Jane Austen? All of Miss Austin's works were there, from *Sense and Sensibility* to *Northanger Abbey*. Definitely odd. True pictured her own library, which consisted mainly of a box of Juliette Benoit paperbacks hidden in her closet like a crate of porn.

She looked at the blue marlin picture. Jackson's story about the contents of the safe smelled like a dead marlin, True decided. *But what is he up to?*

Stacks of papers and books and several newspaper clippings littered the expanse of the desk top. Untidy, but not excessively so. A mug of pens and pencils and a pair of reading glasses sat beneath a battered lamp. A file cabinet whose drawers looked securely and suspiciously locked, was topped with a printer and fax machine and a couple of photos. In one picture, a smiling, tanned teenaged boy held an enormous fish and beamed his pride into the camera. The boy's eyes were dark, but there was no mistaking that smile. He had his father's smile.

Wedged in the corner of the frame was a snapshot, curling at the edges. It was the dated image of a studious-looking teenaged girl. True guessed this to be Jackson's daughter, Evelyn. Another, smaller frame held the picture of a curly-headed toddler dressed in a jack-o-lantern costume. She wore a demure, self-conscious smile. True picked it up to get a closer look, smiling at the adorable child, and was reminded of her own granddaughter, though Mary Kate was anything but demure and self-conscious.

Jackson located the leash under a bed where JuJu had evidently left it and returned to the kitchen. Amazingly, his dog was sitting, staring intently at True who was in the adjacent study next to his desk. She was holding the picture of his granddaughter, Evie. Was she snooping in his things? Invading his privacy? Damn women and their nosiness …

When he'd worked himself into a full-blown case of personal insult and outrage, he caught sight of the expression on True's face, which was anything but curious and prying. True was smiling at the picture, probably thinking of her own granddaughter who would be about the same age as Evie.

He took in the curve of her mouth, the thick hair tucked carelessly behind one ear, and the delight in her dark, shining eyes as she looked at Evie, and it all drained out of him. He stood there for several seconds, relishing the absence of all that inappropriate, unjustified angst and irritability, relishing the sight of True enjoying the sight of Evie.

"Her name is Evie. She's my granddaughter, and I've never met her. Like I said, I was married and divorced a long time ago. Two kids. I haven't seen Evie's mother—my daughter—since, well … since a long time. If we're any kind of family, I guess it's a dysfunctional one."

True thought of her mother, and decided that she and Jackson were at a sort of dysfunction junction, both presently attempting to sort out the past in the hope of brighter, more functional futures for themselves and their progeny.

Jackson walked over and sat on the edge of the desk. "I've been writing to Evelyn—that's my daughter—for a few years, trying to reconnect." He smiled at the picture. "She sent me that about a year ago. I guess you could call it progress."

True was touched that he was confiding in her, especially since, according to Jane E, he never talked to anyone about his past or his children. Was this new openness on his part simply because she had been so forthcoming with him earlier? Or because, like her, he was at this dysfunction junction? Maybe he was just tired of keeping it all to himself, and she was available to listen. Right place, right time. Who knew?

Undecided, she didn't know what to say, didn't want to pry, didn't want to make him regret opening up to her. She looked back at the picture and true to form, said the first thing that came to her.

"She's adorable, Jackson." She smiled at him. "And she has your eyes, lucky girl."

"Well, let's just hope that's all she got from me," he said, grinning at True.

"You didn't ask for any advice from me, but …"

"Uh, oh. Here it comes," he teased.

"Sorry."

"Don't be. I want to hear what you have to say."

"Just that I admire you for trying."

"And the advice?"

"Don't give up. It would be a shame for Evie not to know you. Keep trying."

"Thank you. I intend to, Ms. Cowley. I definitely intend to."

He didn't move from the desk, but continued to look at True with … what? True wasn't sure what the emotion was behind that look, but she was pretty sure it was something good.

JuJu, fed up with this human bonding, gave a yelp of misery, as if to say, please stop talking and take me out! And so they did.

When they arrived at True's back door, Jackson said, "Do you know how to lift an elephant with one finger?"

"Uh, why, no, I don't" answered True.

"It's not easy. First you have to find an elephant with one finger."

"Oh … That's … very cute," said True, smiling politely.

"It's for your grandson." said Jackson.

"Oh," she said again, the relief apparent in her voice. "Thanks. He'll love it."

JuJu, who had been dancing around the end of her leash suddenly settled down. She cocked her head to one side, ears perked. She watched Jackson and True as if there might be another piece of microwave bacon in her immediate future. But it was True who received the treat. Jackson leaned over and very softly, very slowly, kissed her cheek.

"Good night, True," he said.

When True had gone inside, and he'd heard the click of the back door lock, Jackson led JuJu down their familiar path toward Oak View. As usual, he allowed her to stop and sniff and relieve herself again and again. Soon the moonlit eaves of the old cottage came into view through the oaks and palms and pines.

At the edge of the side lawn JuJu suddenly stopped her sniffing, her ears perked, her intelligent eyes serious. Jackson looked toward the house and thought he saw a flash of light. He cursed softly under his breath. He wasn't in the mood to get into it with Bertie or the Honeychurches or whoever might be creeping around the place looking for God knew what. Maisy would disapprove of this dereliction of duty—after all, he'd promised to keep an eye on things. But playing detective just wasn't the same without True.

He smiled to himself, realizing that he hadn't had that much fun with a woman in a long time.

He gave JuJu's leash a gentle tug. "C'mon, girl. Let's go home."

As Jackson let himself into the back door, his phone began to ring. There was only one person who would be calling him at this hour. A glance at the caller I.D. confirmed that it was indeed Holly Varjak and that the Belle Hill grapevine was humming at a break-neck pace.

"Hello, Holly," he said amiably as if it were mid-morning instead of midnight.

"You son of a—"

"Holly, could you hold on a minute while I take JuJu's leash off?" said Jackson, keeping the annoyance out of his tone.

Maybe a few seconds would cool the woman off. Maybe not.

"Okay. Now what's the problem, Holly?" Though he had a pretty good idea.

"The problem is you're involved with that ditzy neighbor of yours, and it seems I am the last to know."

Suddenly Jackson was very weary of Holly Varjak. It took everything he had not to simply hang up the phone. But he knew from a boatload of experience in such matters that hanging up on the Holly Varjaks of the world resulted in anything but escape.

"Holly, I'm not involved with Ms. Cowley. She's a nice lady who happens to be the niece of an old friend of Maisy's. It's called being neighborly."

"Neighborly? Ha! I'd call it convenient. The vulnerable, little widow right out the back door. Come on, Jackson."

"I don't do vulnerable, Holly. You should know that by now."

"Actually, it occurs to me that I don't really know you at all."

Here it comes.

"We've been dating for months and I really don't know a thing about you. I just don't get you. As a matter of fact, I don't get this whole damn town."

Jackson had never understood why Holly had come to Belle Hill. His impression that she wouldn't stay long was part of the attraction. She was smart, funny, beautiful in that plastic way so many of them had nowadays, and was different from the available locals. He liked different.

But had he misjudged her? Mistakenly put her in that rare category of woman who can enjoy a casual relationship without taking it to the next level? It seemed as if he had. Because the relationship had run its course as far as he was concerned, and he was ready to let it die an amiable death. Holly appeared to be anything but ready to end things. Or maybe she was just peeved it wasn't ending on her terms. Which he had hoped it would. He hated these break-ups, most of which he had initiated through the years.

And this is why you don't do vulnerable, he reminded himself. He had opened himself up to True Cowley in some way he didn't quite understand himself. The idea of having the break-up conversation with True was not something he could even think about.

"So what do you have to say, Jackson?"

About what? He hadn't been listening. "I have to say I'm sorry if I upset you, Holly. I was honest with you from the beginning. I'm not in the market for anything serious."

"Oh, yes. You were brutally honest. I guess I thought things had changed. But people like you don't change, do they?"

"I guess not."

Holly hung up the phone.

Jackson took a deep breath and let it out. He hated it for Holly. He really did. But a wave of relief washed over him.

By this time True had checked her email and sent Jackson's joke to Tommy. She slipped between the sheets, too tired for even one chapter of her book. Thoughts of Jackson's secrets (and lies) concerning the safe warred with memories of the night he had seen her dismay and impulsively wrapped his arms around her as well as the gentle kiss he'd given her that evening. To say she had a good feeling about him was an understatement. But the duplicity concerning his income (which was none of her business, she reminded herself) and the secrets of the safe threw a great big red flag over her positive feelings for him.

Besides, she had not been widowed a year yet, had not even sorted out her feelings about Burkett. She was getting there though, and she would not let loneliness or fear or any other emotion-run-amok let her get involved with anyone, least of all Jackson Bean with his questionable source of income, his obvious dishonesty and his back-breaking pile of emotional baggage.

True Cowley was doing just fine all by herself. She was sure of that. Well, pretty darn sure. But just to make herself feel better about it all, True put her cheek against the warm inside of her arm. And since there wasn't a train passing through Belle Hill at that moment, she imagined the whisper of faraway wheels on a distant track and followed it into the darkness where she floated off to sleep.

23.
A Fish out of Water

"All appears to be in order. Yes, very orderly," said Bertie, peering at True with those strangely questioning eyes of his. Not for the first time True pondered Bertie's weird orbs. Was this failure of Bertie's lids to properly cover the tops of his irises simply a stubborn stain in the Wallace gene pool or the result of some freaky birth trauma? A leftover childhood habit, perhaps, like thumb-sucking?

True forced herself to abandon this fruitless cognitive detour and focus on Bertie's words, but then it occurred to her that had it been fifty years prior, she and Bertie would be occupying her French provincial twin beds. The desk at which they sat inhabited approximately the same area in which she had slept the nights and afternoons away as a toddler.

She had repositioned the desk into what had been her old bedroom. It was a sunnier, bigger room and away from distracting filing cabinets and copiers that sucked the wonderful Oak View ambience from the back office. So True had found the lovely escritoire gathering dust in a back hallway and wrestled it here where her view was roughly the one she'd had as she lay in her bed as a child. This was not only more pleasant but highly conducive to conjuring up memories sleeping in Oak View's shadows.

The May morning was warming up, insects buzzing more lazily than they had an hour earlier. The smell of just-cut grass out on the golf course intensified in the sunshine and soft air and drifted through the house's open doors and windows. A hint of perspiration formed on Bertie's face as the breeze released his comb-over, setting the hairs dancing above his owlish eyes. He fidgeted with a jacket button.

True felt sorry for him. It was the kind of sympathy she had for an unlucky earthworm languishing in the sun on the pavement or a lizard caught between screen and window pane. She always picked these creatures up and transported them to their natural habitat. With a minimum of effort, she saved them from a slow demise, easily transforming their little, creepy-crawly lives from hell to heaven in an instant. True found these experiences extremely rewarding.

Bertie cleared his throat. True's mind snapped back to the present moment. As she often did in these situations, she simply smiled pleasantly, as if to say, yes, I'm listening.

"As I was saying, I have not a small amount of concern, uh, concerning the Baxter-Baker reception.

"Baker-Baxter," True reminded him. "Baker is the bride."

"Right, right. There seems to be some problem concerning a punchbowl? A punchbowl problem, you might say?"

"Oh, yes, the problematic punchbowl," said True, trying to infuse her voice with a seriousness the problem did not deserve. "Well, the bride's mother refuses to take part in the reception unless the Baxter bowl is there, too."

Bertie nodded as if this were a perfectly reasonable reaction on the part of Mrs. Baxter.

"It seems that this Aunt Tudie, who doesn't get along with anybody, is holding the punchbowl ransom until she gets an invitation."

"Oh, my," said Bertie. "My, my …"

"It gets worse," said True. "Aunt Tudie has put the punchbowl up for sale." At this point, True got tickled by the absurdity of it all and just managed to get the rest of her sentence out. "On eBay."

Even Bertie had to give up a small smirk at this, which set True into full laugh mode, which set Bertie to twittering uncontrollably through pinched lips. True hadn't thought it possible, but was, of course, delighted to see this other "wild" side of her boss.

She noticed Bertie was alarmingly red in the face and

perspiring profusely. Was he so uptight that he'd rather suffer a heat stroke than remove his jacket? True insisted on getting him a glass of iced tea from the kitchen. When she put the glass into his damp hand, their fingers touched. Bertie was now looking more doe eyed than owl eyed. He smiled demurely at her and sipped the tea.

"Delicious," he said, almost whispering. "Absolutely delicious."

"Good," said True, all business again. "Hopefully the punchbowl problem …" The mere mention of the Baxter bowl had her face twitching, but suppressing the giggles, she continued. "Hopefully, the problem will work itself out. I'll keep you apprised of the situation, though. Now, what else is on the agenda?"

Bertie was still making goo-goo eyes at True between sips of tea, but he managed a peek at his notebook.

"We have the Belle Hill Bibliophiles summer murder series," said Bertie in his new, whispery voice. "Let's see, now. The third Thursday evening in June, July and August."

He named the dates (twice) for True, who took notes though she already had them on her calendar.

"I believe Jane E is in charge of the food which she will coordinate with the evening's setting and theme," said True. "One is set on an island in the Bahamas, one in the English countryside and one in an Italian villa. Jane E will do a great job."

"Oh, I have no doubt, no doubt at all on that score. You're planning on attending, I assume."

True hadn't thought about it, but said, "Of course. If you think I need to."

"Yes. And I plan on being here also." He smiled coyly at her as he disclosed this info, then morphed back into his nervous, little self. "I hear these murder mystery parties can get a bit, well, out of hand. People running about, hiding in closets, that sort of thing." Bertie dabbed at his dime-slot mouth (one of B True's more colorful descriptions of people afflicted with too-small, thin-lipped mouths) with his napkin and actually winked at True!

She was completely put off.

"Well, there are no closets in Oak View." This fact came from Maisy who had entered the room just in time to witness the wink or she wouldn't have believed it.

Bertie leapt to his child-sized feet and bowed in Maisy's direction.

She waved him back into his seat and said, "Just go on with your meeting. Sorry I'm late."

But Bertie insisted on a rehash of the punchbowl report and details of the murderous third Thursdays coming in the summer.

"The Bibliophiles report that they are sold out of tickets for all three events already. Oh, and the Honeychurches will be there, gratis. The bibliophiles think they will add a certain, uh, panache is the word they used, I think. I expect Jane E knows to add them to her numbers."

There were other, more mundane matters to address (the ordering of new chairs, a minor plumbing problem in what True now thought of as the turtle's powder room and new signage for the parking area), but no one mentioned eerie lights, or Al the Electrician, or Bertie's and True's and Jackson's unplanned meeting at Oak View the night of the Honeychurches' drunken soiree.

As Bertie headed off in the direction of his beloved library, Maisy shook her head with a wrinkled smirk. She poked True in the arm and said, "Bertie's sweet on you, True. How'd you manage that?"

True shrugged. "I gave him a glass of tea."

"Got to be more to it than that."

"Well, I shared a laugh with him."

"Ahh," said Maisy.

24.

Luncheon is Served

True put Grandmother Hunter's silverware (Camellia, by Gorham) alongside B True's fine English china (the name of which no one can remember). It is a lovely floral pattern, if a bit overdone in the pansy department. A bunch of pink-tinged, yellow Peace roses from the florist, greenery from the yard and those lemony linen napkins True had found in Savannah when she and Burkett attended the regional orthodontic convention finished the job. Though the meal wouldn't be fancy, it was the first luncheon served in True's new home, and she felt that it merited the use of the family heirlooms and pricey roses. True paused to admire her handiwork. She had removed all three of the Queen Anne table's leaves, making it a perfect fit in the sunny Belle Hill dining room of Jackson Bean's cottage.

After much deliberation, True had decided on Cuban fare for lunch with new friends, Jane E and Bobbie Roberts and old friend, Maisy Downey. She figured some of her south Florida/ Cuban recipes might be a novelty for renowned caterer, Jane E as well as for Maisy. And Bobbie, of course, who had never been south (or north) of Belle Hill.

For starters, there was shrimp marinated in citrus juice tossed with just-ripe avocado and shaved red onion. Spicy pork, saffron rice and black beans rounded out the menu. In spite of the budgetary requirements of her "phase three plan" True had become very friendly with the gourmet grocer, Mr. Geo Manetti, who managed to find a loaf of Cuban bread at her request. Mango tea, made up and ready to pour was something he kept in stock.

All three guests were lavish with their compliments as they finished the flan True had prepared for dessert, but the biggest testament to the meal was that when they were done, as B True would've put it, there was nary bean nor bread crumb left.

Claiming she'd overeaten and therefore was in need of a digestive nap, Maisy left the three younger women. True was sure the sweet old thing just wanted True to be with women her own age, to allow friendships to grow unfettered by generation gaps.

True and Jane E and Bobbie discussed local politics and the best of Belle Hill shopping. They were finishing off the last of the mango tea when the conversation turned to books which in turn brought them around to Juliette Benoit's latest effort, *Peril in Portofino.* It had been thoroughly discussed at the book club meeting a few days prior, but was still a fairly hot topic. The consensus of the group was that though the book was one of Benoit's best, it was the author, herself that was most intriguing.

Ms. Benoit was never seen—not a book club appearance, not a book signing, not an interview—which led to endless speculation as to her actual identity. Now that *Peril in Portofino* (Benoit's first work in twelve years) was on the shelves, the interest in the woman was building again. Most assumed Juliette Benoit to be nothing more than a *nom de plume* used by another, perhaps more "literary" author who preferred not to be linked to the escapist though lucrative fare of Bailey Jones adventures. Others said the author was as deficient in personality and charm as she was adept at plotting and description, and that publishers simply used this negative to their advantage, keeping the woman under wraps while piquing readers' interest with the author's anonymity.

"Nothing but a publicity stunt," opined one of the more outspoken book club members. "You know, to make her as mysterious as her books. Why, I bet she can't even speak French!"

To prove her point, another member had produced an old article about the enigmatic Benoit. It stated that according to very reliable sources, Juliette was indeed of French descent.

But she had been born and reared in southern Louisiana. Upon hearing this news a collective sigh of disappointment escaped the group. Cajun French lacked the cache of Parisienne French, to say the least.

"Wouldn't you just love to know who she really is?" said Bobbie.

"I don't think you'll have to wait much longer," said Jane E. "Things aren't like they were when her last book came out."

"You're right," said True. "With everyone online talking about anything and everything and the popularity of this new book, I don't see how she can keep it a secret."

"Well, even if I don't find out, I'm glad she's back to writing Bailey Jones adventures," said Bobbie. "They're so much fun!"

The conversation eventually segued back into local doings and Oak View in particular.

"That reminds me," said Jane E, "I had a meeting with Bertie yesterday. He's acting very strangely."

"So what else is new?" asked Bobbie.

"No, I mean strange even for Bertie," said Jane E. "True, he kept asking about you, asked me if you were alright—you know, financially and everything. Did I know if you felt like Oak View was your home. Stuff like that. And whenever he mentioned you, his voice got all whispery. Really weird." Jane E shook her head, then shrugged in incomprehension. "Anyway it seems that the battle over the Baxter bowl—" Jane E turned to Bobbie and filled her in on the punchbowl saga before continuing. "It seems that Bertie is worried the contretemps, as he refers to it, over the punchbowl could escalate into a row at the reception and damage the pristine—because that's what it is you know, absolutely pristine—reputation of Oak View. It was just too much. I assured him that we could host a mud wrestling tournament at Oak View and brides and their mothers would still be lining up at the door, but he's determined to be upset about it."

"So what's the latest on the punchbowl?" Bobbie wanted to know.

"When the invitations come out, if there's not one in Aunt Tudie's mailbox, she's putting the bowl and all twenty matching cups on eBay. The thing is worth a fortune, according to Mrs.

Baxter, and she's offered to pay twice what it's worth, but Tudie won't sell it to her."

"Good Lord," said Bobbie. "Why doesn't she just crash the reception like the Honeychurch girls do?"

"Oh, I think the battle is half the fun for the Baxter women," said Jane E.

"Okay," said Bobbie, "There's got to be more going on in this burg than a couple of nuts fighting over a punchbowl. Any affairs, divorces, unplanned pregnancies? Don't you know anything, Jane E?"

Jane E laughed at her friend's unabashed interest in everyone else's business. "Well, I did hear that Holly Varjak has tended her resignation."

True inhaled a sip of tea and started to cough.

"Really?" said Bobbie. "She's leaving? She's only been here a year or so."

"It seems a hot, visiting professor from Boston has got her thinking about heading up east."

Jane E and Bobbie both looked at True, waiting for her to stop coughing and comment on this development.

True cleared her throat. "That's interesting," she said in her most offhand manner, but she could feel her face turning red.

Having received the anticipated reaction from True, Jane E and Bobbie looked at one another and smiled.

"I never could figure out what she saw in Belle Hill and little, old St. James College," said Jane E.

"Well, I know," said Bobbie. "Jackson Bean. She met Jackson at the Derby. He was up there covering the races, don't you remember? And they were at the same party. That's when she started coming down here."

"I kind of remember that," said Jane E, "but surely she didn't move here just because of him."

"I think that's exactly it. You underestimate the charms of that cousin of yours, Jane E, and for all her sophistication, Dr. Varjak is the kind of woman who always has to have a man—and an exciting man, at that."

"Jackson used to be exciting, traveling all over and everything," agreed Jane E, "But he's slowed way down." She rolled her eyes to the heavens and added, "Thank you, Jesus."

"I'll bet he looked pretty good to Holly, hob-nobbing with the Derby bigwigs, talking horse talk and swigging mint julips. I can just picture it."

True was determined not to take an interest in all of this speculation concerning Jackson Bean and Holly Varjak, though as Maisy had pointed out, where there's smoke, there's usually a spark of truth. Could it be that Holly had no motives in her exploration of Oak View other than professional ones, as she had claimed? True doubted it. Was it possible that a smart woman like Holly would jump into a risky relationship before the ink had dried on her divorce papers? Would a woman with a PhD move halfway across the country because she'd fallen for a man with more baggage than Delta Airlines? True added these to her ever-increasing pile of unanswered questions and forced her attention back to the light chatter of Jane E and Bobbie.

25.

A Month for Reunions

Hey, True, did you hear what happened to the clumsy magician? He was driving down the street and turned into a driveway. Pretty funny, huh? Mom says we'll be at your house soon. M. Kate is already getting homesick. In case you don't remember, she's a big baby.

True looked at the computer screen and sighed. She was starting to empathize with Katie as far as Tommy's jokes were concerned. And though it was more likely that Tommy was the one experiencing premature homesickness, what if either—or both—of her grandchildren just couldn't stay in Belle Hill for an entire extended visit? True shook her head. *I just can't worry about it*, she told herself. She had lots of things planned—even a day camp three mornings a week so Tommy and Mary Kate could meet other children their own age. She didn't want her grandchildren going into shock while making the adjustment from their roller coaster lives to life with True in Belle Hill. Going from seven action-packed days to three seemed like a good plan. True sighed. She had prepared as best she could. It would be fine. Just fine. She turned her attention back to the computer.

Hey Tommy and Mary Kate,
I can't wait to see you both! We're going to have lots of fun. There won't be time for home-sickness. Besides, you can call home whenever you like.
Here's a joke from Mr. Bean—he's my landlord.
A French fry walks into a bar and orders a beer. The bartender says, "Sorry, we don't serve food here."
Tell your mom I'll call later. Love, True.

As True was logging off, a knock and a bark came from the general vicinity of her back door. Had to be Jackson and JuJu.

"Hi, there. I was just sending your French fry joke to Tommy." True unlatched the door and rubbed the wriggling JuJu behind her ear. "Come on in."

"I've come with an invitation," said Jackson, stepping across the porch in two long strides. "But I don't want to put you on the spot. If you turn me down, believe me, I'll understand." He grinned at her, adding, "And I'll try not to take it personally."

"Sounds intriguing," said True, expecting to be included in another evening of canasta.

He eased himself onto one of True's pine breakfast-room chairs and surprisingly, JuJu sat at attention beside him. "I might as well just spit it out," Jackson said. "It's my high school reunion. Jane E's catering, and I can't get out of it." He grinned at True, his eyes the Mediterranean at its bluest. "I might just be able to stand it if you're along."

Like Bobbie said, Jane E's cousin was nothing if not charming.

"Oh, gosh, a reunion." True had only attended one of her own reunions, the main result of which was a sad reminder of how little in common she had with her old friends. She'd never darkened the crepe-paper festooned door of another one.

"Yeah," said Jackson. "There's nothing worse than going to someone else's reunion, but then I thought it would be a good way for you to meet some more of the local gentry. It's this Saturday night—a dinner dance at a house on the river."

"This Saturday?"

"Short notice, I know. I wasn't going, but well, Jane E kind of twisted my arm."

True had to admit that she would probably go to anything shy of a cock fight if Jackson invited her. And there was the disturbing realization that if she declined his invitation, some other woman—Holly Varjak, for instance—would jump on it like fat-free chocolate.

"Okay," True heard herself say.

"Really? Great. Pick you up at seven." His knees creaked alarmingly as he rose from the chair. He winced and shook his head. "Damn knees."

JuJu scrambled to her feet, but instead of making a break for the door, merely stood wriggling in a paroxysm of self control.

"You know who is certainly minding well these days," said True, giving a subtle nod in JuJu's direction. Mentioning the dog's name might just be the straw to break her fragile constitution.

"Yeah," said Jackson proudly. "We've been working on things." He paused a moment, then continued. "Which reminds me, I heard from my daughter, Evelyn. She's bringing Evie here."

"Wow. That's great."

"I'm a little nervous about it. I haven't had much experience in that department."

"You'll make a great grandfather."

"Grandfather. I wonder if that's what she'll call me. Do you think I should choose a name?"

True laughed, wondering what on earth he might come up with. "Why don't you let Evie decide? So when are they coming?"

"In the next few weeks. As it turns out, Evelyn and her husband are moving to Florida—not far from Vista Palmas, as a matter of fact. She and Evie will stop here on the way, spend a night or two. It's hard to believe. After all this time and now..." He shook his head, lost in his own thoughts for a second or two before looking back at True. "I'd like you to meet Evelyn."

"I would love that."

"Okay, then," he said, visibly encouraged by the idea. "I guess this is the month for reunions."

"So it is," said True.

"Don't forget. Saturday night." He flashed that grin at her again. "And it's a date."

Good Lord. A date.

The idea literally made True dizzy. She could hear the blood rushing around in her head. Or was it just the sound of B True and Burkett simultaneously turning over in their graves?

26.

And the Crowd Goes Wild

True spent the rest of the week meeting people at Oak View, shopping for an outfit for Saturday night, getting things ready for her grandchildren's upcoming visit, shopping for an outfit for Saturday night, getting her hair colored and cut, oh, and did I mention shopping for an outfit for Saturday night?

I'm acting like it's my junior prom! she thought, slipping a white silk shift over her head. She wriggled out of the white shift and reached for a peach linen outfit that was the epitome of that oxymoronic dress code directive, dressy casual.

The whole town would be buzzing about her date with Jackson Bean. She could just hear Al the electrician telling the church ladies all about it. But True was determined to follow the strategy she'd outlined for herself in her Phase Three Plan. There was no room in Phase Three for shallow emotions such as false pride or worrying about the opinions of others (dead or alive).

Or self-deception, she reminded herself. She and her landlord were overdue for a heart-to-heart chat. True would not embark on a friendship (much less, something more serious) with a gambler—or worse! No matter how charming he was, no matter how his desire for a relationship with his daughter and granddaughter tugged at True's soft heart, no matter how that smile of his made her feel sixteen again, no matter how blue his eyes were.

There was also the subject of True's mother. Jackson had promised to help with the search, but had turned up little in the newspaper files he'd supposedly researched. Maisy insisted that in the end it was a quest for True and True alone since "the truth often lies in the journey rather than the destination," and Jane E, for all of their intimate conversation, was not especially forthcoming. Everyone had been hospitable to Belle Hill's prodigal daughter, but most had discouraged True in her search. When she'd mentioned this to Jackson, he'd deftly changed the subject. But knowing that Jackson was preoccupied with his own familial problems, True sighed and resigned herself. Her own mission would have to wait until after Evelyn's and Evie's visit.

When Jackson appeared at her front door on Saturday night, he was attired pretty much as usual, except that he was wearing saddle shoes and a letter sweater (with a moth hole in the sleeve) over his golf shirt.

For a guy who hates reunions, he's really getting into the old school spirit, thought True.

At least he didn't smell like mothballs. As a matter of fact, he smelled great—like pine soap and clean laundry and well, like Jackson. And the way he was looking at her? Every hour of primping and shopping, every penny over her budget was worth that.

"Ms. Cowley, you are looking especially lovely tonight," he said. "I think I might just have a date with the prettiest girl at the prom."

"Why, thank you, Mr. Bean. You're looking very, uh, sporty yourself."

He held out the pocket of his sweater—the one with the football letter. "Oh, this old thing?" he joked.

True laughed, took his arm and headed for his truck, which was still glistening from a run through the car wash.

True did feel good about her appearance. The peachy linen skirt and blouse, new sandals and jewelry, as well as fresh manicure, pedicure and hair color set off the tan she'd acquired in her walks around St. James' campus. Her fairly regular adherence to her Phase Three diet and thrice-weekly Pilates class was paying off. She hadn't felt or looked this good in ages.

"Wow, this is some house," said True when they turned into a drive lit with an embarrassment of hurricane lamps. The stucco structure looked like an enormous wedding cake glowing in the distance. Every light inside of the place seemed to be on. In addition, there were spotlights accentuating a hodge-podge of roof lines. More lights glowed in the palms. This was a house worthy of Vista Palmas at its worst, True decided.

"Who lives here?" she asked as Jackson opened the door for her.

"A guy named Dwayne Bond. Made a lot of money in car washes." He nodded toward the truck. "I contributed to the cause before I picked you up."

"I think I met him at the Withers-Moore wedding," said True.

"Did he give you the double-O-seven routine?"

True laughed, remembering. "Yes, he did. It was kind of funny."

"Oh, he's a riot, old Dwayne is," said Jackson, and True sensed one of those macho rivalries that went back to high school. As a matter of fact, True would be surprised if "old Dwayne" weren't sporting a letter sweater himself.

They mounted the steps and crossed a back porch chock full of thickly upholstered, faux-wicker furniture and entered the Bond lair through enormous glass doors etched with palm tree designs. The wide hall reminded True of the time she had gone with a friend to the furniture mart in Miami. Only there had she seen as much bamboo, rattan, teak and palm gathered in one place. A bar was set up on the front porch which faced a wide bend in the river. More opulence from this view boggled her brain as Jackson handed her a mojito.

"Kind of brings back fond memories, doesn't it?" he said clicking his glass to hers in a toast to the night they had spent with the Honeychurch girls.

"Yes—as much as I can remember of it," said True, surveying the scene below.

The steps before them led to a succession of decks that eventually led through the palm-and-oleander-laden yard to a large pier and pavilion on the water where a boat that was well into the yacht category sat like a miniature, floating version of the house. Its name, *Happy Hooker*, was proudly emblazoned on its stern.

Jackson suggested they pay their respects to Maisy, who was there on a "fortune-telling gig." Several tents had been decorated with green and white (school colors?) ribbons, giving the scene a carnival feel. Even Maisy's tiny yellow and gold tent was strewn with green and white streamers.

A band was playing *Sweet Home Alabama*. This toe-tapper can usually be counted on to get things moving at any party, especially one south of the Mason-Dixon Line. And not surprisingly, it's a fool-proof ice-breaker at all festivities in the Heart of Dixie a.k.a. the great state of Alabama.

The dance floor, placed invitingly between the music and the water, was beginning to fill up. As True and Jackson approached Maisy's tent, True noticed that most, if not all of the fifty to sixty year old crowd looked as if they'd found their outfits in B True's attic.

"Jackson, is this a costume party?" *Or do your contemporaries all have really bad taste?*

"Uh, yeah, it is. But it was optional."

True looked around her. "Are you sure?"

"Well, it was actually, dress like your favorite decade or some damn thing. Since your favorite decade could be the present one, the whole costume thing becomes optional, right?"

Relief at not having to wear a costume was over-riding her dismay that as the "new girl" True was going to stand out after all—for being out of costume as well as having a date with Jackson, the school quarterback/heart throb back in the day. But then she took note of his moth-eaten get-up.

"Then why are you wearing a letter sweater that is—although adorable," she teased, "… definitely not of this decade?"

"Jane E dug it up. She even had it cleaned. Said I couldn't eat unless I wore it. I hope you're not disappointed—about not wearing a costume, that is. It was bad enough dragging you to my reunion without asking you to come up with a costume."

"No, I'm not disappointed. Costumes aren't exactly my thing. And you're right. If you had told me, I would have stewed over it. I just hope I'm not the only one in regular clothes. The organizers of these things get irritated when guests don't go along with the plan, you know."

The disjointed feeling True had lived with for as long as she could remember—the one that made her feel like she was in the wrong place, in someone else's dream almost—washed over her as she looked at the odd little world of fifty-ish Belle Hillians. For the millionth time she wondered what it would be like, what she would be like at that moment in time if she'd never left.

But it wasn't the where, it was the who that mattered, she reminded herself. Home is where the heart is and all that. Was her heart here with these strangers in their poodle skirts and leisure suits? In Vista Palmas where friends moved in and out like the tide, and she had to schedule an appointment to see her family? Some other place she had yet to discover?

She was spared further speculation on the befuddled state of her emotions by the approach of a two men. One was in a clerical collar, one in a green and white football uniform, complete with shoulder pads. Understandably, football guy was sweating profusely. Besides their costume choice and perspiration output, the men were identical.

Jackson nodded to them rather formally. "Dwayne. Wayne." He looked at True. "True, this is ..."

But before he could finish, Dwayne had his helmet off and under one arm. Tilting his head with a smirk he made the familiar gun shape with his free hand.

"I believe we've already had the pleasure. I'm Dwayne Bond, Ms. True, and this is my brother, Wayne. He's the good-lookin' one, hah, hah, hah."

Wayne winced and held out his hand.

"Hello, Dwayne. Nice to meet you, Wayne," said True. Looking at the brothers she felt an overwhelming desire to laugh. She could feel it in her eyes, then in her cheeks, like the time Burkett had talked her into smoking pot, and she'd laughed in the house mother's face. She clamped her lips together and made herself think about world hunger.

"Why thank you, Ms. True. We'd love to see you at Big Welcome Baptist. Any Sunday. Here's my card." And he palmed the card into her hand as if he were slipping her something illegal.

"Dwayne, I take it you were on the football team," she said, slipping the card into her pocket.

"Yes, ma'am. Wide receiver. Had a hell of a job makin' your date look good. Hah, hah, hah." And he gave Jackson a macho punch on the arm.

Jackson scowled.

In an attempt to keep things light, True said, "That uniform looks brand new, Dwayne."

"Oh, it is. I had it made special for the party. Cost me a fortune, but what the hay, you can't take it with you, can you? I got a new ball, too. Thought Jackson and I might run a few patterns, see if we still got what it takes."

"Oh, no." Jackson said. "I—"

"Well, look what's cruisin' our way," interrupted Dwayne, forgetting all about football for once. "That Dr. Varjak is one Cadillac of a woman." He winked at True. "Fully loaded, too."

Holly Varjak, all got up like Joan Crawford a la *Mommy Dearest* on a wire hanger rampage (her shoulder pads were bigger than Dwayne's!) and hours ahead of the rest of the crowd in alcohol consumption was lurching toward Jackson.

"So you're not involved with the little neighbor who's too good to even wear a costume, huh?" Holly spat the words out.

About this time Maisy was having the usual problems with her crystal ball. Its eerie green glow had diminished to a putrid flicker. She shook it. When that didn't work, the old lady held it in one hand and pounded it with the other. The ball popped out of her hand and sailed out of the tent, rolling to a stop at Holly's feet.

A snicker escaped Dwayne Bond, which only enraged Holly more. She picked up the ball and screamed, "I followed my rainbow to this damn town. And for what? There're no decent men, there's no pot of gold. Ha! Not even a few loose coins." She narrowed her eyes at Dwayne and Jackson and snarled, "I'm sick of you illiterate bumpkins and this whole anachronistic backwater."

"Whoa," said Dwayne. "Somebody call a dictionary."

More snickers ensued from the gathering crowd of illiterate bumpkins. Holly's face was turning purple, and she was swaying dangerously on her vintage platform heels. She slung the crystal ball with amazing accuracy at Dwayne's head.

Unfortunately he had not put his helmet back on. But it

didn't matter because Jackson (whose reflexes were still pretty darn impressive) snagged the ball before it made contact with Dwayne's unprotected skull.

Holly, now beyond furious, charged at Jackson, slurring what sounded like, "Give me that ball!"

"Hey Jackson," yelled Dwayne, "Goin' wide!" And he took off across the lawn toward the river.

There was an evil grin on Jackson's face even as he took Holly's tackle. He let go a spiraling crystal ball the likes of which have never been duplicated. It settled into Dwayne's outstretched hands as he reached the river's edge. Cradling the ball to his chest just before his foot caught in the loose soil, he plunged into the water. Seconds later he stood dripping and muddy but smiling as he held Maisy's pulsing, radiant crystal ball above his head.

The crowd went wild.

Thankfully, the locals were well past sophomoric concerns such as who was in costume or who chose which decade. (Excepting Holly, of course. But her date, a terrified music professor, finally relented and took her home.) To True's relief, several other people had chosen the present decade and were dressed more or less normally.

Holly's surprise tackle resulted in grass stains and another hole in Jackson's letter sweater, but he didn't seem to mind. It gave him "a good excuse to take the damn thing off" was how he put it, but True noticed that he folded it carefully and gave it an affectionate pat before returning to her side.

Dwayne retired his soaking jersey. At least for the evening. After a quick shower, he returned to the festivities resplendent in lavender polyester. Was the suit a back-up plan for the party or an actual part of his wardrobe?

Maisy's crystal ball continued to function on high-glow for the rest of the evening. Everyone waiting to have their futures told took this as a good omen. Who would've guessed that river water is the best remedy for a finicky crystal ball?

Jane E's food—gourmet drive-in fare, she called it—was fabulous, of course. The band was the hottest thing coming out of Atlanta and played everybody's favorites from every decade.

True knew she was in real danger of falling for Jackson Bean when he got Maisy out on the dance floor to *Shake Your Bootie.* It was a sight to behold. A full compliment of horns blared in the background as Jackson jitterbugged with his octogenarian auntie. Though still attired in her gypsy fortune-teller get-up, she managed to shake her tiny bootie all over the place.

The band was famous for its lead female singer. When she started to sing *At Last,* True turned to Jackson and said, "I love this song. She sounds just like Etta James, doesn't she?"

"Well, that was a little before my time …"

But he smiled at True, took her drink gently from her hand and placed it with his on a nearby table. "Would you like to dance, Ms. Cowley?" he asked.

"I would love to dance, Mr. Bean."

Jackson took her in his arms, and just when True thought there was nothing that could feel any better, he held her closer, pressed his hand into the small of her back, wove his fingers through hers and pressed his lips softly into her hair.

Lights twinkled in the trees, and the moon shone on the river. A soft breeze and the laughter and conversations of good friends floated through Dwayne Bond's outrageous garden. And True Cowley felt like the queen of the prom. At last.

27.

Ties that Bind
(or Wedding Myth # 7—
The Comfortable Tux)

Wedding Myths:
1. *Rain on your wedding day is good luck.*
2. *You are not losing a son/daughter, but gaining a daughter/son.*
3. *This is a bridesmaid's dress you can wear again.*
4. *A disastrous wedding and/or reception and/or honeymoon guarantees a disaster-free marriage.*
5. *A year from now no one will remember (fill in the blank).*
6. *You'll come to love that about your mother- (father, son, daughter, sister, or brother) in-law once you know them better.*

•

The fabrications listed above comprise an abbreviated list of wedding myths perpetuated by frantic wedding planners lying through their teeth to hysterical brides and their mothers because if there was ever a time for the little white lie, this would be it. Usually only one or two myths are sufficient to slide through a down-and-out snake-bit wedding, but in the case of the Baker-Baxter nuptials, Zola, aka the bridal warrior, was juggling all of the above platitudes and even coming up with a few of her own.

As the wedding party approached Belle Hill Methodist Church a bolt of lightning ripped through a fifty-year-old pine tree, sending its smoldering carcass crashing across the lily and rose bedecked entrance to the church.

"Aren't we lucky it didn't fall on anyone," Zola trilled into Mother Baker's ear.

"It's a sign from the Almighty!" yelled Aunt Tudie through the smoking pine boughs.

Mother Baxter brandished a small, white pill and popped it triumphantly into her mouth. Even Tudie was no match for Xanax, by God. But Tudie, undeterred, merely pointed to the leaden sky and smiled. Zola and Tracie Ann followed Tudie's gesture toward the roiling heavens, and Zola whispered platitude # 4 into Tracie Ann's ear.

Tracie Ann, fortified by the battle of wills with Mother Baxter, which she had won (after all, Ford was in the vestry waiting to plight her with his troth) managed a serene smile. To the young bride's credit, she stepped from the white limo which was festooned with pink carnations (her mother's favorite), took a deep breath, pictured Ford and herself on a sunny Bahamian beach and headed gamely to the church's side entrance. She gathered her wind-blown bridal finery around her and traipsed to the back of the church, waving sweetly to the guests already seated in the pews. Even Mother Baxter was impressed with her poise.

As the orchestra cranked up the strains of Handel's *Water Music* and Tracie Ann made her anti-climatic second entrance, a couple of overzealous groundskeepers decided to try and clear the front entrance before the ceremony's end. Their intentions were good, but you know what they say about good intentions and the road to hell. In this case, the hellish result was that the violins and trumpets and choir Mother Baxter had insisted on— actually, just about the entire service—were drowned out by the sounds of a chainsaw.

When the workmen were done, the sad remains of the bouquets that had adorned the church doors lay tattered and crushed. Pine sap was everywhere, ruining everybody's best outfits as they hurried out, intent on making it to the reception before the impending storm. (Hunnicutt Lee, proprietor of Magnolia Cleaners, was heard cursing into the night for weeks after the event—pine sap and silk make for the worst of dry cleaning challenges.) But it did smell nice, the crushed roses and pine mingling in the heavy air.

The heavens opened as everyone arrived at Oak View. Within minutes the grounds were inches deep in water. Flowers drooped, shoes were ruined and everybody's hair looked a sight—especially the Bakers, who, if you remember, are really into big hair and hairspray.

The band, rightly fearing electrocution, refused to play and headed back to Nashville. Though Jane E had learned to read the weather better than Bart Snow, the local TV meteorologist, and had moved all of the food inside, the humidity was so heavy that you couldn't tell the crackers from the dip.

Tudie, demon that she was, held up a limp watercress and walnut spread finger sandwich and cackled maniacally, reiterating her assessment that it was a sign from God. She then told anyone who would listen (everybody) how Mother Baxter had tricked Mr. Baxter into marrying her by becoming pregnant with Ford. At this point in the festivities, Mother Baxter gave the ring bearer a twenty and her last three Xanax with instructions to drop them into a fresh flirtini and deliver the concoction to Aunt Tudie. She then took her place next to the Baxter Bowl, protecting it from defilement (two groomsmen had already been caught attempting to spike its contents), regaling old ladies with its history and giving out her punch recipe less one ingredient. It only took minutes for the cocktail to work its magic. Aunt Tudie became positively angelic. For the fifteen minutes prior to her disappearance, that is. Not being the types to look gift horses in the mouth, no one looked for her, of course.

The horrified clean-up crew discovered her curled into a fetal position in the claw-footed tub. She was hidden from view by the shower curtain. To this day no one has owned up to any knowledge of how this came to be. An ambulance transported her to the emergency room where she was reluctantly revived. Everyone knew what to expect from Aunt Tudie with a Xanax and flirtini hangover. And she didn't disappoint.

Of course, True Cowley had been pressed into service. When four inches of rain are forecast on a wedding weekend, all hands are needed to stay afloat, so to speak. She donned her oldest shoes and a dress of an unknown, man-made fiber, and reported for duty.

There was a surprisingly good turnout. The Honeychurch girls in their usual identical wedding attire were there, snagging stale crab claws and rubbery shrimp. They reminded True again that the past should be left alone, and "tsk tsk" her grandparents had nothing (except that Sheraton sideboard).

Jackson, like the rest of Belle Hill, never missed a wedding or a funeral. He was there in his soaked tux, tugging at his sodden tie, but looking handsome as ever. And when True's synthetic duds sagged and her energy flagged and she'd slipped into the back hall to catch her breath, there was Jackson with a grin and a pretty green drink in a martini glass.

"I know how you feel about drinking on duty," he said, "But I thought you could use this. It's called a basil gimlet—Jane E's invention." He looked first over one shoulder then the other. "I'll stand guard. If any busy-bodies show up, just hand it to me."

True laughed and took the drink.

"Wow, this is delicious," she said.

And it was. And it and Jackson Bean were just what she needed to get her through the rest of that miserable night.

Ford and Tracie Ann made their way carefully down the slippery steps of Oak View as the remaining guests threw clumps of rice at them. The young couple's flight to the Bahamas was cancelled. Due to the same freak tropical depression that ruined Tracie Ann's and Ford's special day, the resort where they were to spend a week cavorting in the sun had been flooded and was closed for repairs.

They were forced to slip away to the Whispering Pines Motel for their wedding night. The rest of their honeymoon was spent in New Orleans, which is only a couple of hours down the road. It was not exactly the stuff of their dreams, but New Orleans is a pretty good Plan B.

The great thing about the Baker/Baxter disaster was as time went on, it seemed Tracie Ann and Ford were a sure bet for a life lived happily ever after, thereby ensuring the veracity of wedding myths. True figured that for years to come, Zola and her counterparts would be heard comforting hysterical brides and their mothers with a recitation of wedding myths backed up by the story of Tracie Ann (nee Baker) and Ford Baxter.

28.

Unringing the Bell

There was not an inch of air between Evie and her mother as they sat upright and uneasy on Jackson's porch swing. Glasses of lemonade sweating in the morning sun and a plate of sugar cookies (sent over by Jane E to sweeten the awkward meeting) sat between Jackson and his daughter and granddaughter like a barrier.

Evie stared at her grandfather with those blue eyes so unnervingly like Jackson's own. Evelyn looked as if she regretted the decision to come at all. To say that things were not going well would be an understatement. Just when Jackson felt that it couldn't possibly be worse, JuJu, who was banished to a back room, began to bark. Insistently. Jackson had not thought it possible, but Evie's eyes grew even wider, and she moved even closer to Evelyn.

"I don't like dogs," she said.

But JuJu was not to be thwarted. She kept up her barking until Jackson said, "I'll just go check on her."

In preparation for this very situation, Jackson had hired a trainer and per her instruction, increased his daily "obedience workout" with the dog to two-a-days and stretched these to an interminable hour each. Still, as E-day (the day of Evelyn's and Evie's visit) approached, JuJu persisted in her "self-control issues" and stubbornly refused to acknowledge Jackson's alpha status in their relationship. So master had locked dog in the bedroom.

But even as JuJu had failed again and again to obey Jackson's

184 Margaret P. Cunningham

commands, it seemed to him that she sensed there was more at stake than mere dominance. At times Jackson would shake his head and sigh in frustration during their training sessions, and JuJu would still herself, cock her big head to one side and stare intelligently at Jackson, and he could have sworn there was empathy in those amber eyes. As exasperating as she was, Jackson loved the dog's perseverance, her resistance to being molded to human standards. But it had to be. Such was the nature of the canine/human relationship. Man must be the master, or it simply will not work.

JuJu was now scratching furiously at the doorframe. Jackson silently cursed her chocolate hide up one side and down the other as he approached the rattling door. He slowly turned the knob, ready to grab JuJu's collar before she could hurdle herself into the cookies and lemonade—into Evelyn and Evie, if she had her way.

As he cracked the door, JuJu shoved her head quietly yet persistently through the opening. Jackson was reminded of a foot-in-the-door tactic of an overzealous Bible salesman. But amazingly, JuJu was sitting. It was as if she were actually awaiting her master's command! Jackson looked into her eyes, and somehow he knew. She wouldn't let him down.

"Oh, Dad, she's beautiful!" said Evelyn. "We've never had dogs. Because Evie doesn't like them," she added in an impatient tone.

Evie looked at her mother and pressed her little lips together.

JuJu sat quietly next to the swing and allowed Evelyn to stroke her head and back. She didn't try to jump into the woman's lap or even slobber all over her. Jackson began to wonder if someone had tranquilized the animal.

"Her fur looks soft, Jackson," said Evie.

JuJu and Jackson smiled at Evie. "It is soft," said Jackson. "You can pet her. But you don't have to," he added.

Soon Evie was petting the dog. And the dog continued to behave. Jackson was so relieved at this turn of events that he even let his granddaughter feed his dog one of Jane E's sugar cookies. This was a big no-no according to the trainer.

Evelyn wanted to see the neighborhood, so they walked JuJu

through the woods, stopping to show Evie the grotto before coming to Oak View. Jackson gave them the grand tour, then sat on the patio with Evelyn while Evie investigated the fountain and caught tadpoles in a jar he'd found for her in Oak View's kitchen.

Were the planets in alignment that day? Or fate on their side? Or was it simply due to some fortuitous quirk of their shared heritage that father and daughter found themselves in the same emotional place on that particular afternoon in the garden at Oak View?

Whatever the reason, they began to chat, casually at first and discovered they shared a genuine rapport. Soon they were venturing into the past which they discussed without malice. Jackson found that he could talk to Evelyn about Barbara. And Jack. It was the first time he had been able to discuss the failure of his marriage and the loss of his son with anyone. She understood. She felt what he felt. He'd lost his son. She'd lost her brother.

There had been problems in Barbara's and Evelyn's relationship. Barbara wouldn't hear of Evelyn having anything to do with her father or any of those dysfunctional Alabama Beans. Eventual realization of the folly in this course of action resulted in Barbara allowing Evelyn's brother, Jack, to come to Belle Hill, to get to know Jackson. At this point in her life, Evelyn was too bitter and rebellious to try and get to know her father. When Jack died, Barbara had found strength in her faith and her second marriage, but not in her daughter. Evelyn had felt as alone as Jackson had.

Now Evelyn's marriage was in trouble. And her relationship with Evie was beginning to mirror the one she'd had with Barbara. In an attempt to salvage her family, Evelyn and her husband were starting over. In Florida. A new job. A new life, she hoped. Lots of good counseling had her mending fences. She and her mother were getting along. She wanted to know her father, wanted Evie to know him. She wanted Evie to have a stable family.

She had confided all of this to her mother who said, "The year Jackson spent with Jack was the year my son grew into a man. His best year. I only had my son, the man for a few weeks before he died. Now that you're beginning to work through your problems, becoming the woman you were meant to be, you want to know your father. You'll be living closer to him, too." She sighed and looked suddenly older to Evelyn. "Jackson has always won at everything," she said. She smiled grimly and added, "And with very little effort."

"It's not a game, Mom," Evelyn had said, starting down their old adversarial path.

But she'd managed to change direction, to reassure Barbara, and that, Evelyn said, had been the real beginning of Barbara's and Evelyn's "new and improved relationship."

Jackson looked at this remarkable young woman who was his daughter, who was turning her life around, mending fences, becoming focused and all of those meaningless clichés that acquire great meaning when one sees them in action.

He looked over at Evie who "didn't like dogs" yet was decorating a docile JuJu with gardenias and "powder puffs" (mimosa blossoms). This was the big kahuna of second chances, he told himself. He couldn't undo the past, unring the bell. He couldn't get those years back, but a window of opportunity was sitting in the wall he had constructed around himself.

He was almost sixty years old, and he was going to shake things up, by God. He wanted what Evelyn wanted—a family. He pictured True laughing in the moonlight, saving turtles and taming dogs, trading jokes with her grandson. And he knew. He was in love.

Of course there was a fly in this pie of good fortune. Jackson Bean would have to give up his secrets.

By the time Jackson and Evelyn tucked Evie into bed that evening, the little girl was talking nonstop to "Jackson." That's what she had decided to call him, and the more he thought about it, the more he liked the idea. He didn't feel old enough to be called Grandpa or some damn thing anyway.

The next morning True was as ready as she would ever be for Tommy and Mary Kate's visit. Jackson was busy showing Evelyn and Evie around town before taking them to lunch at Maisy's for a reunion with the rest of those "dysfunctional Alabama Beans." True was still a bit stressed from the wash-out at Oak View the previous weekend. What she needed was a good, long walk.

The day was pleasant, but humid, promising rain as True set off in the direction of St. James cemetery. She wandered down the paths between the markers and flowerbeds in the direction of the Hunter graves. As she approached the stand of camellia bushes near her family's final resting place, True heard a familiar voice coming from the other side.

"Listen, Bertram," Holly Varjak was saying, "I'm leaving this afternoon, but I expect you to cut me in if you find it. No, I don't think there's anything at Oak View. What? I'm at the cemetery. I thought I'd try one last look while I was here, but this thing has wild goose chase written all over it … Because the woman was crazy—that's obvious from the book … If it's anywhere, it must be buried with them, because I've looked everywhere there are Purple Dawns. I hope I never see another camellia bush. Just remember, if you find it before the others, I still get my cut. I'm not above a little blackmail, Bertram. You wouldn't want to lose your precious job and Oak View … Oh, I'll stay in touch. You can be sure of that."

True heard Holly's footsteps fading into the gravel path as she walked away.

"Wow," said True.

She walked around the camellias to the bench near her mother's grave and sat down. Clouds covered the sun, and a breeze that smelled of rain danced across her family's graves. True went over the conversation she'd overheard, sure it was Holly's voice, and also sure that the Bertram Holly was threatening with the loss of his "precious job and Oak View" had to be Bertie.

And Holly mentioned a book and a crazy person and the "it" she was looking for. True tried to keep it all straight, but it was starting to jumble together in her mind—which threw her into a mild panic and increased the confusion. She would give anything for a pen and paper to jot her thoughts down. She took a stabilizing breath as instructed in chapter two of her grief manual and started again.

Holly and Bertie. Looking for something. Something of value, since Holly referred to her "cut" of it. Something that they learned about in a book. Or from a crazy person. A crazy woman. That was buried with … him? No, she said them, buried with them. With her grandparents? And it was something to do with camellias, with Purple Dawn camellias. What has to do with Purple Dawn camellias? Camellias and …

"Of course," said True out loud.

Camellias and coins. They're looking for coins. *But Grandfather Hunter's coin collection is long gone. Or is it?*

There was something else. What was it? She closed her eyes and replayed Holly's words in her head, trying to organize the Mexican jumping beans of her thoughts.

"If you find it before the others," Holly had said.

So other people were looking, too. Did they all know about the others? Like some reality show treasure hunt? Was that what they were all looking for at Oak View? Suddenly scenes from the old movie, *It's a Mad, Mad, Mad, Mad World* were flickering through her head. She pictured Bertie, Holly, Carver, the Honeychurch girls, Al the Electrician, maybe even the church ladies from Big Welcome Baptist, maybe even Jackson, racing around Belle Hill in the night, armed with flashlights and maps and shovels looking for Purple Dawns and coins.

"Purple Dawns and coins." She said aloud. "And who is the crazy woman, and what book are they talking about?"

Thunder rumbled. The breeze picked up. Determined to write down her thoughts and avoid getting caught in the downpour, she said a silent good-bye to her sleeping family and hurried home.

True stepped onto her back porch as the first drops of rain materialized, reciting the facts of Holly's phone conversation until she found a piece of paper and a pen. She made her list. But her mind was so jumbled with people and their secrets, with families and their clutter of love and betrayal, that she couldn't think straight. True slipped the list into the top drawer of B True's federal slant-lid desk. She had to give her brain a rest.

Besides, like Holly said, this has wild goose chase written all over it.

29.

Entrainment

There is a delightful phenomenon of nature known as entrainment, Maisy had said. Two rhythmic beings gradually altering until they are in the same rhythm. Like pendulums. And crickets.

And some lucky people, thought True.

When True went to Jackson Bean's house to meet his family, she took a book on south Florida flora for Evelyn and a child's book of gulf coast seashells for Evie. She showed Evie pictures of her own grandchildren and told her about Florida. The child watched True as she spoke, her fine, earnest blue eyes—Jackson's eyes—taking in every nuance of True's conversation.

It was as if Evie knew True's story as well as True knew Evie's. True could remember being four years old, treading the waters of change when she hadn't yet learned to swim. She remembered it like it was this morning instead of decades ago. The child seemed aware of this, in tune with True's empathy.

This little person and I are in a kind of rhythm, thought True. *We are in sync.*

Evelyn, however, was a different story. True sensed Evelyn's irritation with her random thoughts and meandering mind. She seemed piqued, possibly even jealous of the easy rapport between True and Evie, perturbed when Jackson's eyes lingered on True.

But then, she doesn't know my story and doesn't know how I fit into Jackson's world, True reminded herself. She forged ahead, determined to be—if not friends, then at least on good terms with Evelyn. And at some point in her visit, True realized that Evelyn had let down her guard, had let True in a bit. Before long the two women had at least grown comfortable in one another's presence.

The planets continued their amiable alignment, fate was grinning from ear to ear and there were nothing but blue skies as far as anyone could see. Jackson and his daughter and granddaughter were closing the gap by leaps and bounds. At the end of the two-day visit, the farewells were reluctant and fond. Jackson promised to come for a visit, help them get settled, go shelling with Evie, take them all fishing, whatever! Anything, it seemed, but letting go of his secrets.

Soon. All in good time, he told himself.

Evelyn and Evie made a quick stop by True's before heading to Florida. Evelyn knew she'd been unnecessarily cool to True in the beginning. You know what they say about old habits, and Evelyn's defensiveness was still gasping for life.

True told Evelyn she thought Florida would suit her. And she meant it. She certainly knew the area, and she had a pretty good read on Evelyn. It would be a good fit.

As luck would have it, Katie arrived with Mary Kate and Tommy and their luggage and book lists and schedules and organic odds and ends (who knew there was organic dental floss?). Evelyn was embarrassed about the timing of her drop in, and tried to slip away, but once Katie found out that Evelyn would be living a mere thirty minutes away from her in Florida and that they were both marathoners, she insisted that they exchange email addresses and cell numbers. What with Evelyn in dire need of friends in her new home, and Katie always happy to have someone's life to organize, they both were happier for having met.

Once Evelyn was on her way, True gave Katie and the children a quick tour of her new home. Katie was surprised at how small the cottage was, but had to admit to its charm. Her mother's quirky ways as well as True's antique furniture and funny treasures—that had caused Katie no end of consternation —seemed perfectly charming in this place. And like her mother, Katie was beguiled by the little neighborhood in the woods.

"It's like a village of doll houses," she said when True took them for a long stroll after lunch.

Tommy and Mary Kate seemed happy with their tiny rooms, intrigued by the grotto and thrilled with the "five and dime" in the shopping area near True's house. They loved the outdoor shower, which True had almost forgotten about, and insisted on taking all of their showers there.

Another bonus for Tommy and Mary Kate was living near JuJu, who amazingly, was still in "good dog" mode when Jackson and the lab stopped in for a quick hello. Having learned what an ice-breaker a well-behaved dog can be, Jackson had bathed JuJu and taken her through her obedience paces before the visit.

True insisted Jackson stay for a glass of tea. By the time the glass was empty, Jackson and Tommy had traded jokes (Tommy's were better than Jackson's), and he'd shown Mary Kate a magic trick and his recent pictures of Evie. Katie was relieved to see that her mother had a nice, reliable landlord and neighbor. Add to these positives Jackson's easy manner, killer smile and lovable lab, and you can see why his work was done in under twenty minutes.

Katie's plan was to stay only until Mary Kate and Tommy felt comfortable in their new surroundings. Figuring this would take less than a week, she used the time to get everyone organized and "on schedule." True relied heavily on the deep-breathing and motivational techniques in her mini-library of self-help literature (and snatches of *Peril in Portofino*, which she was rereading) to get her through Katie's rigorous schedules and lists.

Katie visited the day camp where True had enrolled the children in three-day sessions. Coast Camp, as it was called, included tennis and swimming as well as trips to museums and galleries. There were even "nature nurture eco-trips" that took the campers up rivers, to barrier islands and into the delta "where the gators made the ones in the Everglades look downright puny," said the camp director, winking at Tommy. Though Katie thought Coast Camp "a bit laid-back," the children loved it and couldn't wait until their first day.

True took Katie on the same route Maisy had taken True the day after Burkett's funeral, although at a safer speed. Katie visited the little cemetery with True, interested for the first time in the Hunters and the Cowleys she had never known. She got to know Maisy. She even helped with an impromptu event at Oak View.

Jackson took them all to lunch at a seafood restaurant where they ate fried crab claws and drank sweet tea on a deck cooled by bay breezes and the shade of live oaks. More than once True caught Katie watching her and Jackson Bean, though Jackson wisely spent most of the time entertaining the children, getting to know Katie and inquiring about the area where his daughter and granddaughter were moving.

"It's on a small bay. Mostly old summer cottages." Katie said. "A quiet place, but nice."

In the evenings, Katie, being the proverbial captive audience, sat on the porch after the children were in bed and visited with her mother. She spoke warmly of times they'd shared in Vista Palmas, admitted that the garden had suffered from the absence of True's green thumb and even confessed that she'd taken her mother's standing offer to baby sit for granted.

"No one is as good with Mary Kate and Tommy as you are," she said.

She acknowledged that Belle Hill and Jackson's cottage suited True.

"And Mom, I think your landlord has a thing for you."

She grinned at her mother. "He's pretty hot."

True laughed this off, but admitted to Katie that she thought Jackson was very nice. Then she agreed that he was indeed, extremely hot, which had them both giggling like teenagers. True couldn't remember the last time she'd laughed with her daughter or when they'd had such a comfortable conversation.

Though it wasn't long before Katie grabbed up her laptop, the time they spent together made True realize how much she missed her daughter and how much Katie needed her. She began to wonder once again if she had made the right decision in moving to Belle Hill. So one night—just for curiosity's sake, she told herself—she got on her own computer and scanned the condominiums and cottages for sale in Vista Palmas, Florida.

There was one condo for sale in the city's Old Town area. The "virtual tour" showed it to be a charming place with a view of the water. True could see herself there, but quickly forced such notions out of her head. It was way out of her budget.

Luggage was stacked as neatly as a completed Rubik's Cube in the back of Katie's hybrid SUV. A mini ice chest packed with cooled mineral water was placed on the front seat beside her laptop and self-help CDs. Addresses were plugged into the GPS.

Katie checked her watch and smiled. She was five minutes ahead of schedule. Time for one of those leisurely good-byes her mother was so fond of. True saw Katie glance at her watch, felt a spurt of irritation but let it go with a sigh of resignation.

She and I are like the hare and the turtle. Or is it tortoise? I wonder if there's really any difference.

"Oh, Mo-om," Katie said in a little sing-song voice one might employ when addressing dawdling children (or demented senior citizens), but True was determined to take that high road B True had always advocated.

"Sorry, sweetie. I was just thinking how organized you are. Thanks again for helping me over at Oak View."

"You're welcome, Mom." Katie smiled fondly at her mother and gave her a hug. "It was fun."

Suddenly True didn't want her to go. They were certainly different, and this would not change. But the distance True had put between them had both hearts growing fonder. Katie had a softer way about her these days that actually bordered on patience. True was less sensitive to her daughter's brusqueness. They were a long way from entrainment, but like Maisy said, it's a gradual thing.

30.
Love (and betrayal) in the Afternoon

Soon True and her grandchildren settled into a loose routine. On the days they attended Coast Camp Mary Kate and Tommy were pretty well exhausted. Upon returning home, they were happy to find a comfortable spot and do some summer reading. They each made new friends and were invited to play dates which True reciprocated. Everyone's favorite activity on these afternoons was a walk to the five and dime where they watched the tanks of fish and cages of parakeets and picked out jigsaw puzzles to work on.

They baked cookies which they always insisted on sharing with "Mr. Bean" who could be counted on to bring JuJu by for a visit in the evenings. Most times he accepted the beer True offered him and stayed for dinner or took them out to the place on the bay where they all had sweet potato fries and entirely too much fried seafood.

Not long after Tommy and Mary Kate had emailed their parents and flossed with their organic floss, they drifted off to the conversation and laughter of True and Jackson, which floated in reassuring murmurs from the porch. And when Jackson headed home on these evenings, if the children weren't around, he allowed himself a chaste peck on True's cheek. But sometimes his lips would catch the corner of her mouth, and his eyes would hold hers, and when he wished her sweet dreams, his voice would grow soft, the sound of it like a caress.

Between the time spent with Tommy and Mary Kate and evenings with Jackson Bean, True rushed back and forth to

Oak View. The summer murder mystery dinner series was the last big event before the fall wedding season, and True had underestimated the planning time it would take. But she was determined not to let her responsibilities at Oak View detract from precious hours with her grandchildren.

She scheduled meetings with Bertie (who seemed more smitten with her than ever) and the Belle Hill Bibliophiles (who had whipped themselves into an anticipatory frenzy based on the previous year's success) while Mary Kate and Tommy were at camp or on play dates. Though they would occasionally walk JuJu to Oak View and the grotto and the cemetery, True did not spend a minute of her "quality time" with the grandchildren talking about work. Which seemed like a good idea at the time.

On the evenings when the children were sleeping or otherwise occupied, Jackson and True cooked and listened to music and talked. Jackson taught her to play poker, assuring her that he never bet more than "peanuts." She consistently beat him at Scrabble. They briefly discussed books. Briefly, because True changed the subject when it looked as if the conversation were drifting to the land of books-I-meant-to-read-but-just-never-got-around-to.

Judging from Jackson's library, it was obvious that he was much more well-read than she. Besides, True knew herself. She would inadvertently blurt out the title of some innocuous tome or get the characters' names confused in the classics she had managed to get through. In her opinion, it was best not to go down that illiterate little path just yet.

One evening, however, she observed Jackson shifting positions on her sofa.

"Everything okay?" she asked.

"There seems to be something under here." He reached beneath him and extracted True's long lost copy of *New York Nemesis* by — who else? — Juliette Benoit.

"I've been looking everywhere for that!" she said before remembering her claims of disdain for such "lite lit."

"Oh, what the heck," she said. The effort and guilt of denying her favorite author were getting downright tiresome.

"Jackson," she said, "I have to come clean. Juliette Benoit is my favorite author."

"Really?"

"Really."

Jackson was decidedly less vocal about the subject of the mysterious Ms. Benoit and the woman's "annoyingly alliterative" titles than he had been before. There was no teasing. No put-downs about the literary quality of the books.

He simply said, "I've never understood the popularity of these books. What is it you like about them?"

"Here," she said, opening *New York Nemesis*. Let me read you just a bit …"

When she was done with the opening pages in which Bailey Jones finds a briefcase of government bonds near the Central Park Conservatory Garden, she said, "Now doesn't that just make you feel like you're right there in Central Park? And you know something exciting is going to happen, that Bailey Jones is at the beginning of another adventure!"

When Jackson didn't answer, True said, "Besides, I've always wanted to travel to these places, but never have. I've only seen them through books."

"Why?"

"Why what?"

"Why haven't you traveled? I mean if that's what you wanted to do?"

"Well, Burkett could never spare the time, and I didn't have anyone to leave the children with … Oh, I don't know. I guess it was easier to keep everyone happy and just live vicariously through Bailey Jones."

True shifted on the sofa to look him in the eye. She was biting her lip in that determined way she had. Jackson loved it when she did that and wondered how long it would be until he could have her to himself, unchaperoned by Mary Kate and Tommy.

"But I have these frequent flyer miles, tons of them, and ever since I read *Marseilles by Monday*, I've wanted to go to France. As soon as I can save some money for a hotel and the rest of it—and get some answers about my mother—I'm going."

"Who would you go with?"

Jackson held the question in those mesmerizing eyes of his as True's thoughts wandered back to a seaside table like the one in her dream. The one near the Mediterranean. She could almost smell the salty air, feel the breeze, see the waves winking at her in the noonday sun. She pictured Jackson there. She pictured herself not running after some elusive thief as she had in the dream, but there with Jackson, sharing a meal, planning the rest of their day, their week, their future.

"True?" His voice was quiet and deliberate, bringing her back to the present.

"What?"

"Who would you go with?"

"Oh. Who would I go with." It came out as a statement rather than a question.

She looked at him again and was tempted to admit that just being with Jackson Bean was an adventure in itself and that she couldn't imagine anyone more interesting or more fun to sit by the Mediterranean with than him.

"Well, I haven't really thought about that," she said. "Maybe Jane E and Bobbie would go with me ..."

"Sounds like a great idea." He pressed his lips together and said, "I've got to get going." Then, in response to the confused look on True's face, he added, "My column's due tomorrow."

Before she knew it, he was out of the back door. True watched his tall frame disappear into the woods.

Was it something I said? she wondered.

•

True didn't see Jackson the next day or the day after that.

It was definitely something I said. But what? Nothing. It's him, not me. Not me not me not me! She let out a tired sigh. *And why am I attracted to secretive men who gamble?*

Because that's what True had decided was the obvious solution to the mystery of Jackson Bean. Either that or he was a highly overpaid sportswriter with such an inflated opinion of his column that he kept his computer and who knew what else in a safe.

She knew no more about him than the day he'd first shown up on her doorstep. Well, except that he was the only child of doting parents who didn't have much in common except him. That his father had what Maisy referred to as "a bit of a wandering eye." That his favorite meal was fried trout, cheese grits and jalapeno cornbread—which he cooked for her and her grandchildren—and now it was her favorite meal, too. That some of his fondest childhood memories were of times spent with his grandfather "right here in this house." That his voice and his smile and his vulnerability lifted her heart a little more each time she was around him.

But she was determined not to be swayed by all of this. The two Jackson Bean-less days had cleared her head, thank God. By now he'd probably moved on to greener pastures with some Holly clone—one untethered by grandchildren, recent widowhood and an unresolved past. She sighed. The children would be leaving in a week. The first murder mystery soiree would be behind her. She would then devote all of her time to coins and camellias and finding Nick's journal. And she would finish that book on navigating the first year of widowhood (the time of greatest challenge to one's mental health, according to the subtitle).

Though she now had the golf dream (where Burkett missed the putt and lost his fortune) infrequently, and her increased understanding that Burkett's need to gamble was based on his own lack of self-esteem, she still did not feel that she had gotten to the "end of that particular tunnel."

With Mary Kate and Tommy on one of Coast Camp's all-day excursions to the nearby Audubon Zoo in New Orleans and her meeting with Bertie more than two hours away, she took off her clothes and wrapped a bath towel around her. The thought of Jackson in his greener pasture, whoever she might be, had her sniffing back tears.

What True needed was a new experience of her own. The best she could come up with was an outdoor shower, but it would have to do. She gathered a travel bag of toiletries (which included a bar of lavender soap like Bailey Jones and the missionary used in *Mission in Montmartre*) and headed outside.

The primitive enclosure was fairly large—approximately six feet square—and made of wooden fencing. There were boards for shampoos and razors and hooks for towels. A mirror was attached to one wall for shaving. The walls were higher than the top of True's head and there was barely a foot of space at the bottom, thereby ensuring privacy for the tallest woman or the smallest child.

True stepped in and closed the door. It sagged so that she had to struggle to get the rusty bolt to slide into place.

"Whew," she said, wiping perspiration from her head and tossing her towel over the now-secure door. "This better be good."

And it was. The sun on her body, the sky peeking through the trees above, a breeze rustling the banana leaves and caressing her skin—it was heaven.

I can't believe I haven't been using this everyday, she thought, rinsing the shampoo from her hair. She reached for her razor and noted the added benefit of actually being able to see what she was shaving—if she positioned her leg in a patch of sunlight.

As she turned off the water, she was aware of a rustling in the bushes nearby. It was probably just JuJu. Which meant there was a good chance Jackson Bean was also in the vicinity. Well, she would just wait it out. There was more rustling, this time very close. She looked down and there was the dog's big chocolate head, peering up at her from beneath the shower's enclosure.

"Shoo!" she whispered.

JuJu gave a happy bark in response. And now the darn dog was inching her body into the shower.

Good grief! She's going to get herself stuck, thought True, and she tried to push the animal back out.

But JuJu wanted to play. True knew that labs are known for their fearlessness and will happily risk getting stuck—if they even think about it—for a few minutes of play. So True sighed and helped her canine buddy the rest of the way through the tight squeeze.

"Now what?" True asked the dog. JuJu now seemed intent on getting out of the shower.

Wrapping the towel around her, True grabbed the bolt and... nothing. It wouldn't budge. And its rusty edges were hurting her hands. She took her towel off and tried to protect her fingers with it as she pushed with all of her might. It occurred to her that the children never bothered to lock the door. There was no telling how long it had been since the latch had been used.

"Well, I got it in, I should be able to get it out," she said to

JuJu whose wet nose was now poking around her thigh.

But she couldn't get as much as a wiggle out of the bolt. There was no way she could get herself out the way JuJu had entered, but maybe, just maybe she could get over the top. She wrapped the towel around her again, commanded JuJu in her sternest voice to sit, and pushing her lavender soap to one side, stepped up on the board so that she could peer over.

Jackson Bean was just yards away, looking directly at her.

He smiled as if he'd met her on the street and said, "Hi, True. You haven't seen JuJu, have you?"

She was getting ready to lie to her smug landlord when JuJu, upon hearing her master's voice, barked in reply.

"As a matter of fact, she's right here. She came in while I was taking a shower."

"So how do you like it? Showering outdoors, I mean."

"Oh, I love it. Except I don't usually shower with dogs."

Jackson came closer. "JuJu! C'mere, girl. Come on. Get out of there. Damn dog is a pain in the ..."

True's arms were getting fatigued from holding herself up, and her towel was sliding off.

"Uh, she can't get out," True explained. "She almost got stuck coming in."

"Damn dog," Jackson muttered again. "I'm sorry. I didn't realize ... Would you just let her out of the door? I'll stay here."

True looked into Jackson's calm, expectant face, caught a quick glimpse of herself in the shaving mirror as her towel slid to the floor, and started to cry.

"I can't get the door unlocked," she sobbed. "It's stuck!"

Emotions jumped across Jackson's face as he attempted to sort out the situation. A frown of confusion and sympathy was at odds with the laugh forming in his eyes and the smile twisting his mouth. He raised his hands palms up as if to ward off her hysteria.

"It's okay, really. I'll get you out. Really, it'll just take a minute or two."

"How?" True howled. "How are you gonna get me out?"

JuJu barked as if to say, *Yeah, how?*

"Just let me think about it. I'll be right back."

True dropped back to the shower floor and could have sworn she heard a stifled laugh coming from Jackson, but it was followed by a cough so she wasn't sure. She sniffed the last of her tears away, turned the water on and washed her face. Using the shaving mirror, she combed her fingers through her hair. Next she secured the towel around her once again and picked up the tube of Lavender Fields After-shower Body Oil. But instead of rubbing it onto her legs and arms, she squeezed the oil on the bolt. She wiggled it a bit, shouldered the sagging door upward and added more of the oil. The bolt slid free and the door swung open to reveal Jackson Bean hurrying toward her, a can of WD-40 in his hand.

JuJu trotted out (looking very pleased with herself) found a patch of sun and plopped down for a snooze.

True held up the tube in her hand. "I used my lavender bath oil. I didn't think of it before."

Seeing True there in a pink towel with her dark, thick hair curling around her face, her skin tanned and shining in the lacy sunlight, smelling of lavender … well, it was just too much.

Jackson tossed the can of WD-40 into a nearby azalea bush and stepped right into the shower. He took the stunned Widow Cowley in his arms and kissed her like he'd wanted to from the first day he'd seen her. (Okay, so that happened to be at her husband's funeral, but it was what it was.) And she kissed him back! She kissed him like he was the love of her life. She kissed his mouth and his neck and his mouth again. She looked into his eyes.

Jackson ran his hands down her back and kissed her mouth, her neck …

"Wait!" gasped True, lifting his head in her hands.

Oh, no, Jackson moaned to himself. But he managed a smile. "What?" he said, with as much tenderness as he could muster under the circumstances.

"I am not doing this, Jackson. Not until I know what it is you're hiding." Though her eyes were filling with tears again, True's voice was low and calm, and he knew she would not be dissuaded.

It was almost more than he could stand. God, he was too old for this. However, he was determined not to lose this woman.

He stepped away from her, looked her straight in her lovely brown eyes and said, "I love you, True. I want you in my life. Whatever you want to know, I'll tell you. But you've got to trust me, just a little while longer."

At hearing this addendum to Jackson's profession of love, the tears spilled down her cheeks.

"No." True picked up her sodden towel and attempted to wrap it around her one more time. "You can tell me now or … or never." When he didn't reply, she pushed by him, slamming the door behind her.

Jackson stood immobile in the outdoor shower as the screen door of his grandparents' back porch slammed shut.

"What the heck just happened?" he asked himself.

•

True revisited the shower scene in her mind again and again as she dried her hair, absently applied make-up and pulled on a mismatched skirt and blouse.

I love you, True. I want you in my life.

Honest words or …?

True could still feel Jackson's mouth on hers, his hands … She grabbed her purse and her bag of Oak View folders and headed out of the rarely used front door so as not to run into her landlord who might still be lurking around the shower.

Taking the long way around, she found herself on the path to the grotto. There was a half-hour or so before meeting the annoying Bertie, so she decided to sit in the calming presence of the Blessed Mother and her endless rosary.

True looked into Mary's face and decided she appeared happy. As a matter of fact, she looked as if she might be saying the Glorious mysteries today. As far as True could tell from where she sat on the old bench, Mary was close to the fifth and final decade on her beads. That would be The Coronation celebrating Mary's reunion with her son when she is crowned Queen of Heaven. True sighed. It was the happiest of happy endings.

Surely Burkett was in heaven. Though he had betrayed her trust, she reminded herself. She sent a prayer to Mary to intercede on her (and Burkett's) behalf to her son, then gathered up her things and rose wearily to leave this place her mother had loved so.

A place she might leave her precious journal? The very book Holly had alluded to?

Absolutely. But where? If it were here, it would be unreadable after all this time. True walked slowly around the grotto, and as she did, the more convinced she became that her mother might have had a hiding place somewhere in the pile of rocks.

True remembered her mother writing in the journal as her small daughter played in the nearby woods, remembered taking her mother's hands as they walked home to Oak View. Her empty hands. Nick must have left the journal somewhere in the grotto. There could be a loose stone, another space somewhere. *Or I could have read one too many Bailey Jones novels?*

It was time to meet Bertie, so she forced thoughts of journals and secret spaces in the grotto out of her mind, took one last look at the Blessed Mother in her beautiful robes, which caused True to look down at her own yellow plaid skirt and pink striped blouse and navy pumps. All she had been able to see was Jackson Bean's face when she threw on her clothes.

Oh, well. At least it was Bertie she was meeting. He wouldn't notice if she showed up in Dwayne Bond's lavender leisure suit. Remembering the party at the Bond Estate made her smile. Made her think of Jackson and his letter sweater. Before she could stop herself she was back in the shower, kissing Jackson. *I have got to stop thinking about him!* she told herself again and again as she approached Oak View.

Not only did Bertie not notice her unorthodox outfit, but he greeted her as if she were draped in Vera Wang. He rushed to her as she entered the front room of the house and took her hand in his damp one (rather passionately, if you want to know the truth).

"True, you are looking lovely today. Quite lovely."

"What did you say?"

"Uh, I said that you are looking especially lovely today."

Jackson Bean and his dog had come very close to depleting True Cowley's rather large reserve of patience. This little pile of baloney was the tipping point for True.

"I do not look lovely, Dr. Wallace."

Bertie took his hanky from the pocket of his seersucker

suit and mopped at his brow. He forced his lips into a panicky smile.

"Oh, please call me Bertram."

"My clothes don't even match!" hissed True. "I am tired of all this, this ..." She searched for a sufficiently dramatic word. "... mendacity!"

"Mendacity?" Bertie's round eyes seemed to float in their sockets. "I have not been dishonest. No, not dishonest, per se. I would never, ever do anything to upset you. I think you're ... you're wonderful!"

Now it was True's turn to be confused. Was this yet another profession of love? Two in one afternoon? Well, she wasn't having any of it.

"I'll tell you something, Bertram. I am upset. And you are dishonest. What about your little arrangement with Holly Varjak?"

True had no idea what she was talking about, and she might very well be tipping her hand. Now that "Bertram" knew she was on to him, she might never find out what he was up to. But the whole cat-and-mouse thing was making her tired.

"Well, Bertram?"

To her horror, Bertie began to cry. No, make that wail, bawl and blubber the likes of which True had never seen. It was a terrible sight. The stuff of nightmares.

"God help me, God help me," he moaned and dropped onto a rosewood settee right there in the front room.

True stood before him, her face impassive, her arms folded defiantly across the bosom of her pink striped blouse. She tapped the toe of one navy shoe. And waited.

"I did it for Oak View. No one loves her, sees to her needs as I do. Oak View belongs to St. James. Where I can ..."

"Pretend she's—it's—yours?" said True.

"Yes, as it should be. It was my ancestor who built this house, you know. He named it Sunrise."

"What?" True dropped her arms, forgetting her anger.

"Yes. Horace Wallace, my ancestor, and a great man. It was Horace the third—a dishonorable scoundrel—who sold my birthright and ran off to California. With the cook!" At this revelation, Bertie started to cry again.

True dropped to the settee beside him.

"Wow," she said. "So you and Jackson Bean are …"

"Cousins."

"Wow," she said again. "And you and Holly were looking for …" She hoped since he was in full confession mode that he would fill in the blanks.

"That's right."

He blew his nose into his tear and sweat sodden hanky. True tried not to grimace in disgust.

"That's right," he said again. "We were looking for the will. And the treasure, for lack of a better term. Everyone was." He let out a palsied sigh and True almost felt sorry for him. "But I'm sure you know all about that," he continued. "It's the cause for your sudden return to Belle Hill. We are well aware, my dear. Well aware."

True frantically tried to piece the fragments of this puzzle together as Bertie spoke. She didn't dare interrupt him or ask a question, for to do so would tip him off to the fact that she had only the slightest clue as to what he was talking about.

Bertie's shoulders slumped. Another sigh escaped him. He shook his head slowly. True's boss seemed to be running out of steam—and info! She had to get him cranked up again. Mimicking his sighs and sorrowful head shaking, she said. "And Holly… I mean, whoa."

"The woman is a cobra," cried Bertie, his voice high and quivery. "Once she found Gertrude Hunter's journal in the rare book vault, it was the beginning of the end. She was not even allowed in the rare book vault. I am among only a handful of people who are granted access."

Bertie's side trip down ego lane gave True time to still her wildly beating heart, focus on her breath (a la chapter nine of her grief manual) and sort through her racing thoughts.

The journal of Gertrude Hunter—True's mother—had been in the library all along? But how long? Had Bertie found it there? Or put it there? Or found it in the grotto? Somehow True couldn't see Bertie poking around the dusty, dirty grotto with dishonest intentions under the very nose of the Blessed Mother. Obsequious twit that he was, Bertie was not comfortable operating outside of the rules. Or getting his little hands dirty.

"You have to believe me, True. Holly was after the treasure—whatever it was. I personally doubt very much that it even exists. And finally Holly, viper that she is, agrees. There is no will, no treasure of any kind. We have all been on an elaborate wild goose chase." He sighed again. "My goal, though misguided my methods may have been, was to ensure unparalleled guardianship of this house, of Oak View." He hung his small head. "And yes, to ensure my continued delusional proprietorship of Sunrise."

It was all True could do not to shake and slap Bertie, drag him to the rare book vault in St. James' venerable library and snatch her mother's journal from its climatically controlled shelves. But recalling that well-worn adage about catching more flies with honey than vinegar (a favorite of B True's despite True's argument that no one in her right mind would want to catch flies), she twisted her face into what she hoped was a smile and said in a non-threatening tone, "Just to make sure I have my facts straight, Dr. Wal... uh, Bertram, you actually found the journal."

"A mason in charge of shoring up the grotto discovered it in a space beneath the statue of Our Lady. Thinking it was of some value, he brought it to the library. St. James library. I was a young librarian then—just a lad, really—and had just been granted access to the rare book room. Quite a feather in so young a cap." He paused and smiled, savoring the memory. "As I am sure you are only too aware, in the journal there is mention of a will and the promise of prosperity and security. But it is written in obtuse verse, gibberish, really. Forgive me, True, but your mother was … troubled. Extremely troubled."

True checked her watch. If she hurried, she could make it to the library and back home in time to pick up Mary Kate and Tommy. After a day-long field trip with a busload of sweaty kids, the counselors became very unhappy campers if forced to hang around beyond pick-up time. However, True didn't dare give Bertie the opportunity to destroy the journal and claim that it was True who was delusional.

"Alright, Bertie we are going to get that journal, and on the way you are going to explain who all of the others involved in this little treasure hunt are and just how they came to be involved."

When Bertie hesitated, True said, "Maybe we should call Maisy."

As they walked along the twisting paths of the campus, they passed classrooms and labs, tennis courts and dorms and students hustling to classes. And Bertie sang like the proverbial canary.

The Honeychurch girls had known True's mother, Nick Hunter and True's grandparents from childhood, having grown up as their neighbors. Like Bertie, they hoped to find the will and destroy it so as to keep the status quo at Oak View (the hub of their social life, not to mention an unending source of free meals). They, too, had heard that Nick's father had left his daughter and granddaughter well provided for. They were aware of the Hunter women's preoccupation with Purple Dawns, old man Hunter's obsession with coins and Nick's penchant for riddles and puzzles.

"When no money … money or assets, that is … turned up after Nick Hunter's death, they deduced, as we all deduced, that the old man's coin collection—there was no record… no record whatsoever of its sale in the stacks of papers left in the house… that the coins were hidden or buried near a camellia bush. Or its facsimile."

"Facsimile?"

"Yes, facsimile, such as a painting or book or some such artifact."

"I just can't believe those two old ladies would try to steal my inheritance," said True.

"The Honeychurches rationalized that by engineering a romance between you and your womanizing landlord—from all appearances he has quite an income—you would not need your inheritance." Bertie shook his head. "They're getting a bit batty in their old age. Quite batty, I'd say. At least they have that excuse. That Neanderthal, Al …"

"Wait a minute," said True. "Al from Al's Electric was involved?"

"Unfortunately, he was working in the attic and overheard the Honeychurch girls talking about wills and treasures. He also had access to the Big Welcome Baptist Church ladies' grapevine—an invaluable source of gossip and speculation. They and Al were sure there was a ghost—voodoo spirit, I think it was—guarding Oak View. That kept Al from venturing into Oak View at night."

"How do you know all of this?" asked True.

"Holly caught Al and two of the church ladies snooping through the basement one afternoon. She forced the truth out of him."

"Good Lord. What about Carver?"

"I have no idea. None whatsoever. But it is probable, very probable, indeed that he was privy to more than any of us, being so close to the Hunters and having complete and total access to Oak View as well as the cemetery. It wouldn't surprise me if he hasn't already found that coin collection as well as the will. If they do indeed exist.

"It would also be to his advantage that the house remain in the holdings of St. James. Looking after things at Oak View is part of his job description. If our beloved benefactress, Maisy Downy should predecease him, he could be out of a job."

True left Bertie sweating like a guilty piglet despite the frosty atmosphere of the rare book room. She was dying for a quick peek at the journal, but was already late picking up the children. So she hugged the precious pages to her and ran home as quickly as her navy pumps allowed.

31.

Rest in Peace

"Hey, True. Do you know what happens when you throw a blue rock into the Red Sea?"

"Um, it turns purple?"

"No, it gets wet!"

"That's a good one," said True as she tucked Tommy in. "Try not to dream of sharks and stingrays, okay?"

She had rushed the children through dinner, looked over the treasures they'd found on their field trip (shells and sand dollars for Mary Kate; a starfish and a giant crab claw for Tommy), handed them each a book and popped them into bed, all the while eyeing the journal peeking from her bag.

True got comfortable, poured herself a glass of wine and opened the journal. There was bad poetry—lots of it. Some of the writings were, as Bertie pointed out, completely unintelligible. There was an interesting section headed *Man of My Dreams; Father of My World.* This heading was followed by a list of seven names. Each of these was followed by a question mark.

There was Johnson Beaudreaux, whose boat Nick had been enjoying the night she'd died. True had already looked him up. He'd died childless several years after Nick. Most of the other names were unknown to True, but they had obviously been altered. Some first names had no vowels or the last names consisted of what was probably the first few letters of the names.

There were two that made her scalp tingle. George Washington (had her mother been completely delusional?) and

Wil. Jac. Bean. True knew Jackson Bean's father was named William Jackson Bean. She grew light-headed with the idea that she could have been kissing incestuously in the shower that very afternoon! True moaned and fell dramatically into the sofa cushions.

"Hey, True, you okay in there?" It was Tommy.

"Fine, just fine," croaked True.

Oh, why had she opened this can of worms? Her mother was a nut, and True had fallen for someone who might not only be another gambler, but her half-brother!

Despite the woozy feeling in her head, she fixed herself another glass of wine and turned to the next page in the journal of horrors.

He who bends unto himself a joy ... That poem again. There were drawings of camellias and hibiscus. Star hibiscus is what her mother called them. True suddenly remembered them growing in a ditch in the woods by Oak View. She had gone there with Nick quite often. Her mother would pick the leaves. Not the flowers, but the leaves which she dried in the basement. True could see them there on the long table next to her grandmother's camellia books.

Must have herbal qualities of some sort. She made a mental note to look it up.

On the last pages there were references to wills and coins guarded by *The Sunrise's Purple Dawn for TrueMyWorld,* but True couldn't make "heads or tails" of it. Wedged in these final pages was a small black and white photograph of a young woman. True turned it over. Cousin Maisy was printed on the back.

True had the feeling that she had seen this person—this young version of Maisy somewhere else. But where? She got Nick's photo album and flipped through the pages, scrutinizing the old pictures. The woman was not there. As she sat sipping her wine and thinking, her eyes fell on her copy of *Peril in Portofino*—the one Maisy had given her.

With a shaking hand, True turned the book over. She placed the photo from the journal next to the picture of Juliette Benoit. It was not the same picture, but she was certain it was the same person. And unless there was another Maisy in her mother's small world, it was Maisy Downy.

True turned these revelations over in her mind, all thoughts of wills and inheritance swept away. She placed her mother's strange journal into B True's federal slant-lid desk with the tiger maple interior, turned the antique key in its lock and looking over first one shoulder then the other, placed the brass key behind a tea canister in her kitchen cabinet. She reminded herself of Jackson Bean, hiding books away so suspiciously. She had to ask herself, *Could he possibly be as innocent of wrongdoing as I?*

Ha! Not a chance, she thought.

No, she had to face the unpleasant truth. Her innocent search for her mother's story had led her to a hotbed of deception, hypocrisy and… and mendacity. Like Big Daddy in *Cat on a Hot Tin Roof,* she had formed an attachment to that word.

Even Maisy was not who she seemed—which was the final straw, the felling blow, the … True sighed. She had run out of not only metaphors, but patience with these … people.

No wonder B True had never come back to this town and never allowed True to return. No wonder Burkett and his family were so quick to cut their ties to this place. In contrast to the players in her mother's story, Burkett emerged as a prince! Well, not a prince, exactly, but at least as an okay human being—with issues. True didn't understand it, but seeing the underbelly of Belle Hill had a sudden cleansing effect concerning her feelings toward Burkett.

She forgave him. She gave up the need to understand his actions and for better or worse, simply forgave him. Then she grieved for her husband, for her daughter's father, for her friend through it all. She cried, had another glass of wine, and grieved some more.

She awoke with her face stuck to *Peril in Portofino.* There was a small puddle of drool on Maisy's picture. As she wiped it off, she forgave Maisy, too. Why should Maisy tell True that she was the face behind the pen name of Juliette Benoit when she'd kept the secret for all of this time? The more she thought about it, the more exciting it was. To think, she was a friend (not to mention, distant relation) of the famous Juliette Benoit!

True's head was muddled. Her muscles were cramped from falling asleep on the sofa. It was time to call it a night. She crawled into bed and waited for the sound of the train. But she was asleep as soon as her cheek came in contact with the soft inside of her arm.

She was back on the eighteenth hole, watching quietly as Burkett lined up his putt. But something was different. This was no longer the weary, middle-aged man of her nightmares. This Burkett looked about nineteen years old, like a man with a lifetime ahead of him. And the way the setting sun glowed behind him, he seemed downright celestial.

Burkett glanced from the ball to the hole once, twice, then tapped the ball sending it curving away, then toward the cup. Plop. And for the first time in her life, True thought that the sound of a golf ball finding its home was a lovely sound.

The small gallery was cheering, but True still heard a man's voice behind her say, "It's a shame he didn't have any money on that one."

Burkett leaned over and retrieved the ball. He started toward the men's grill, but stopped. Turning, he waved to his wife, smiling at her just like he used to at the Phi house.

"Hey True, I'll see you later, okay?" he called. Burkett stared at her for a while as if fixing her in his mind, then walked toward the clubhouse.

32.

Curiouser and Curiouser

After breakfast, the children begged to visit Jackson and JuJu, so True sent them to his house with an offer to walk the dog. An hour or so later they returned with JuJu straining at the end of her red leash.

"Let's walk her to Oak View. I need to check on some things," said True as they headed out. "Oh, by the way, what did Mr. Bean have to say?"

"About what?" said Tommy.

"Well, I thought he might have, you know, sent his regards or something."

"We just played with JuJu and looked at pictures of Evie and her mother on the computer," said Mary Kate.

"Oh. Okay."

Once they were in the garden behind Oak View, True noted the stream that ran through the golf course. She followed its path with her eyes through the woods. That had to be the ditch where she had gone with her mother to pick leaves.

Tommy and Mary Kate were used to their grandmother's abrupt changes in direction, conversationally and otherwise. They stopped with her, waiting for her to come back from wherever her thoughts had taken her.

"Oh, sorry," she said cheerfully. "I'm in the mood to explore. Let's see if we can find the beginning of that stream."

Soon she had them all stomping through the underbrush beyond the side garden of the house. Sure enough a spring bubbled up through the soil. The area that was the origin of the stream was low and wet. Swampy things grew here that did not grow anywhere else in the area, but True didn't see any of the lovely red star hibiscus plants.

"What are we looking for, True?" asked Mary Kate.

"Big red flowers—hibiscus that are sort of like the ones by the pool in Vista Palmas."

"Well, I don't see any," said Tommy, obviously bored with this excuse for an adventure.

"I took up all them plants after your mama died."

"Oh, hey Carver," said Mary Kate.

"You know Mr. Jenkins?" True asked.

"Jackson introduced us," said Mary Kate. "He's making me a swing to take back home, aren't you, Carver?"

"Yes I am. Swings is my specialty."

Am I the only one who isn't buddies with this guy? wondered True. As far as she was concerned, he was as weird as the rest of the denizens of her neighborhood. She seemed to be alone in her opinion, however.

"Carver, can we talk?" asked True in her strongest no-nonsense voice.

While the children and JuJu played with a tennis ball Carver produced from the pocket of his overalls, he and True sat in the shade on the patio.

"Miz True," Carver began.

"Please, Carver, call me True."

She tried to keep the irritation out of her voice.

It is I who should be calling you Mr. Carver since you are so much older than I, thought True.

He smiled and seemed to relax. "True, me and your mama were friends. She was older than me. She was a lady. And she was white. It was the fifties. I think you old enough to remember them days. That friendship could a got me killed in some places. Not in Belle Hill. Folks was different here, but still, my mama worried herself to death over it. Said Miz Nick was just being rebellious having a colored boy for a friend. Besides, she knew the truth." Carver shook his head. "I hope you won't take offense at this, but I was in love with your mama. I knew it was wrong. For a lot a reasons, but I could not help myself. I would a done anything she asked. So when she asked me to smoke the pot—that's what it was, but nobody knew it back then, and it was growing in with the star hibiscus what look just like pot with flowers, I said sure."

True remembered smelling marijuana here and there on her college campus. Oddly enough the aroma always had a nostalgic effect. At the time, she figured that this was one of the odd effects of "the killer weed."

Other children smell blueberries or Chanel No. 5 or baby powder and get nostalgic. But then their moms hadn't spent their children's formative years tiptoeing through the cannabis. True now recalled the smell of the sweet smoke out on the golf course at night and in Oak View itself after her grandparents' deaths.

"What happened? When you smoked the pot, I mean."

"Your grandmother heard us laughing like hyenas in the woods, knew something was up, but didn't know what. That kinda put a end to me and Nick spending time together, though. Lord knows, it was for the best. Still … like to broke my heart. We stayed friends till she died, but it was never the same."

"Carver, why didn't you tell me this the first day we met?"

"Nick was your mama. I was close to you, too when you was a little girl—made you a swing and taught you how to use it. I know you remember that, but all the same I'm just a old, black stranger to you. And this might be the twenty-first century, but we ain't exactly in California where anything goes. I guess I had to test the waters first. I always start out distant with white folks." He grinned at True. "After all these years, I still can't figure 'em out."

True laughed. "Neither can I, Carver. Especially this crowd around here."

"I ain't no world traveler or nothing, but I been around enough to know folks is folks. Some good, some not so good, every place you go."

Carver had taken a chance, being honest with True about his feelings for Nick—something that still might not go down too well with some of the locals, though they would likely blame Nick. True's instincts told her she could trust Carver. This was backed up by Maisy's high opinion of the man. She made the decision to take him into her confidence.

"Carver, do you know anything about my grandfather's will—a later will, I mean that was never found? And something of value that could be hidden around here?"

"I know the same stories everybody else does. I've been all over this place fixing, things, working the grounds. Like I'm the only one knew about the pot growing in the woods. I pulled it all out. I didn't want folks saying Carver Jenkins planted that stuff. Didn't want the college kids finding it either. Anyway, I ain't never found a will or coins or nothing like that. They all sure asked me 'bout it, though."

"Who?"

"Half the people 'round here—Dr. Bertie, the Honeychurch ladies, that crazy 'lectrician, Al, Dr. Varjak, even some of the ladies from over to Big Welcome. They all running round here looking, thinking they the only ones." Carver shook his head again. "It would be funny if it wasn't downright pitiful."

"If Maisy knew all of this, why didn't she put a stop to it?"

"You know well as me that Maisy got her own ways. And she know things other folks don't know. I ain't kidding on that. People think it's a joke when she tell fortunes. I know it ain't. She a good person, too. Gave me that house I live in. I been living right here in the middle of the white folks all this time. Even back in the sixties when everything was going on, we all got along. Course we always been a little different right long the coast here, all kind a folks coming and going. Most a my kin live a ten minute walk from here—did even in segregation days. Worked in the white folks' houses right behind 'em. You go fifty miles in the wrong direction, you think you back in segregation days, though."

"So it was different here?"

"It was better here than a lot a places. Now I'm not saying the whites asked me to Sunday dinner or nothing, but we got along. Now I take supper with Jackson and some of the others," he said, nodding his head. "I have my kin over to barbecue at my house. Works out okay."

True told him about finding the journal and how Bertie and Holly had seen it, too.

"I'd like you to look at it and tell me if you can make any sense of it."

"You sure you want to go opening this up?"

"Yes. I'm too far into it now. I just hope you don't mind me dragging you into it."

"No, it's time. Like Maisy told me, secrets stay in dark places. Every now and then you got to throw open the doors, air things out. I think she know what she talking 'bout." He smiled at True. "As usual."

"Thank you, Carver. Why don't you walk back with us and look at the journal. I'm cooking hot dogs for lunch."

"With chili?"

"The works."

After lunch, True left Carver on the front porch with a glass of tea and her mother's journal and photo album. She sneaked a peek at him now and then as she piddled around the kitchen. He turned the pages slowly, and True saw him take the napkin from beneath the tea glass and dab at his eyes again and again. Was this really better than letting secrets fester in their dark places? Was she no better than Nick, involving this man in her problems?

When Carver was done, he placed the books on the kitchen counter. His eyes were red from crying.

"Carver, I'm so sorry. I should never have involved you in this."

"No, you did right. Looking at that picture album, I was like a boy again, remembering all the excitement of being round your mama. Reading that journal, I was seeing Nick through the eyes of a grown man. And …"

"What? Carver, please be honest with me."

"You sure?"

"Yes, I'm sure."

"Well, your mama was crazy as a bedbug. I see it now. And you know what? It has set me free. I am free of that woman's hold on my heart. After all this time. Carver Jenkins is free at last."

"Really?"

"Yes, and from the bottom of my happy heart, I thank you for that."

True let this settle for a minute and said, "So, you couldn't make sense of the journal?"

"There ain't no sense to make." He looked around and lowered his voice. "She was smoking the hibiscus when she wrote in that journal is my guess."

True sighed. She now had to add pot head to the list of her mother's frailties. Whenever one of B True's family members or friends was similarly afflicted—usually with alcohol or prescription meds or just "bad nerves"—her aunt referred to them as fragile. Well, Nick Hunter was about as fragile as they come.

True locked the journal away feeling like Alice in Wonderland where things only got curiouser and curiouser.

33.

Whodunit?

Though there were many unresolved issues in the shadows of Belle Hill, True didn't worry about their resolutions as she once had. And though the sound of the train and the feel of her arm in the night were still things of solace to her, she no longer had the golf dream.

However, when the pressures of the day or too many muddled thoughts kept sleep at bay, it was Burkett's smile on that final round that soothed her. The look on his face after he'd sunk that wagerless putt and the sound of his voice as he promised to be with her again was the way she would remember him from then on. She had climbed her mountain of doubt and grief, and made it to the other side. And she was grateful.

The frenzy of preparations for the first of the summer murder mystery dinners swirled around her, but True thought of the peacefulness in Burkett's face. His calm aura was contagious. And so she checked off her list of duties and let the others fret. True concentrated on more important things such as making the most of her last few days with Mary Kate and Tommy. They went to movies and the beach. They had a sleepover with their new friends from camp and the neighborhood. They played with JuJu, and visited Jackson (who never sent his regards to their grandmother). True even chaperoned the final field trip into the delta where the promised huge gators lurked in the dark water.

On the eve of the mystery dinner, True simply told the children she had a function at Oak View. She wasn't comfortable talking about murder as a game with them. When she showered outside and the hot water released the smell of lavender and memories of Jackson's mouth on hers, she simply put him out of her mind. Sort of.

When the sitter called in sick at the last minute, True was glad she had decided not to bring up the subject of murder at Oak View even if it was all in fun. She reluctantly left Mary Kate and Tommy with a movie and her cell number, promising to return as soon as possible. After all, she would be minutes away and could probably hear them if they yelled for her.

Oak View was awash in tropical ambiance. Pots and baskets of tropical vegetation sat everywhere. Tropical music—heavy on the steel drums—echoed from the ballroom. Banana daiquiris, Yellow Birds (an island concoction made with coconut rum) and pina coladas were on their trays in preparation for happy consumption. Cans of Kalik (the primo Caribbean beer) had been iced down in an old skiff on the back patio.

Dinner was actually a bounty of heavy seafood hors d'ourves. Boiled shrimp, fried shrimp and barbecued shrimp kabobs as well as minced crawfish, oysters on the half shell, fried oysters and oysters Rockefeller were arranged amid palm and banana leaves on the dining room table. These delicacies surrounded a breath-taking centerpiece of white orchids overflowing from a clay pot. Women were given hibiscus blooms for their hair. It was all quite over the top.

There were the actual participants who had gotten letters telling them of the parts they were to play. They were given outrageous names befitting their occupations or personalities (which helped everyone remember who was who). These people were in 1920s era costumes and had arrived an hour earlier than the other "guests" who had paid half of what the principle participants had forked over for this evening of frivolity and mayhem. They were also encouraged to dress accordingly.

By the time True arrived in white linen, the principles had rehearsed their parts and been advised of the importance of strict adherence to the "rules of the game" by Mary Lou Lassiter, the chairwoman of the Bibliophiles Second Annual Summer Murder Mystery Dinner Series. Any violation would result in automatic expulsion from the game and forfeiture of the chance at the grand prize (five hundred dollars and free admission to all subsequent murders).

After the rest of the guests arrived and had gotten into the spirits and appetizers, the murder of Dame Felicity Knott was discovered. (The part of Dame Knott was played by Maisy Downy who could always use a nap halfway through the festivities anyway). Felicity Knott was the miserable matriarch of the Knott clan. She had lived in single-minded determination to make all of the conniving potential inheritors of her immense fortune work for his or her slice of the Knott pie.

Her body was discovered on Oak View's one comfortable sofa by her son, Sir Harry Knott, the overbearing "Lord of Knott Manor" who had rented out the entire Caribbean island of Canubia to celebrate his 60th birthday.

In true Agatha Christie fashion, the aroma of bitter almonds emanating from the victim resulted in quick deduction that she had died as a result of cyanide poisoning. But Whodunit?

Her son, Sir Harry, whose own business ventures were headed down the drain?

His part is played by Dwayne Bond.

Lady Knott?

Lady Candy Knott is the wife of Sir Harry and mother of Ida, Lola, Lilly and Harry Jr. (aka Art Deco). Lady Knott came from the wrong side of the tracks, married above herself, and sadly, is still no better than she should be. Poo Honeychurch plays the part of Lady Knott.

Ida Left?

Ida is a thrice-divorced, hard-hearted marriage counselor on the verge of bankruptcy. She is the eldest daughter of the deceased.

Flora Honeychurch plays the part of Ida Left.

Lilly Gilder?

Lilly is the baby of the Knott family. She is a twice-divorced, notorious gold digger on the hunt for husband number three. Lilly, an obsessive spender and pathological liar, hasn't the patience to wait around on her grandmother's inheritance. Martha May, a pillar of Big Welcome Baptist Church plays Lilly.

Lola Bido Knott?

Lola Bido is the only looker in the family, but unfortunately, a big tease. She is played by Dwayne Bond's newest girlfriend, Victoria.

Dang Foo?

Dang is the devoted but challenged Asian man servant of Sir Harry. When the original participant dropped out, Bertie Wallace was pressed into service (and embarrassingly type cast) in the role of Dang Foo.

Art Deco/Harry Jr.?

Art is an interior decorator and Sir Harry Knott's only legitimate son. He constantly flirts with the specter of disinheritance because of his unorthodox lifestyle and the fact that he changed his prominent name to Art Deco once he'd discovered his true calling in interior design. The part of Art is reluctantly played by Wayne Bond (his brother bought the ticket for his twin brother as a gift).

Fairley Strange?

Fairley is Sir Harry's business partner. Everybody agrees he is a very weird guy. He is played by Bob Roberts, good sport and husband of True's friend, Bobbie.

Nefarious Johnson?

An ex-con with soul, Nefarious is the illegitimate (but favorite) son of Sir Harry. He is played by none other than Jackson Bean. True thought this might be another case of type casting and tried to avoid making eye contact with Nefarious/ Jackson.

Maisy was just coming off a fortune-telling engagement at the Little Sisters of the Poor lawn party. She had stayed late to finish everyone's fortune. After all, the Little Sisters could use every dime she could earn for them. As she left, Sister Mary Vanda, whose wimple was covered in a pink web of cotton candy (she always ran the cotton candy/candy apple booth.) stuffed a holy card bearing the likeness of the Blessed Mother into Maisy's hand.

"God bless you, dear," said Sister Mary Vanda with a tired smile.

Maisy stuffed the card into the pocket of her gypsy skirt, drove like a bat out of hell to Oak View and just made it in time to "pass away" on the goose down sofa in the entrance hall before Chairwoman Mary Lou Lassiter let out the blood-curdlingest scream anybody could remember. This was the traditional signal to "let the games begin" and to get everybody in the "mood for mayhem." True thought she'd never seen anything so corny, but had to admit that it did get everyone's attention.

Remembering the holy card Sister Mary Vanda had given her, Maisy pulled it from her pocket. But before she could read the note on the back, Chairwoman Lassiter rushed over, still panting from her game-commencing shriek.

"Maisy, until this murder is solved, you are not to move," said Mary Lou. "And whatever you do, do not talk to any of the suspects!"

So Maisy closed her eyes and got comfortable on the sofa. She just wished she'd gone to the ladies' room one more time. She was about to doze off when she felt a tug on her hand. Opening one eye, she saw Flora and Poo Honeychurch bending over her.

"It's a clue, I tell you," said Poo, snatching at her holy card.

"Maisy, is this a clue?" whispered Flora, but Maisy held tight to the card and played dead as instructed.

•

Another series of events was taking place at the home of True Cowley. As Tommy and Mary Kate sat obediently eating popcorn and watching their movie, they heard a bark at the back door. It was JuJu, of course, who was lonely and bored to begin with before getting a whiff of possum in the back yard. This being too much even for the new, well-behaved JuJu, she had pushed her way through the screen of Jackson Bean's porch. After chasing the possum all the way to the Honeychurches, the smell of popcorn and the sound of children's voices claimed her attention. She raced to True's back door and issued her most demanding bark.

"I think we should take her home," said Tommy who was itching for an excuse to be outside on this balmy summer evening.

"True said not to go out," said Mary Kate. "We should keep JuJu here."

That's when they heard it—a horrible scream coming from

the direction of Oak View. JuJu's ears perked up.

Before Tommy and Mary Kate knew what was happening, the dog took off like a shot. The children looked at each other, eyes big as two owls', and raced into the darkness after the dog. JuJu, who could outrun a jaguar, was on the golf course sparring with an armadillo by the time the breathless, sweating children got to the end of the path.

Tommy and Mary Kate stood where the tangle of underbrush met the edge of Oak View's manicured side yard. The woods were full of lightning bugs and crickets, the lawn strewn with moon shadows. Jasmine and magnolia and pine smells were heavy in the air. A tiny breeze stirred the trees and sent a chill up the children's damp, little spines. It was a perfect night for a murder.

Tommy took his sister's hand and with a warning finger to his lips, led her to a clump of Formosa azaleas. They sat on the ground looking through branches while Tommy wondered how in the heck to save his grandmother from the diabolical murderers skulking about Oak View.

In the meantime, Flora and Poo waited until Maisy was snoring, which took about four minutes—an octogenarian who's been telling fortunes all afternoon is no match for goose down stuffed upholstery. While Poo stood guard, Flora slipped the holy card out of the old lady's fingers. Maisy opened one drowsy blue eye and gave Flora the meanest look she could muster, but Flora merely smiled and left the corpse in frustrated repose.

"I could sure use a smoke," Flora said loudly and nudged Poo toward a door to the outside.

The game was afoot as they say, but amid incriminating revelations and red herrings timed to keep things hopping, Poo and Flora slipped out onto the side porch. Holding the holy card up to catch the light from a nearby window, they examined it carefully.

"Okay," said Poo. "This is a lovely likeness of the Blessed Mother being assumed into heaven surrounded by a halo of stars, celestial clouds and golden rays." She sighed. "So beautiful."

"Try to say focused, sister," said Flora. She fired up a Salem.

"Turn that card over. There's something written on the back. Got to be a clue."

Flora read the message aloud. "May the good Lord reward you and his light shine upon you from above your plentiful table. S. M. Vanda."

"Lady Knott must have written this just before she succumbed to the poison," said Poo.

There was a squeal from inside Oak View followed by drunken laughter.

"Let's go out to that bench, so I can smoke and think in peace," said Flora.

"It has to have some significance," said Poo, once they were seated. "I mean the corpse was clutching this holy card in her fingers, for God's sake."

She gave a small shiver in spite of the evening's warmth then inspected her polished nails in the moonlight. The two women fell silent, each turning the note's words over in her mind trying to attach some meaning to them. Flora took a drag of her cigarette, then let the smoke out in a slow stream. She watched it float in the night air and disappear into Spanish moss hanging from the oak branches above them.

"Must be a code of some kind," said Flora.

"Oh, I hope not," said Poo. I'm terrible at that sort of thing."

Flora ground out the remains of her cigarette on the leg of the bench and tossed it into the azalea bushes.

"But we've got to figure out who killed Lady Knott and get that money," she said.

"Well, I'm not getting anywhere sitting out here in the moonlight breathing second-hand smoke," said Poo. "I'm going back inside."

When Tommy was sure the old ladies were gone, he carefully pushed some branches aside for a better view.

"Did you hear that, Mary Kate? There's been a murder in there all right. But why isn't anyone upset about it?"

"I want to go home and call 911," said Mary Kate.

"Are you kidding? We might get True in worse trouble. Besides, this is pretty exciting."

Sitting in an azalea bush getting cigarette butts thrown at her was not Mary Kate's idea of excitement.

"I'm going home," she said.

"By yourself? With a murderer running around?"

Mary Kate sighed and tried to get comfortable.

Tommy watched the people through the open windows of Oak View. It was like watching a play, he thought. Every light seemed to be on, illuminating the house's interior and the oddly-dressed party-goers who would alternately convene, cocktails in hand, then disburse to snoop about and have quick, intimate conversations with one another.

As he watched, someone came out of the shadows behind the side porch. It was Mr. Bean. He had been watching the two old ladies, too.

Tommy was so relieved to see Mr. Bean that he almost ran out from his hiding place. After all, Jackson would want to know about JuJu getting out. As he tried to decide, Jackson slipped through the door, and Tommy lost his chance. Not to mention his nerve.

He could see Jackson through the windows. He was trying to talk to someone. As the lady turned toward the window, Tommy could see that it was True. But True didn't talk to Jackson. She shook her head and walked away.

"Something isn't right, Mary Kate."

But when he looked down, his sister was asleep in the grass, her thumb in her mouth, her face resting on her arm.

There was a sudden flicker of light. It was just the two old ladies back for another smoke. The glowing end of Flora's cigarette danced in the darkness until the women emerged into a puddle of moonlight. They passed into the darkness again before sitting down on the stone bench. The little breeze started up again, throwing shadows across the patch of white shine that was Poo's hair.

"Now that we have a few more clues, we should be able to find out who did the murder," said Flora. "We're the only ones who have the holy card, so we stand the best chance of getting that money."

"Okay, we know the dead woman is Dame Felicity Knott. And that she had just found out that her estranged son, Art Deco was having a fling with her lover, the gardener. I bet she was going to disinherit Art once and for all."

"And we know that the gardener had access to arsenic. He used it to kill vermin in the greenhouse."

"Yes, and it was the greenhouse where he raised the Vanda orchids—just like the ones in the centerpiece on the dining room table!" said Poo, coughing and waving smoke out of her face.

Flora took another drag on her cigarette. "What does that have to do with anything?" she asked.

"The message on the back of the holy card was signed Vanda and says *may His light shine on your plentiful table.* The Blessed Mother's halo of stars reminds me of all those circles around the chandelier above the table."

"I don't know, Poo. That's pretty far-fetched."

"Got anything better?"

"Not at the moment. And the card does say, 'May the Good Lord reward you.' That must refer to the five hundred dollars!"

Poo shook her head sadly. "So Art killed his own mother. Makes you kind of glad we didn't have children, doesn't it?"

"Get a grip, Poo."

"You're right." Poo grinned at her sister. "I guess I did get a little carried away."

"Alright, let's go get our money," said Flora.

She ground out her smoke and tossed it over her shoulder, barely missing the sleeping Mary Kate.

Tommy watched the two old ladies hurry back inside. Again, Mr. Bean walked from around the side porch. As luck would have it, just as Jackson slipped through the door, JuJu trotted up. Her tongue was hanging out and she was panting blissfully from all of her nocturnal escapades. She dropped to the ground next to Mary Kate, issued a small sigh and closed her eyes.

"JuJu, stay," whispered Tommy.

He could stand the suspense no longer, so he crept up onto the well-lit front porch and squatting behind the closed panels of the jib windows, peeked into the dining room. If he were caught, he would blame it all on JuJu, he decided.

Inside, Chairwoman Mary Lou Lassiter called everyone (except the corpse) into the dining room where she announced that the Honeychurch girls had simultaneously come up with a solution to the mystery of who murdered Lady Felicity Knott. The murderer's name—Art Deco—was written on a piece of paper which they had given to Mary Lou.

She unfolded this missive and waving it triumphantly over her head, she trilled, "We have a winner! As a matter of fact, we have two winners, who will split the five hundred dollars. Both have an open invitation to attend all subsequent summer murder mystery dinner parties." (Like they wouldn't have come anyway is what everyone was thinking, but they were good sports and kept this to themselves.)

Next was the moment everyone was waiting for. The corpse was awakened and brought into the dining room so that she could hear how the clever deduction was reached. Chairwoman Lassiter looked very confused when Flora Honeychurch started alluding to clues on the holy card, but Maisy caught Mary Lou Lassiter's eye and with a discreet shake of her head (that everyone else took to be palsy), silenced the chairwoman.

After all, this isn't an algebra test where the steps of the solution are as important as the correct answer, Mary Lou rationalized.

When Flora got to the part about the money and the prize and how the stars comprising the Blessed Mother's halo were like those funny circles in the medallion around Oak View's chandelier, she suddenly stopped and stared at the medallion. You could practically see the light bulb pop on in her brain.

"What?" said Poo, following Flora's gaze. "Oh, my Lord," she said. Another light bulb fired up.

And one after another—first Bertie, then Martha from Big Welcome Baptist, then the Bond brothers and finally, True— looked to the ceiling and figured it out. Not the puzzle of Felicity Knott's demise—nobody cared about that any more —but the mystery of Nick Hunter's obsession with coins and camellias and what happened to old man Hunter's valuable coin collection.

True let her mind float back to a night almost fifty years prior. Oak View was being repainted, and the trompe l'oeil depicting vases of Purple Dawn camellias was still damp in the upper corners of the room. The dining room was empty except for drop cloths and cans of paint and spackling and an enormous wooden ladder. She remembered waking to sounds of jazz playing on her mother's record player, to the smell of marijuana in the air. She had walked through the big hallway to the dining room and sat in the shadows to watch her mother.

Nick stood on the painter's big ladder way up at the top, her red hair wild like fire in the glow of the chandelier. Her cigarette sat in a tiny ash tray next to a pile of coins, a saucer of spackling compound and a teacup of paint, all crowded on the ladder's flat top. Nick was sticking the coins onto the medallion with spackling, then carefully painting over them with a small brush. The coin designs in the medallion were real coins.

The odd little group of Belle Hillians either hadn't known or had forgotten about the paintings of camellias that had once adorned the corners of the dining room. That's why they had been snooping around real camellia bushes and pictures of Purple Dawns. They had been searching high and low for Grandfather Hunter's coin collection. Just not quite high enough, thought True. Now they all stared in confused amazement at the ceiling above them. All except Jackson Bean, who watched the pretty, befuddled face of True Cowley. And Maisy Downy who looked knowingly from Jackson to True.

Bertie Wallace cleared his throat authoritatively, but then didn't really know what to say. He was in charge of Oak View, but like the others, admitting to the possible existence of a fortune in coins spackled into the medallion surrounding the chandelier would be tantamount to an admission of… well, to all sorts of things ranging from unorthodox to unethical to downright illegal. The silent, stunned crowd stared at him. In a rare moment of clarity, he saw himself as they did—a frightened, owl-eyed little man in a rented Chinese coolie costume. He opened his mouth to speak, but nothing more than a whoosh of hot air escaped him.

"Well, congratulations to the Honeychurches," said Maisy, saving the deflated Bertie. "And since this is a night of mystery, I would like everyone to know that we are on the verge of solving the puzzle of the strange lights seen in here at night. My sweet nephew, Jackson Bean has agreed to stay here tonight, and in the morning all will be revealed."

She said the all will be revealed part in a spooky, melodramatic voice and everyone laughed nervously.

"The bar is open for another hour," said Mary Lou Lassiter,

"So please stay and enjoy yourselves."

Though most of the game players were half in the bag, they all took Mary Lou up on her offer and headed to the nearest bar. True and Jackson and Maisy stood alone in the dining room.

"Maisy … " True began, but the old lady interrupted her.

"Do you trust me, True?"

"Of course, but …"

"Then be patient just a bit longer."

True looked at Jackson who had made the same request of her. He looked tired and sad, and she missed him more than ever.

Maisy smiled at True and Jackson. "Patience, my dears. As I promised, all will be revealed."

True looked up at the curlicues and circles in the medallion and sighed.

"Okay," she said. "Now I'm going to say god night to Mary Lou Lassiter, and get home to Mary Kate and Tommy."

Because of Maisy, Jackson was facing a long night in Oak View. True Cowley was treating him like a case of the pox. These damn women are killing me, he thought. But he had to smile because he couldn't think of two people he loved and admired more.

Hearing that his grandmother was headed home, Tommy scuttled across the porch and down the steps. He found Mary Kate curled around JuJu and sleeping soundly. The big dog was almost invisible in the darkness and did not move a muscle until Tommy woke his sister.

JuJu guided the two children quickly and quietly through the woods. Tommy and Mary Kate dashed through the house and into their beds, pulling the sheets over their clothes and falling immediately to sleep. Even JuJu had had enough excitement for one night and headed home.

Minutes later True arrived. As she blew kisses to her sleeping grandchildren from their bedroom doorways, she was too exhausted to notice that Mary Kate's foot peeking out from beneath the covers was still clad in a dirty pink tennis shoe. Happy that the children, at least, had enjoyed an uneventful evening, she fell into bed without even brushing her teeth.

•

The next day True dropped Mary Kate and Tommy off at a friend's house for a farewell swim party and lunch. As she watched the children and their friends loaded down with towels and goggles and flip-flops, she knew she would miss playing the role of the young soccer mom. But she had to admit that at her age, it was exhausting. She waved good-bye and counted her blessings that it was not a full-time job.

When she pulled up in front of Oak View, she saw Maisy's silver Miata parked next to the battered truck of Al (from Al's Electric). She hurried into the house and found Al on an extremely high ladder positioned beneath the dining room chandelier. He had a small knife and was working on the medallion on the ceiling. A small pile of whitish shavings littered the floor beneath him.

Maisy Downy (attired in pink yoga pants, matching sweat band and a bra top) and Jackson Bean (needing a shave and wearing the same clothes he'd worn to the mystery dinner) and a man True had never seen before were seated at the dining room table. This had been pushed to one side to accommodate Al's giant ladder. The top of the table was covered with a drop cloth. The man True didn't recognize was cleaning and inspecting a pile of coins as Bertie (who had regained his "all pomp and no circumstance" persona) and George Washington Carver Jenkins looked on.

The men rose from their seats as True entered. The stranger was introduced to her as Dr. Benning, an old friend of Jackson's.

"True, do you remember me telling you about a man I did an article on who was a numismatist? Well, it was Dr. Benning, here. He's the one who told me about the 1927 Double D Eagle coin, like the one on your grandfather's grave."

"Okay," said Al, "this is the last one. Woo, you ain't gonna like it, though."

He handed it down to Carver who handed it to Dr. Benning. The man shook his head sadly as he cleaned it with a cloth. When he was finished, he flipped it onto the table with the rest of the coins. Maisy picked it up.

"Al, are you sure this is the last one?"

"Sure as shootin'. Woo, it's hot up here. Okay if I get down now."

"Might as well," said Maisy.

As Al climbed down, Maisy smiled grimly at the coin. "It's nothing but a Mardi Gras doubloon—the kind you catch off the floats in Mobile."

"Could it be … like a collector's item, real old or something?" asked Carver.

"Afraid not," said Dr. Benning.

"We thank you for coming, Dr. Benning," said Maisy. "I'm just sorry it was a bit of a wild goose chase."

"Not at all, Maisy. There are some wonderful coins here. Maybe as much as ten thousand dollars in value. Of course I'm disappointed not to have found the Double D Eagle—I would love to hold it in my hand before I die—but it's just an old man's dream."

He said his good-byes and left.

True told them how the memory of her mother putting the coins in the ceiling had come to her the night before and that she was sure the coins had been her grandfather's.

"Then they belong to you," said Jackson.

"Oh, I'm afraid not," said Bertie. "I'm sorry Ms. Cowley, but this house and all of its contents were left to St. James College."

It seemed that Bertie's infatuation with True had turned sour after she'd exposed him and gotten her mother's journal from him. And they say women are fickle, thought True.

"Now, just a minute," said Jackson, but True interrupted.

"No. He's right." True turned to Bertie. "Dr. Wallace, I would like to buy a few of the coins back for my grandchildren, though. I'd like them to have something of their great grandfather's."

"I will certainly take it up with the board," he said. "And use all of my influence to see that you get them at market price."

"Why you little …" Jackson began, but this time Maisy interrupted.

"We're all tired. We'll discuss it later. Bertie, I have the list of coins Dr. Benning has catalogued for us. I trust you will put them in a safe place."

"Oh, yes. Yes, indeed. I intend to put them in the vault in the rare book room immediately."

He gathered up the coins, placed them into a box and taking

pains not to get within striking distance of Jackson Bean, hurried away.

Al slapped a hand to his chest. "Woo, that Dr. Bertie is somethin' ain't he?" He threw a goofy look at True. "All heart, he is. Okay, if y'all don't need ol' Al, I got to be goin'. Problems over to Big Welcome. Electric chimes done shorted out again."

"Just one more thing, Al," said Maisy.

And she told him about the solution to the mysterious lights in the house, how it was simply car lights bouncing off the mirrors of Oak View.

"I know people are wondering. Would you mind explaining it to anyone who asks?"

"Sure thing. Wooee. How about that?"

Al was tripping over himself to get out and share this news flash with the ladies of Big Welcome and anyone else he met along the way.

"Well, the whole town should know in about twenty minutes," said Maisy when he'd left. She turned to True. "I'm sorry, sweetie. I was sure that double eagle coin was in the medallion. That's why I had Jackson guard it all night." She looked at Jackson. "Go home, sugar." She wrinkled her nose. "You could use a shower."

34.

Fond Farewells

True was happy to see that both Katie and her husband, Parker, had come to pick up the children. Katie had warned Mary Kate and Tommy that Parker was busy and not sure he could get away. So when both parents got out of the car, the children were beside themselves with excitement.

True and Tommy and Mary Kate had spent the morning fixing a pot of gumbo for their farewell supper. The mindless busy work and interaction with the children had kept True's mind off of the events at Oak View. She was determined not to let the Belle Hill crazies interfere with the last of her vacation with Tommy and Mary Kate.

By the time the dinner hour arrived, the gumbo was just right. The children made a passable salad all by themselves, and True heated up crusty loaves of French bread from Manetti's gourmet grocery.

Parker turned off his Blackberry when they sat down and declared the meal a feast when they were through. Katie kept her nutritional concerns to herself. There was no discussion of organic versus non-organic and not the first comment about calories or carbs or sodium or any other dietary bugaboos. True was thankful for miracles, and realized that Tommy had not told a joke all night—or for the last few days, now that she thought about it.

"I've decided not to be a comedian when I grow up," he said when she questioned him about it.

They all breathed a sigh of relief.

"I'm going to be a detective," he said.

"Not me," said Mary Kate. "Stake-outs are no fun!"

"Now how does a five year old know about stake-outs?" her dad wanted to know, but Tommy shot his sister a look and she said, "Oh, I learned about them from Tommy. He read about it in a book."

They were still laughing and talking about Tommy the P.I. as they cleared the table and prepared dessert.

Even the nights are warm during south Alabama summers, but after dinner, True turned on the fan and they sat on the porch with their bowls of vanilla ice cream which she had topped with Chilton County's best peaches. There were crickets and lightning bugs and white flowers floating in the moonlight—one of those nights a child might remember even when she is a grandmother herself.

True had decided not to speak of hidden coins or journals, or deceptive friends and neighbors or her doomed relationship with her handsome landlord, but she couldn't help asking Katie if she'd been in contact with Jackson's daughter, Evelyn.

Katie had indeed taken Evelyn and her family under her wing, as True hoped. The new friends were practicing for an upcoming marathon together. Katie and Parker had gone to a baseball game with Evelyn and her husband, and Evie would be taking ballet lessons with Mary Kate in the fall.

"So, where is Mr. Bean?" Katie wanted to know.

Are you referring to Mr. Jackson Bean, the heart stealing, shower seducing, secret keeping person who, by the way could also be my half-brother? Omigod! Could be your half-uncle?

This is how True was tempted to respond to her daughter's question, but this was not the time to go into her convoluted relationship with the mysterious Mr. Bean, so instead she said, "I think he's been busy."

Katie gave her mother a look that said she knew she was being had. She started to say something, but changed her mind. It occurred to True that Jackson may have mentioned their relationship to his daughter, Evelyn who in turn may have discussed it with Katie. Her own daughter might know more about Jackson's intentions than she, herself did! The whole thing was giving her a headache.

"Mom, are you okay?" asked Katie with such concern that True had to fight back the tears.

"I'm just getting emotional at the thought of you all leaving," she said. This was the truth.

"Do you regret moving here?" asked Katie.

"Truthfully? Yes and no. It's been hard—in many ways, but I think it was the right decision for me. Something I had to do. I hope you understand."

"Truthfully? No. But I understand the feeling that you have to do something. So, don't feel guilty. We just miss you."

"I know, and I miss you all, too. But I'll come to Vista Palmas soon, and we'll have a long talk. I want to tell you about your grandmother and her parents. About your dad. Things we need to talk about. The kind of things I wish someone had talked to me about."

The next morning there were tearful good-byes, but True could tell that her family was ready to get back home. And truthfully—there was that word again—she was ready for a little solitude. She walked back into the kitchen and realized that she was exhausted. The house was a bit too quiet without Mary Kate and Tommy. But it was also nice.

She fixed a cup of coffee and went out to get the mail. Among the junk and the bills was a postcard bearing the Technicolor front cover of *Peril in Portofino*. On the back was an invitation to a book signing and reception by the author—in two days' time, no less. True had to read it several times to be sure she wasn't missing something. Surely, the now-semi-famous Juliette Benoit (aka Maisy Downy), was not coming out of the literary closet in True's very own neighborhood bookstore, Belle Hill Books-n-Things right here in little, ol' Belle Hill, Alabama?

She remembered the old lady's melodramatic words. "All will be revealed."

It's about time, thought True. *I don't know how much more of this boring, small-town life I can take.*

She was trying to decide what to wear to the book signing and wondering if anyone else—Jackson, perhaps? Or Jane E?— knew of Maisy's alter-ego, Juliette Benoit when the phone rang.

Well, speak of the devil, thought True, when she heard Jane E's voice.

"Hi, True. Listen, I heard about that twit Bertie claiming your inheritance for the college. Everyone knows those coins were meant for you."

"Jane E, a lot of those people were prowling around Oak View hoping to find them and keep them for themselves. At least Bertie wanted them for the college."

"I wonder what Bertie would have done if he'd found them first—you know, without half the town looking on. Besides, hell hath no fury like a weasel spurned."

"What do you mean?"

"Listen, True. It was obvious that Bertie was... shall we say... smitten with you. It's also obvious that you're smitten with Jackson, whom Bertie has always been jealous of. I think that little weasel figured that claiming the coins for St. James would get him in good with the board—which it will, and with Maisy—which it didn't—and get even with you. I'm telling you, Bertie is pathetic."

"Wow," said True, trying to process this, but she simply could not think in a straight line. "It's obvious that I'm smitten with Jackson?"

Jane E laughed. "Fraid so, friend. The good news is that my hot cousin is also crazy about you. And I couldn't be happier. You're good for him, True. I think he's finally rid himself of all that baggage he's been carrying around. Now, I have to start cooking for a bat mitzvah over in Cloverton, so I can't hang on the phone. The reason I called is to see if you got your invitation to the book signing."

"Yes, I did."

"Okay. I promised Maisy I'd have you there. She said it's really important. Oh, and how's this for odd? She said to tell you to wear what you wore to the reunion at Dwayne Bond's house and to remind you that things will be revealed or some such nonsense. That old lady is up to something. I can always tell." Jane E sighed. "Of course, she's always up to something. Anyway, I'll pick you up at six sharp. Be ready. Bye."

Okay, so Jane E doesn't know that Maisy is Juliette Benoit, but that still leaves my secretive landlord, Jackson Bean. She thought back to Jane E's comment concerning Jackson's feelings for her which took her back to the romantic episode in the shower.

Get over it, she told herself. *You cannot get involved with another dishonest man, baggage or no baggage.*

35.

All is Revealed

True and Jane E were among the first to arrive at Belle Hill Books-n-Things for the invitation-only signing. True felt a bit overdressed in her peach linen ensemble, but her main concern was Maisy's forthcoming announcement.

Maisy, in readiness for her big moment, was dolled up in a black mini-skirt, white ankle boots and a ruffled, hot pink blouse. Jackson Bean wore his usual outfit of khaki pants, top-siders and a blue polo shirt. He sat in the back row of chairs, reading glasses perched on his fine, straight nose. An elderly man True had never seen before was seated next to him.

Jackson must be here in some official capacity with the Belle Hill Courier, thought True noting the legal pad and pencil resting on his knee.

True steered Jane E to the other side of the room where they sat in the front row.

By the appointed time of six-thirty, the tiny bookstore was packed. The mostly female voices were shrill with anticipation. It reminded True of the time her class visited the turkey farm just before Thanksgiving. Heads swiveled and necks craned to catch a glimpse of some sophisticated stranger who might be the mystery author.

All of the players in True's recent drama were there—Bobbie and Bob Roberts, the Honeychurch girls, the Bond brothers, several of the church ladies from Big Welcome and of course, Bertie Wallace. Carver was there looking quite dapper in a sports coat. Even Al was there tinkering with the microphone attached to a podium at the front of the room. The only one missing was Holly Varjak who, if you remember, had headed for the hills up east somewhere in hopes of yet another fresh start.

Finally, the attractive, middle-aged owner of the store, Harriet Honeychurch Downy, stepped to the microphone. The cream of the Belle Hill crop were so far out on the edges of their seats, True feared they might start falling off. Harriet Honeychurch Downy was trembling with excitement. After all, this was quite a coup for a small-town bookstore. Getting the scoop on the latest literary newsflash was thrilling enough. But the following morning this miracle would be topped off with a very lucrative cherry. Juliette Benoit in all of her glory would be signing—and selling—the stacks and stacks of books overflowing the stock room of Belle Hill Books-n-Things. You'd be trembling, too.

"And now, I would like to bring Maisy Downy to the podium."

Surprise, surprise, thought True.

Confused murmurs issued from the crowd.

Maisy stepped behind the podium, but only her head was visible. She hadn't got herself dolled up to be hidden behind some podium, so she came back out and yelled to the expectant crowd.

"Thanks to all of you for being here. I know you're all about to pop to know who Juliette Benoit really is, so with no further ado, I would like to introduce our own very talented friend and neighbor…" She paused here for maximum effect. "My nephew, Jackson Bean."

"Oh, my God," said Jane E. "That son of a— He never said— Oh, good grief."

True of course said nothing because she was in shock.

Jackson Bean took his place at the front of the room. He grinned at the crowd, who one by one began to clap until Jackson/Juliette was receiving a standing ovation.

Jackson thanked them all for coming, thanked them for buying and reading his books and said he hoped they'd had as much fun reading them as he'd had writing them. He then turned to look directly at True and Jane E, who mouthed an obscenity at him.

"When I wrote my first Bailey Jones adventure, *The Problem with Paris*, I let my Aunt Maisy read it. She liked it and insisted on sending it to a publisher friend of hers."

At this point, Jackson introduced the stranger who had been sitting next to him in the back row.

"This publisher who has published all of my books, by the way, liked the story but thought we'd sell more books if the predominantly female readers thought it had been written by a woman. He suggested a female pen name and came up with Juliette Benoit. I figured no one would take me seriously as a sportswriter if they knew I'd written a romantic mystery with a female protagonist, so this appealed to me, too. I supplied an old picture of Maisy for the cover. It was kind of a tribute to her for helping me get the book published.

"You might be wondering why, after all this time, I decided to come clean. There are lots of reasons—the Bailey Jones books have an established readership, the latest book, *Peril in Portofino* has done especially well and people are curious about the author and frankly, I am getting a bit bored with the secrecy."

Jackson took a deep breath and let it out before continuing. "But the real reason is that I heard someone read a few pages from one of my books. I liked how it sounded. She told me how much she'd enjoyed her vicarious journeys with Bailey Jones, and for the first time, I was really proud of the work I'd done." Jackson turned to look at True. "She has also taught me something about the damage secrets can do, about the importance of facing up to who you are, where you come from and most importantly, where you are going. There is a poem called *Waking* by Theodore Roethke that I never understood, especially this line— *I learn by going where I have to go.* Thanks to her, I now know exactly what Mr. Roethke was talking about. I just hope that she can forgive me for taking so long to come to my senses."

True was smiling, tears brimming in her eyes. She jumped to her feet. "Oh, I will!" she said. But then a terrible thought occurred to her, and the smile faded. She chewed her lip in that way that Jackson found so adorable. "You are talking about me, aren't you?" she said.

Jackson grinned at her. "I am definitely talking about you."

And with that, Jackson walked over to True, took her in his

arms and gave her the Hollywood kiss of all Hollywood kisses. As you can imagine, by this time all of the females and most of the males in Belle Hill Books-n-Things had goofy smiles on their faces and/or were sighing and/or dabbing at their eyes. Jackson's publisher and Harriet, the bookstore owner were practically high-fiving each other over the unexpected bonus of Jackson's declaration of love and admiration for the attractive, flustered woman in the front row.

Jackson signed copies of *Peril in Portofino* until his fingers cramped. An embarrassed True Cowley, a very happy Maisy Downy and even the publisher were asked to add their signatures to many of them as well.

Jackson Bean admitted that he'd hoped to one day be signing copies of his biographies of sports figures or a compilation of his columns from a major newspaper. But if there was one thing he had learned, he said, it was that a surprise ending is often the best of all.

36.

One More Revelation

After promising to call Jane E the very next day, True walked home with Jackson Bean. As they strolled along the sidewalks of St. James campus, Jackson did indeed, reveal all.

"True, I knew about Burkett's gambling problem, and I didn't blame you for being suspicious of me. I didn't care what the busy-bodies around here thought, but I couldn't stand you thinking I was into something … unsavory. When you asked me why I kept my computer in a safe, I saw everything for the farce that it was. I called my publisher and said I was coming clean about being Juliette Benoit. He was fine with it, agreed that with the popularity of *Peril in Portofino*—there's a movie option on it and everything—people would want to know more about the author. But he made me promise to let him decide when to make the announcement. I agreed not to tell anyone until then."

"I admit I was suspicious," said True, "And then when Al said something about your friends from the Delta …"

"Al the electrician? He's the worst gossip in town. And that's saying something. Listen, those guys I hunt and fish with are just what they seem—good, old country boys who love the Delta. You don't find better guys."

"So you really made your living from writing?"

"Not exactly. The book business has been good to me, and I make a little off of my column, but my parents left me some money. I've had good luck with investments—mostly real estate. That's how I've been able to travel and write and pay child support through the years. So, is there anything else you would like to know? After all the years of keeping secrets, I'm kind of enjoying this."

"Jackson, there is one other thing. But it's something I have to tell you. In my mother's journal, she mentions your father. I think we could be … related."

"Related?" The meaning behind her words slowly sank in.

"Yes. Your father and my mother …"

"Good Lord, it's no wonder you were avoiding me. I hoped you wouldn't find out about that."

"Then it's true?"

"Sort of."

"How can it be sort of true?"

They stopped walking, and Jackson turned to face her.

"I'll try to explain. After you came to town, Maisy and I had a long talk. She knew no one would open up to you about your mother because … well, because she had lots of problems. But Maisy knew you would find the truth. She said you deserved to find the truth in your own way, is how she put it."

Jackson shifted back and forth a bit, thinking how best to put things. Finally deciding there was no gentle way, he said, "She told me there was talk that my father had had an affair with Nick. But she told me something else. My father had mumps, I think it was, as a young man. He was not able to have children."

"So you're …"

"Adopted. And he could not be your father."

"Really? You're adopted? That's wonderful!"

"I'm glad you think so." He smiled at True. "It was kind of a shock, but in the light of recent developments, I'm pretty happy about it, too."

True sighed, and it was a contented sigh. "I guess my search is over. I know Nick's story. Her death was a tragic accident."

"But what about your father? You don't know who he is."

"I don't think anyone knows—or ever knew—including Nick. And you know what? It's okay. Knowing her story is enough."

They had stopped at the entrance to the woods. True looked back at Oak View where memories floated across the grounds and porches, through the rooms.

I know this place better than anyone, thought True. *And for that reason, it will always be mine.*

Jackson put an arm around her shoulders, reminding her that it was time to leave the past, return to the present and focus on a very promising future.

"Let's go home," he said.

•

Jackson put on some French music. He opened a very good bottle of French wine. A coffee table book of French impressionists was open on the sofa. Leaving True immersed in all things French, he took JuJu for a quick walk.

"So, Monsieur, what's up?" asked True when he returned.

"Well, I've been thinking of setting my next book in France. That was the setting for the first one, and in a way I'm starting over—letting everyone know I'm Juliette Benoit and everything."

He sat next to True on the sofa and kissed her neck. Then that spot just behind her ear. He murmured into her ear, "And of all the places I've visited, I think Paris is the most romantic."

"Really?" True managed to say.

"Yes, really." He kissed the corner of her mouth. "As a matter of fact, if I were to plan a honeymoon …" He kissed her slowly on her mouth. "… I think Paris would be my first choice."

"Um," said True. Then his words made their way into her brain. She sat up very straight. "Did you say a honeymoon?"

"Yes. A honeymoon."

True smiled at him. "But who would you take?"

"Well, I thought my wife would probably be a good choice."

"Oh, I agree." She giggled. "But you don't have one."

Jackson put on a sad face. "That is a problem. I agree."

And before True knew it Jackson was down on one creaking knee. "True, I don't have a ring yet. But you're the one I want to spend the rest of my life with. In Paris or Belle Hill or anywhere. As long as you're there. True, will you marry me?"

"Yes, yes, of course I will. I love you, Jackson Bean."

The next morning as they had their coffee in Jackson's kitchen, True said, "Do you mind if I keep my own name?"

"Don't want to go through life as True Bean? I don't blame you."

"There's one other thing. I insist on buying our tickets to Paris."

"I thought you were broke?"

"Well, I have all these frequent flyer miles. I had to put Burkett's funeral on my Visa."

When Jackson stopped laughing, he said, "True, there is no way I'm letting Burkett's funeral miles pay for our honeymoon."

True sighed. "I understand. It's just that I was starting to enjoy my independence. It's important to me not to be so dependent on anyone again."

"True, there's one more thing. I was going to let Maisy fill you in since she cooked up the whole thing. But I think she'll understand if I tell you now. Come with me."

She followed him into the study where he slid the marlin picture to one side, opened the safe and removed a gold disc which he placed into her hand. It was a twenty dollar gold piece. The color was a bright orange gold, and it felt unusually heavy on her palm. On its surface was a bald eagle flying over the sun. True turned the coin over. The reverse showed Lady Liberty holding an olive branch.

"What is this?"

"That is the 1927 D Double Eagle your grandfather left for your mother and you. That is why he left the house to the college. This coin is very rare, True. Dr. Benning has verified its authenticity. One of these recently sold for almost two million dollars."

"But how?"

"Let's just say I found it in my yard. And unlike Bertie, I intend to see that it goes to the person who was meant to have it."

It took True a few minutes to process it all.

Finally she said, "You put the Mardi Gras doubloon in the medallion. To replace this. But how and when?"

"Let's just say that if Maisy happened to find the doubloon in her pocket and brought the spackling and paint to me in the wee hours of the morning and if I had put my stepladder on the dining room table and spent half the night digging out coins until I found the Eagle and then the rest of the night putting them all back, I wouldn't admit it because Maisy and I would have decided to take full responsibility for the whole thing."

"But Dr. Benning—"

"As far as he knows, I found the coin in my yard the day after the murder party. He knows the story of your grandfather and will vouch that it was probably lost by your mother—possibly when she was visiting my parents."

"But these stories have to be authenticated. No one will believe this."

"No one can prove otherwise. There are several of the 1927 Double D Eagles unaccounted for according to Dr. Benning. The one in your hand is one of them. The coin is yours, True. It was your grandfather's. He bought it, and he left it to his heirs."

True looked at the coin. She grinned at Jackson.

"Good Lord, Jackson. We're rich!"

37.

One More Wedding

True Cowley and Jackson Bean were married by the Reverend George Baker on a sunny, almost-cool October Saturday morning at St. James Church. Jackson's and True's daughters attended their parents. Tommy was the ring-bearer and of course, Evie and Mary Kate were the most adorable flower girls ever.

True wore an ensemble of ivory lace, and everyone said she had never looked lovelier. Tall, dark Jackson Bean was especially handsome in his new charcoal gray suit, white shirt and blue striped tie. There was not a dry eye in St. James church as the couple exchanged vows.

This had nothing to do with the celebration of love and devotion between Jackson and True, of course. It was gratitude that had them all misty-eyed.

What with the mystery of the lights in Oak View being solved and the coins being found, there wasn't much to talk about lately. So it was the fact that little True Hunter of dubious parentage and tragic beginnings had managed to snag two of Belle Hill's most eligible men in one lifetime and return home to claim her birthright that had them whipping out their hankies. They would be telling this tale for generations to come.

A reception followed at—where else? It was not catered by Jane Ellen Jackson so that she could relax and enjoy herself for once. The Honeychurch girls were in a fit of pique over this and refused to take so much as an egg roll home, which was very gratifying to Jane E.

Dwayne Bond and his now-affianced girlfriend, Victoria

were there. According to the Belle Hill grapevine, they had met as a result of Victoria's accident in one of Dwayne's car washes. When she threatened to sue (due to the fact that there was no warning anywhere not to turn your windshield wipers on during the wash cycle), the king himself was called in. By the time Dwayne had seen to her wiperless (but sparkling clean, Victoria had to admit) Volkswagon bug, he had asked her out. After seeing Dwayne's house on the river with the *Happy Hooker* bobbing at the dock, Victoria dropped the suit. The rest is now Belle Hill history.

"Yeah," Dwayne was heard to say, "She's dumb as hell. But God I love her."

True's wedding gift to Jackson was a watercolor portrait of Evie and Evelyn (which she hoped would replace the leaping marlin in Jackson's study). Jackson gave True a small box containing a house key. He'd bought the condo True had been coveting but thought she couldn't afford in Vista Palmas.

"We can spend a third of the year here and a third of the year there," he said as they danced across the floors of Oak View's ballroom. "It'll be fun being grandparents together."

"But what about the other third of the year?"

"I thought you might like to see those places you've been visiting through my books," said Jackson.

True looked into the Mediterranean blue of her husband's eyes and smiled back at him.

"I can't wait," she said.

● ● ●

The End
(and the beginning)

Margaret P. Cunningham

Margaret P. Cunningham's short stories have
won several national contests and appeared
in magazines and anthologies including five
Chicken Soup for the Soul books. She grew up
on her father's nursery in Mobile,
Alabama, where she lives
with her husband, Tom.
She enjoys writing, reading,
gardening and "beaching it"
with her friends and family.

Also by this author:

LILY IN BLOOM
ISBN: 978-1-934912-02-7

CPSIA information can be obtained at www.ICGtesting.com
Printed in the USA
LVOW051338220612

287068LV00001B/309/P

9 781934 912270